■

by Wilfrid Sheed

SQUARE'S PROGRESS

PROGRESS

A NOVEL ■

by Wilfrid Sheed

Farrar, Straus & Giroux ■

NEW YORK

"Tragedy tomorrow, comedy tonight"

—*A Funny Thing Happened on the Way to the Forum*

CONTENTS

1

Last year at Bloodbury

1

Mud along the Thames, mud in the Chancery. . . . Mud in the Jersey flats.

People brought the first spring mud into the bus terminal on their boots; and dragged it over to the newspaper stand, where the crowd bobbed and pecked erratically at the evening papers; foot-painted it around the stand, up the escalators, and into the buses. (Squat fellow with dead cigar piling on more *World-Telegrams*; pale winter-hands flutter and grab.)

The Bloodbury bus jammed, but awfully polite after the subway; people say "Evening, Fred" and "Hello, er, there," and the newspapers open like spring buds, in every workable crevice.

Two men about three inches too much for one seat read the front page exhaustively and experiment cautiously with turning it. A sense of wet raincoats, of bulbous hipbones and the ceaseless negotiation of elbows. But nice and clean after the crosstown bus. Hopes the other won't speak; a rabbity tension about that; but sanctuary in the evening paper, if one can just get it open. (Mortally sick of page one after twenty minutes of strap-hanging, Fred Cope wrenches it open, crunching lightly against his neighbor's ribs.)

The lights go off for a moment. The handful of men who really like to talk are going at it serenely. The rest sit tight, and the motor starts up and they're roaring into abortive day-light; sucked briefly through a tube of tunnel and out again onto the expressionless Jersey highway. The rain has washed off the sky, and even in the Jersey flats and under thick glass, there is a form of spring going on. Life stirs uneasily in the commuters. Meanwhile, Fred Cope has never had so much trouble turning his pages: this other fellow seems to be all over him. "Excuse me," polite grunts, almost words, page two at last. "Peace talks, actress, which is it, jewels or sleeping pills"—a man has a duty to be bored among his own people.

The bus turns off the highway, into a gorgeous improbable bower: a dazzle of brilliant greens in the after-rain light. Points of wetness and light glint on both sides of the mammal bus. By George, Fred has never come across such disruptive breath-ing. Man can't help how he breathes, of course, but a plastic stomach heaving against your arm about every four seconds. . . . Stock market jumps a line, aligning wrong average with wrong company. Crazy market tonight.

Passengers get off in clumps of two and three. They say "good night" heartily, or mumble it, or just swoop silently past. This is a genial, unmenacing driver, and a lot of people come out with good nights who wouldn't usually; but some of them can't talk to any stranger, even a kind one. Fred gets out at Willow Drive and says, "Good night, Charlie, how you been keeping?"

Willow Drive fairly twinkles. Life bursting, drumming, be-tween the cracks in the sidewalk; spring coming on with a swirling, smelling rush. Fred tries to read his paper as he walks. But he still gets the wrong averages because the ground is uneven and he has to settle for quick glances at the solid text. He turns in at the right door, though—the one with the dusty car in the driveway and the most desolate garden, and feels the correct emptiness behind it.

The bit about the newspapers had been silly, why shouldn't he read newspapers? Two letters under the door, neither of them from Stapleton; neither of them from people. (Glossy heart-fund letters—had forgotten about those.) He reaches blindly for the radio and television section—covered with a thin coat of Fred-repellent: essence of Alison. The programs are just the same as last year's, as if he had just left them, sitting dead in the set. *Death City*—very apt. Alison would come from the kitchen at this point and watch him turning on the set.

"*Hello. I'm just turning on the set.*"

"*Go right ahead.*" The contempt would make his fingers stumble. "*Don't let me stop you.*"

No more of that stuff then, ever again. If she came back, it would be on his terms—whatever *they* were.

So quiet now you can feel the carpet under your shoes. Hear the first sound of a car, catch its grumble, passing the house and down the street. *We're going to have you looked at by the TV repairman. You're all made up of tubes. Your birth was a pseudo event.* (He made up things like that for Alison to say, just to keep the conversation going.) *Why don't you buy a canoe, Fred? Or get in some good reproductions? All that newspaper money would float a Matisse. . . .* Alison, the aesthete, there's probably one in every suburb, he decided.

She hadn't been here for a calendar year but she had left some fastidious breath on the air. He felt a touch of the old suffocation. Listen to me, Alison, I can be tranquil and aware with a newspaper: just watch. If she walked in now, by some ass-backward miracle, she would find him fairly wallowing in grossness. Reading the comics, if necessary. No more of her crap. Take me as I am, baby.

"Peanuts" was unusually hard to follow today. Out in the street some teenagers were sitting on the horn in foolish ecstasy, disturbing the delicate concentration. Fred's mother would have said, I've talked to the police about it and they can't do anything; his wife would have said, Oh, let them, for heaven's sake, let them. Alison was "on the side of life"; Mrs. Cope, Sr., was on the *other* side. It didn't matter a damn to Fred one way or the other, he just thought he'd mention it. (Who am I talking to now, he wondered vaguely.) Must try to get in touch with her, though, tomorrow.

Big man in an empty house, moving from the window to the armchair and back, arguing with his own version of what he thought he remembered of his wife.

The phone rang and he put down the paper and lowered the set. (Television *and* a newspaper, my God! You've cut off every avenue!) "Fred, this is Fran, Fran Wilkins, listen . . ." He did, with mild amazement. The telephone also held last year's messages. Fran wanted to launch another premature barbecue this very evening. Thick sweaters and stuttering fingers and laughter with smoke on it, what fun. Fran was the woman who said, "You must forgive us we're crazy," and wasn't crazy at all, it was her tragedy. (Spontaneous barbecues did not add up to craziness—and they were all she had.) But this invitation had a special fascination. It was at last year's party that his—would you call them troubles?—started; this would be a ritual re-enactment of sorts.

"Yes, that'd be fine," he said. No one had asked him out since he'd gotten back from Europe. He had a feeling nobody ever would again. Husbands and wives were like Siamese twins in Bloodbury. Pairs of people in the living room all winter; pairs of people in the garden all summer. If something went wrong, they disappeared in a body. Fred had no idea what really happened to them. "In the cool, cool, cool of the evening," said Fran, "and it will be cool, and I know we're crazy." Fran picking at her tragedy. "Even if we have to chip through the ice . . . the new people next door must think we're quite mad."

He still had half an hour to kill before Fran's thing—and he knew for a fact that you had to kill the little bastards, it was no use just stunning them. Fred turned off the set and threw the newspaper into the wastebasket with a dull clunk. He had supposed when he left Spain a week ago that he would come back to this routine with a resigned zest. The pawkiness of the Paris *Tribune* had been feeding his lust for large newspapers, and he actually bought three of them at the International Airport. He had also discovered in Spain the exact length of those hours that the television set mercifully killed for you, the long, sober, stupid hours of evening. Twenty-four hours made a ridiculous day, in any country.

But the newspaper and the television seemed to have lost some of their mild, benumbing quality this evening. They were not as good as he remembered. He stood and sat and stood again, there was no other anesthetic in the house. Alison's innumerable volumes of Proust, crouching over the hi-fi, reminded him that culture still wasn't the answer. Nothing had so enriched his cultural modesty as a brief attempt he had made last February to get into the Proustian bag. An endless weave of pointless memories, something about a duchess, Alison must be kidding.

He felt a sudden, thin melancholy at being back in America, that would have to do for entertainment. There was no resonance to anything here, no memories of duchesses. It was Fred Cope's spiritual home but that knowledge didn't entirely help. He reached despairingly for the third volume of Proust—he knew it didn't matter which one you started with, as long as it wasn't the first—and resumed for a few minutes his hopeless tryst with Swann and the Duchess.

The gang, Fred's old mousepack, sat in Fran's backyard, as patient as Eskimos around a piece of fish and a twig fire, watching the flame fizzle against the steaks. This was a good way to remember that spring hadn't really come yet. But they would all go through hell for Fran Wilkins because she was so dull and kind.

You got back yes how was it pretty good. (Nobody asked *why* he had gone, it was all too embarrassing.) The Peabodys said how was Spain hot fun cheap and the Mitchells and the Flaxes. Bert Flax looked as if he had seen a ghost, and Fran told him that Bert had had the teeniest breakdown over Christmas but had made a splendid recovery. Par for a Bloodbury winter. Bert looked like a piece of delicate china, and didn't talk much. But then it was really too cold to talk. Fran kept reminding them of the significance of what they were doing, which robbed it of any possible significance. Betty Flax had changed, hadn't she, thinner, older, quieter, dishing out the alpine potato salad and keeping an eye not quite on her husband and not quite off him.

"How does it feel to get back to work?" asked Ernie Peabody with cumbersome tact.

"Feels pretty good, Ernie."

"I hear you people moved into a new building."

"That's right. On Fifth."

"Business must be pretty good, huh."

God I can't stand it. I'll go out of my mind, said Alison, who had followed him spectrally over. *Well, you know Ernie,* he said. *It isn't just Ernie, you talk like that with everybody.* He should never have tried reading Proust, he was getting his tenses all mixed. He was back to last year, and at the same time he wasn't. He looked at Ernie, his face round and white as the moon, and had a physical memory, like a partial stroke, of Fran's last rite-of-spring party; it was suddenly warmer and he was getting the old silly good feeling; he couldn't undertand why his wife was no nervous. The embers were sparking and popping, there was a nice hum of talk, and three drinks were gurgling into dusty corners where the winter mothballs were kept. "You shouldn't drink, Al," he said, "you know it doesn't do the job for you." The dim outline of her head, half made of trees, looked as if it wouldn't take offense. Not great big offense, anyway.

. . . As it happened, you never saw such offense—but that was later. He was getting deeper and deeper into the Proustian fog. Last year, this year. In the flesh he was cold and rather bored, in memory he was warm and vaguely amused. Splendid tinkle of icebooze in last year's glasses, darkness, sizzling fire, women's voices—he used to love these occasions, in those days. Life with Alison undoubtedly had its tense side, keeping your values straight and shiny, and the booze and company helped a man to unwind.

As he sat talking to Ernie, he could feel last year's drinks burbling and slurping across his brain pan, tasting much better than this year's and whispering a richer nonsense: "Bloodbury's all right," they used to say. "Nice people, I mean really nice. Sense of 'sponsibility. American scene, O.K. corny, but if those so-called sophisticates had been in the Army and seen how other people lived . . ." He would get a little peeved with imaginary guys who knocked America, then forgive them on the fifth drink—spirit of nonconformity, *that* was good too. Plur'lism— they have a right to their opinions, he had a right to his. And *that* was part of the American scene, too.

Well, that was the kind of thing he used to think about at parties, and whatever else you could say about it, it did help to work up a glow; the only glow he got now was from remembering what a complete, unadulterated horse's ass he used to be in those days. He must have learned *something* abroad. His present thoughts were probably no more brilliant, but they were better edited—and decisively bleaker. . . . One thing hadn't changed anyhow: he could still think his own thoughts and talk business with Ernie Peabody without any conflict of interest. Here he was, showing Ernie over the new building and, as counterpoint, imagining himself saying good night to Fran last year. It wasn't difficult; after the kind of year he'd spent, you became an amazingly dexterous introvert. He was lost in a maze of flashbacks: like a white mouse, smoking, drinking, stumbling along corridors in a multipurpose experiment.

He wrenched his attention all the way back to Ernie and the flavorless present. There was a glaze of thwarted eagerness around Peabody's eyes, as if Ernie would really rather be talking about something else, but had been ordered not to. Fred glanced around, and got a sudden wild feeling that everyone in the garden would rather be talking about something else and that the whole party was a fantastic exercise in restraint. Ernie's wife, Ann, lurked a few feet away, as if she was ventriloquizing Ernie's curiously formal conversation, and keeping everyone else in line too.

It was quite a change from Spain. There wasn't a beard or an old sweatshirt to be seen. Perversely, Fred almost missed the expatriate smells (irony was like a new toy) and the jungle tension. Those parties always seemed likely to wind up with a drunken scream or a fit of weeping. This one would wind up with "See you, Fred" and a woozy search for jackets.

He didn't want to be the last to leave tonight. The odd man at a Bloodbury party stuck out further and further as the crowd thinned, until by the end he fairly bellowed his status. He could feel people going out of their way not to mention Alison. Fran Wilkins's sister had been dragooned along to even the numbers, but she had stayed holed up in the kitchen all evening, and anyway Fred was feeling lower than he had expected, and wanted the privacy of his car and the night silence. He had become mortally tired of people as such. Bob Wilkins shook hands quite chummily, as if to say "Now you know how *I* feel." Bert Flax said good-by solemnly. There seemed to be a slight impediment in his speech.

Fred stood for a moment with his back to the light. He felt as if he might have something to say that could be of help to somebody. But he knew that for all his new understanding, he had nothing to say, no message. Any wisdom he had acquired abroad was without specific content. He shook another hand, woman's hand. Betty Flax it was. "Good night, Betty." She looked as if she was going to laugh. He couldn't say he blamed her.

He walked to the car, shaking his head inwardly: what people, what a way to live; what existential emptiness, baby. (And Fred Cope was its prophet.) He banged his knee on the door frame and drove away.

2

The white line stayed where it belonged, and the journey was quite swift on the impeccable American roads, three cheers for the impeccable American roads, three cheers for the Tailored Woman. He was still having a terrible time with his tenses. Memory had become one of his most dependable pleasures, and with the smallest encouragement last year rolled itself out for him like a picture rug. Alison sat over there; he sat at the wheel, looking serious until his teeth began to feel false . . . Once, at a time when she was groping for nice things to say about him, Alison had praised him for being stable, so he always acted stable whenever he thought it might help. Right now she was beginning to look a little flushed, so he set his jaw and went stable all over: it gave him something to do, and certainly beat listening.

He had wanted to stay at Fran's and have another drink. But the fire had gone out and everyone else seemed to have disappeared. He got a fuzzy notion that nobody had enjoyed themselves half as much as he had—sometimes it happened like that. Metabolism or something. He sat by the ashes with Bob Wilkins, but you couldn't keep a party going just with Bob. He was one of those invisible husbands you turned to in desperation; Fred was quite willing to talk unabashed clichés by then, but Bob could barely manage even those. Alison was in the house talking to Fran. "Let me freshen your drink," said Bob. "Er, no, I think we'd better be going."

There was a brief, fuzzy jostle under the porch light. Fran and Alison were kissing each other, he wondered about women kissing, how they knew which ones to kiss, thought he might bring this up in the car. "Night, Bob," he said heartily. "Night, er, Fred." Fellow only talks under protest—type of very small man that wears a bow tie. Might bring this up in the car.

Show Alison that he thought about things, too—out-of-the-way things. Fran's "I'm afraid we're crazy" died on the night air and they stumble-shuffled down the steps. He was sorry Alison wasn't as genial as he was. If he had one little fault to find, it was that people had forgotten how to enjoy themselves. Might bring this up. . . . .

"I don't know if I can stand it any longer," she said as he slammed the door on his knee.

"What's that? What can't you stand?"

He couldn't get a good look at her because he was driving, and the lights came and went. Her face was radiant in the ribbons of light, and he couldn't wait to get home.

"I sometimes think you're trying to be not only the dullest man in Bloodbury, although that would be an achievement wouldn't it, but the dullest man anywhere," she said.

"Everybody thinks her husband is best. What about Bob Wikins? Where does he rate for dullness?"

He thought this was a pretty shrewd thrust (the words fell into a small tangle—shrewd thrust stewed thrush trussed shrew —which clogged his mental progress a moment). "Bob Wilkins is a very sensitive man. Did you ever get him on the subject of birds?"

Stewed thrush, hey that's pretty good. "Birds? No. Why in sweet hell birds?"

"Did you ever talk to Ernie Peabody about classical music?"

"Can't say. . . "

"Of course you haven't. Oh, Fred. You never get to meet more than one-twenteith of anybody."

Ho de ho. He could have answered that with laughable ease except that the drinks chose that moment to start dripping into the switchboard making it difficult to coordinate messages. The white line on the road was trying to swing to the right, nothing serious, but it needed watching.

"You get the same little bit drunk, and little bit hearty, and little bit jerky. You know what's going to happen when we get home, don't you? I could draw dance steps."

She went on talking, and he rather got the idea that he wouldn't need the dance steps. He had done something wrong again, and he was suddenly too sleepy to undo it. So he went stable and she talked some more and soon he was in his pajamas and she was talking and he was stably listening and talk and listen and in no time asleep.

The next morning he was pretty sure they'd had an argument as they sometimes did after parties (something about the way he behaved at parties?). Alison was a stimulating woman, that was for sure. He felt obscurely good about that, anyway, and took a cold shower on it; he mightn't make a big production out of welcoming spring, but he knew it was there all right. Alison never got up for breakfast, which pleased him today. He had the house to himself and padded around happily in the fresh sunshine; took the milk off the porch, and it felt cool and looked, well, milky. Just consider something like milk. What a wonderful thing milk is; what a wonderful gift a new day is.

He felt so good that the idea of having a fiery, quarrelsome wife seemed splendidly interesting. Kept a man on his toes. He stable, she fiery, what more could you ask? . . . A cold frost came down, from Canada no doubt, right after breakfast, dragging a load of dirty clouds and frosty currents. He walked to the bus, hugging what was left of his euphoria, hoping it would last till lunch. Preserve it in newspaper. What a wonderful thing milk is, oh my!

The elevator gorged, disgorged. Fred got out at the twenty-third floor. Before him, the desks tapered away to infinity; the big men in white shirt sleeves were already moving slowly up and down the aisles, carrying papers and saying "would you look this over, Herm"; the first olive-skinned secretaries of the day jiggled around the water cooler—transparent blouses with a thousand straps and pulleys for Fred to brood over when the work got boring.

Alison had been mechanically upset when she saw the office for the only time; she thought it was terrible that people should spend one third of their lives in this platinum rinkydink with its staff lounges and its resident psychiatrists and its restfully shaded toilet bowls; and he knew exactly what she meant, in a way; he knew about dehumanization and all that. But there was another side to it, that she didn't understand. Power or something. Gross National Product. Have seen the future, gentlemen, and it works. Here we are—his desk was thirty-third in line, two stops away from an outright cubicle, an embryonic office of his own. Not bad for a becalmed salesman of twenty-seven. 1984, no doubt about it. Terrible thing. But his heart rose a little as he swiveled into his desk; the anesthesia of routine work about to be slipped over his face.

As he made his eleven o'clock survey of the girls at the cooler, he suddenly felt as sentimental as a German beer song about Alison. Golden girl. Very smart, too: *Ja, ja, mein* girl is smart, *mein* girl is—he felt as if he was walking on sneakers; the office knew no real seasons; everyone looked pale yellow from Christmas to Christmas, and yet there it was, spring fever. The water burbled into his mouth like stream water. He phoned Alison at lunchtime to pass on his latest nuance of mood. They had had an argument last night, tipsy scratching after the party. Should he try to find out what it was all about—or wait until she brings it up? Say something insouciant, perhaps, and see where that leads.

The phone didn't answer and he rested it on his shoulder and ate a sandwich and joked with Ed Pilsudski who had brought the sandwich. Polish-Negro, how'd that happen? He wiped the milk off his lip with a paper napkin. Rags to riches, thirty-five desks in two years, what's the secret F. Cope? How do you explain your meteroric rise?

He called again at 2:00, 3:30 and 4:45. It was a nuisance, because he had to get an outside line every time, and there was a policy about private calls, and the operator had a voice full of the policy. Fred was on the borderline prestige-wise, but he got the calls through after a tiny reprimand, and then nothing happened at the other end after all. The afternoon devil got into the building somehow in spite of all the latest precautions, weaving its way through tranquil colors and homogenized air currents. He shouldn't have eaten a salami sandwich, not after last night: and he certainly shouldn't have eaten the pickle on top of it. And why on top of that didn't his wife answer the phone? He writhed like a monk in the desert: his in-tray was so much dross.

They had had this argument, all right, and it was lost one inch down, like a dream. If he could just catch a corner of it, he could drag the whole thing out. She had delivered so many wistful lectures lately that they tended to merge woozily. Was it about his stuffy politics? Yes, he rather thought so. Was it about his stuffy friends and his stuffy job? Yes, no doubt that was in there too. He shouldn't have had the pickle. It was giving him total recall.

He gave it up and buried himself in his paper work for the rest of the afternoon. On the way home, last night's brawl jogged at him again; it seemed to be a compendium of all the arguments they had ever had. And he remembered, now that was strange, a feeling of frozen horror at one or two points. Funny how that had slipped his mind. His jaw locking in the stable position. Alison scalding wistfully, despairingly into him. Alison saying—he had his *World-Telegram* by now, and kept peeping at it to see what was what, and he lost the corner of colored handkerchief, the dream. The gentle, meaningless variety of his work taught you how to give a few minutes to each of life's problems, a minute to his own, a minute to Elizabeth Taylor's.

There was an advertisement on the seat in front of him showing a man striding along with an enormous, nightmare-sized whiskey bottle in his arms; it reminded Fred to cut back through the Bloodbury shopping center and pick up some provisions. It was all so clean and polite after New York (why people complained about Bloodbury he would never really know), and he walked home with a big package, like the man in the ad.

The house was empty and Alison's car was missing. Alison hadn't left any kind of note, so he supposed she was just out visiting. It was part of her thing not to care about time, and she might not be back until midnight. Fine, fine. It meant at least that he could watch television without feeling that he was letting her down. He could read his paper and do a little work and take in the idiot box, and no one would ever know.

He made a drink and took a conscientious stab at reading Churchill's memoirs, and found that he couldn't get very far with the great Englishman: the unbroken print was too much like work. Eight hours of that was quite enough. He read *Time* magazine instead, and the clock hands whirled, as in the movies, from 7:05 to 7:31 to 8:03, and slowly the house began to empty in earnest. He could hear the deafening crinkle of slick paper, like a radio sound effect, as he turned the pages on his second go-through (he wasn't going to leave out "Religion" or "Latin America" this time), and he suddenly knew that Alison wasn't going to come back tonight. His memory, working on its own time and without any encouragement from him, had sorted out some key words and brought them up from the deep. *"I don't think I can take it any more, Fred. You're not even listening now, are you?"* She said the words in such a pleasant voice, and he was in such a fuzz by then, that he thought for a moment that things were all right again. *"It's not your fault, I know,"* she said. Attababy, I knew she'd see it my way, arguments clear the air. Show me a couple that doesn't argue and I'll show *you* a . . . He remembered trying to kiss her and mysteriously missing, and the light switching off and a period of unparalleled confusion ending suddenly in blackness and a cold shower and breakfast and milk and O.K., no need to go through all that.

So she wouldn't be back at all this evening. He was still slightly relieved to have the house to himself. He had so much on his plate at the time that a few tensionless days were more than welcome. Alison would come back, of course, as she had the other two times. He could be glad to see her, with a sense of standing about awkwardly. For two or three days she would drift around like a visionary, very detached and luminous, and then she would snap out of it, and they could start on a new round of tension.

She must have told him where she was planning to go during the chaotic tail of the conversation, and for how long. The very next evening, Sue MacIntyre came over to take her to ceramics class, and Fred found himself groping for a good non-explanation. "She went to her sister's," he said, but he lied badly and Sue backed off wryly, he could tell she didn't believe him. Alison had no sister, you could tell that just by looking at her.

He couldn't ask anyone if they knew where Alison had gone because he was pretty sure she had told *him*. The week shimmied along and other friends came over, and he felt dimly that they were laughing at him because he'd forgotten where his wife was.

Several times during that first week, Fred toyed with the idea of getting mad. Theoretically he didn't care to be laughed at. "The Moose had a terrible temper when aroused" (—his cousin Willy used to call him the Moose). Alison was playing with the Moose's fuse. She didn't seem to realize that his serenity might not just be dullness, but, well, self-mastery. Hey, hey Big Fred— he had this way of kidding with himself that Alison hated. The Moose wasn't the least bit angry.

He was still more or less relieved, five days later and in spite of the creeping embarrassment, to have the house to himself. Relieved from that reflexive gesture of putting newspapers and magazines down as Alison came into the room; relieved from the fear of stumbling into clichés and getting winced at; relieved from having to be at his best with her. Alison was probably the only thing in the world that made him nervous, but boy, she did a job. In a few days the struggle to be interesting would resume; but meanwhile he was free to follow his own bent, go back to patting his stomach and falling asleep on the sofa while the late show glimmered and the beer cans stank gently around him. He bought magazines that he hadn't bought for years and read them without shame.

From the Tuesday when he discovered her absence to the next Saturday, a swinging orgy of squareness raged at his place. On Saturday he drove to Wensley Park and watched the boys play baseball. They were funny-looking boys, some of them big as men, others quite small. They had uniforms with the names of different schools on them and random numbers, and red caps and blue caps, and some didn't have uniforms or caps at all. It was like when he was a boy, none of this damn organization, and he soon got warmly involved. The third baseman of the Montclair-Nutley-Bloomfield High team was, he noted sternly, afraid of ground balls. But the shortstop was pretty good; if Fred had been a big league scout he would have taken the boy's name down. Might take it down anyhow. Send it in somewhere. The Bloodbury Academy-Nutley-Teaneck team hinged on a big, sullen lefthander who pitched, played first base and hit the ball for miles; but he wasn't big league material, his shoulders didn't look right. And you couldn't invest in his personality either.

It was chilly out there, crisp, an early spring Saturday with some leftover winter haze, and Fred had the car windows all the way up. He could hear faintly through the cold glass a whine of chatter coming from the infielders. "Way to go, pitch it in there, easy out." Puffs of smoke formed ardent captions in front of their mouths. "Attaboy, that's the old pepper," Fred heard himself mutter, and froze. What was *he* talking about pepper for?

Mouthing pep cries in an empty car was just the thing to bring back Alison full force. That argument they had had continued to unravel; memory came gliding up with another message: "Apart from anything else, *It isn't fair to you*"—her hair fell earnestly over her eye, that was what he thought was so sweet; was it then that he tried to kiss her? It was very trying the way she kept on talking when she knew he couldn't follow. Her lips were getting thin—kiss them while there's still time, before they disappear altogether. "*I'll tell you what I'll do, I'll stay in New York for a few days*" that was it, that was it! But how many? To try to remember now was just to feel drunk again. "*I'll stay at the whatzit a thingummy and think things over.*"

He shot home through the quiet, stupid streets; some children jumped out of the way wearing the rabbit look. He slammed the car door and ran into the house. The whatzit a thingummy sounded like a hotel. The Delphi was the only hotel they'd ever stayed at together—try that first. "Mrs. Cope checked out last night. She left no forwarding address"—he had got the right hotel, but the wrong day. She hadn't tried to hide, she had remained ironically accessible. For five days, while he was whuffling beer and second-class matter, she had been thinking things out as a serious person should, on her own, in a hotel room. She didn't have his resources for postponing thought. (What kind of a nut must she think I am, unable to retain a simple conversation until morning?)

For a moment the Moose was ambiguously aroused. Fire roared in his belly. He lifted his foot and heaved it at the TV screen: missed it though, grinned sheepishly and settled for the magazine rack.

3

Next day was Sunday—not the gray, drizzly Sunday he could have wished, but another bright green and blue sparkler. He didn't go to church for once, not because of what Alison said about his churchgoing, but because he couldn't face the effervescent crowd at All Souls. Spring coats and all that. Canon Flood asking after his wife. He would lose his half ounce of anger right away, talking to the rosy canon. People saying "How's Alison, how's Alison."

The Sunday papers lay on the doorstep. He tipped them with his slipper, Let them lie. Today of all days, boy. No papers, no TV. Try to think. Think for twelve hours? Sure, why not. Alison's friend, Fletcher Merryweather, thinks, for one. You have to show him his own bathroom, but he thinks. He looked at his watch, five to nine. Think, go on, *you* try it. Head the wrong shape, come on, no excuses. Alison and me, Alison and me what? Alison and me—got *married*. For a moment, he began to wonder if he'd lost the whole process: like forgetting how to talk or how to breathe. He remembered Doctor Romilly's whiskey tenor "Breathe in—no, Fred, you're breathing out," and he suddenly couldn't remember which way was in. Years ago. The time he had pneumonia. Thirteen years old, with the little brown radio going all day long, methodically scrambling the sick people's brains. Breakfast at Sardi's, Breakfast with Don somebody, Breakfast with somebody else—who was that stupid couple?

Sneak up on thinking this way—but already he was stuck, trying to remember radio programs. After breakfast, what came next? The organ music, the motherly women—*Portia Faces Life*—hospital voice, bright, tender, hello everybody toothpaste does he love me yes, in his own queer way I think he does fresh pineapple juice, only 10:30. His mother picking up books with asperity and putting them away. In the one bookshelf they had. So he listened to the radio when he might have been reading. That's where he had gone wrong. Naughty mother. *Inner Sanctum* which was that, Friday nights, *Gang Busters*, Bill Stern—"and the name of that big-hearted, one-legged ping-pong champion was . . . Princess Elizabeth." His cousin Willy's patter. *I Love a Mystery.* "Archie the manager speaking."

Think. The signs that said "Think" didn't know what they were talking about. It was an invitation to chaos. Like Fibber McGee's closet, Tuesday night. Mr. Cope used to stay home for Fibber McGee. He laughed every time the stuff fell out of the closet. A startled sort of laugh, some memory of a real closet opening perhaps.

Oh, come on now. He looked at his watch. Seven minutes was a tiny part of twelve hours. And his free association was only running him backwards deep into the pointless past. He'd be onto the wartime movies if he didn't watch out. ("*Achtung* . . . fil-thy little swine" cut it out now.) He lit a cigarette. Thirty-nine cigarettes, at ten minutes apiece, would take six and a half hours. Six and a half hours divided into—The day stretched off in the endless distance, a roll of gray cloth. It was just Alison's joke about him and the papers, you couldn't really have a craving for something as mild as a newspaper. They were still draped seductively on the porch in their bright skin of funnies. Pick one up and glance at the headlines maybe. Carve twenty minutes out of the eternal day. He found himself starting to get up just automatically. He wanted to look at those damned newspapers. So humiliating, *nobody* felt this way about newspapers.

That brought him at last to the outer reaches of thought. It wasn't the newspapers, said Alison, it was the absence of anything else. He just wouldn't *try*. That must have been after he had kissed the pillow. The light was out, and everything seemed very strange and important in the dark. The pillow, a great gray leviathan, sprawled amorously between him and his wife. If he tried for a hundred years, he couldn't produce a more peculiar arrangement. Alison's lips looked so thin, but they tasted like cotton and horsefeathers as they pulled away. On the other side of the pillow her voice sounded like ice in a shaker. If she ever stopped talking, he would tell her that; might amuse her. . . . But he couldn't wait around indefinitely, and at last he weaved off into black tangles of sleep, leaving her to it.

. . . And yet he didn't quite go to sleep, but hung onto semiconsciousness like a thread, because he didn't want to *offend* her.

"*All right dear,*" he said at one point, "*I'm sorry I disappoint you, but I am awfully sleepy. What do you say we—*" No loving tonight. Much too tired now to wait for a favorable climate. Pity. Take what's left of your mind off it. Sublimate, you fool. Pretend you're playing golf. He could hear her voice from a great distance away, calling him from the clubhouse. "*Why don't you at least get angry, Fred?*" So sleepy and confused. "*Everyone's entitled to their opinion,*" he mumbled.

He played a beautiful approach shot onto the ninth green, with the sand spraying in front of him like gold dust. He had to take this stuff from her because he believed in marriage. You worked at it, the joys and the heartaches. Why did women like to talk so much at night, really should try to answer some of the points she's making tonight, simply too tired to move. And so he slept and listened, anxious to seem attentive, for the sake of the marriage.

He stood up now and decided to make some coffee. That whole sequence had lasted exactly four minutes. Coffee then. He enjoyed an excuse to go out to the sunny kitchen again. Alison had spattered it with burlap and disguised orange crates—it was her rumpus room, her joy of cooking, joy of furnishing, room: you could easily give someone the wrong impression of Alison, couldn't you? If you just went by her kitchen and a few other things, you might expect someone with black slacks and dirty hair. And late meals and burnt food. He shook his head. He didn't want the damn house to himself. He wanted Alison. He guessed he did, anyway. What she called his bovine lust. For the first time in five days. Clockwork Fred. *"O.K., I'm sorry." "And what is the point of saying that?" "I don't know. I thought it might help." "It doesn't, it makes it worse."* Bovine lust foiled again. Even though it was his script.

The coffee hissed and made him jump. *"I don't think I'll ever understand you, Fred." "Wait a minute while I fix the coffee."* For a moment he actually thought there was somebody there. *"You really like Bloodbury, don't you Fred?"* The arrow quivered in his chest. *"You don't care if we never leave, do you?"* He poured the coffee and sat down. The question was two years old at least, so there was no hurry about answering it. It was a test question. *"You like the whole thing, don't you, Fred, physically, the casual calling to order, 'you'll read the minutes, will you Fred?' and then, 'We'll let Fred take care of the refreshments. We'll leave the refreshments to Fred,' you like*

Bloodbury." Well perhaps he liked it better than staying home and watching Alison grow; perhaps he liked it better than fighting his embarrassment over her behavior. Perhaps.

It all went back to their courtship. She was the prettiest girl who had ever taken an interest in him—though not quite the most intelligent, he was catnip to intelligent girls for some reason. No doubt they considered him an intellectual reclamation project. Alison was a great suburb-hater, but then they all were. Not having thought much about it, he supposed he was too—it wasn't something you had to do anything about, in any case. (It was, Alison was to say later, very suburban to hate the suburbs in that particular way.) Anyway, she looked so pretty as she denounced women's organizations that they took on an erotic significance all their own. We might have to live in a suburb for a year or two, she said, but we needn't pretend to like it. Right! They would live as they pleased, she said and damn the neighbors. Right, right! Denouncing the suburbs was the craziest aphrodisiac he'd ever come across.

Well, they did have to move into a suburb—and what a suburb. Bloodbury was the real thing, all dry cleaning and furniture shops; no bars, no restaurants, no places to meet. Even a Montclair man had to readjust downwards to Bloodbury. Alison, of course, refused to join anything, preferring to stay home and make her own clothes; and Fred felt he couldn't join either, after what he'd said. So he found himself with great oceans of saved time to deal with. Alison dug up some ratty-looking friends of her own, a Central European cello teacher, some ceramics buffs and a six-foot-tall abstract paintress, none of which he would have thought possible in Bloodbury; but he never knew where to begin with that crowd, and it made him tense talking to people with foreign accents.

And then she wanted to throw even that up and move into the "real" country. Great idea, of course, but he stalled on it for business reasons. For the same reasons they compromised a little with Bloodbury, they went along. They saw some of his new friends, business people, bus mates, and they kept a reputable living room. Organic furniture, or whatever the hell, was kept to the back of the house. He told her that, just for a while, he had to think of appearances. At that stage, she had nothing special against his job, she took his word that it was a means to an end, and that his end was roughly the same as hers: independence and life-as-a-work-of-art. So they got in some Bloodbury tables and carpets and subdued lighting which gave them at least one room, plus a downstairs bathroom, that you could take *anyone* to.

On his own, he would have gone on tut-tutting about the suburbs and fraternizing with them indefinitely. It was Alison who saw that old Fred was living a lie. The first veil came off after a dinner at the Peabodys three months after they got back from their honeymoon. He just couldn't pretend to himself that he hadn't enjoyed himself that evening: he'd talked a lot, had a jolt of Courvoisier, well, he just felt tremendously good. His guard was down around his ankles. "*I just don't understand people like that,*" said Alison. "*What was that, dear?*" "*They're probably interesting people underneath. Everybody's interesting underneath. But—please don't pat your stomach like that, dear—you look like a Shriner.*" "*Eh? Oh, God, yes.*" "*Their conversation is like somebody saying 'don't look at me, I'm not interesting, I haven't got an immortal soul or anything like that, but we got this rug for a song.'*" He felt flustered, because he couldn't shed the good time quickly enough to agree sincerely. (What was all that about rugs, anyway? Should he say something about rugs?) Instead he said, "*Yes, that Ernie is pretty much of a bore, I guess. But, as you say, underneath* everyone *is interest—*" He felt the eyes on him, for the first time. She didn't say anything then, they were still some months away from a real bloodletting. But he knew something had gone wrong; her sorrowful fanatic's eyes suggested that perhaps his life wasn't quite the work of art it could be. She looked so grave and lovely that he perjured himself and said he'd had a lousy time, but it didn't do him a bit of good.

The last of Cope's seven veils must have come off the other night—she had ripped it off while he was half asleep "*One couldn't even have a real renunciation scene with such an inattentive man,*" she said. . . . To his delight fifty minutes had just gone by in a swoon. He drank the cold coffee and tried to plan his next move. One thing he knew was, she hadn't gone back to Stapleton. You don't leave a Fred Cope just to get back to a Stapleton, Pennsylvania. He pushed the thought away with sly violence: he wasn't going to look there.

In a way, he didn't feel ready to find her yet, though he supposed he ought to look. The thread of sex attraction that each, for some wild reason, held an end of was still intact. But otherwise they were hopelessly alienated. Her electricity intimidated him. He would have to become a new man, a true-blue artifart with a new set of tail feathers. She said he was too fat to change. She said, *I dare you—Just get out. Leave the damn house. Drive the car into the lake. Burn your neckties—See, you can't, you can't.*

He could, of course, in one sense. His unemphatic father, now retired to Florida, had bequeathed him an unemphatic nest egg on his twenty-first birthday, and it had lain untouched for six years at the Bloodbury Corn Exchange; his mother had left him some stocks; he was abysmally secure.

Nobody really did things like that, not even Alison. But he did phone the Delphi Hotel, where Alison had been staying, and booked a room for the night. Too fat, eh? He replaced the kitchen phone, feeling a little surprised by his impulsiveness. Maybe she'd left a clue in the hotel register, or let something slip to a bellboy, was that why he had just booked the room? (She's my wife, of course one has to look for her. Naturally.) He packed his bag with the kind of silent-comedy speed he needed to go through with something like this. Something quite childish and pointless. To be abandoned on the grounds of extreme boredom, well it hurt.

(Apart from anything else, how could you face the judge?) He went whistling across the porch, pausing at the papers, glancing down the steps . . . Without a wife, who needs a newspaper? Chinese saying. . . Part of his brain mocked at him relentlessly, and he sensed himself smiling back at it with a sort of apologetic determination as he scampered over the lawn, with his suitcase clashing against his leg. He didn't know what he was going to do, but he was going to do something. And that for a man of his particular life-style was intoxication enough.

2
Square sets forth

Fred didn't know the times of the Sunday buses and had to wait half an hour on the corner, with his suitcase and his lightly flapping overcoat. Don't get bored already, he told himself grimly, or we're all licked. Use your eyes or something. Who lived in that house, for instance? It looked like a doctor's house, with the prosperous sandstone walls and the spruce gravel paths: the doctor will be a few minutes, step this way and look at his ten-dollar magazines. Next to that was the Merryweathers', of course, all shuttered up for Sunday, but pretty soon now Fletcher Merryweather would be out in his shorts, pushing the mower and trimming the whatthehell azaleas, it was good to notice things, he was excited about it.

All the way into New York he watched the bus window, and took in a whole stretch of highway he had never seen before. There was nothing much to please the eye, but this was a side of life too, the gas stations, lot of Mobilgas sold around here, and the brown what was it straw? bamboo? of the Jersey fens. What kind of people lived around here? he wondered. Swamp people in clapboard shacks. Pig farming. The world was full of interest, when you looked around. (God, all this bustle, where are we rushing to anyway? Those were the things the right people asked.)

Eighth Avenue in its Sunday best. Pawn shops with saxaphones in the window, hardware stores full of window-box tools, chili con carne stands, all dead as Moscow on a Sunday, of course, but latent as hell. He stood at the corner of Forty-second tasting the different flavors, exulting in his discovery. The rich weave of everyday things.

Rust, grit, yellow faces. Abstract of Sunday subway. Rattle and thrust. Long, kinky cigarette butts on the metal steps. Street, sudden explosion of daylight, Sunday faces in the cafeteria window. Montage of Fred on the glass looking at man eating pie. By the time he reached the metal awning of the Delphi, he was just recording rather blankly. That's a hat shop. Brims still getting smaller, I see. And that's a tie shop. Hmm. And here we have a Nedick's.

Did the life-people keep this up all day—recording, vibrating, maybe it was a knack you acquired. He looked at his watch and it was only ten of two. He still had the afternoon to cope with. It wasn't a problem any more, but this was certainly a record day for length.

He checked into his hotel. His wife's name was in the old-fashioned register, in her own hand, and the Bloodbury address next to it. No, he couldn't have the same room, it was occupied—by a Mr. Schneider it looked like from upside down— but he could have the one adjoining. There didn't seem any special point in having a room next to Mr. Schneider, but he took that one anyway, and was soon on his melancholy way with the bellboy. Have you seen my wife, young man? An old hotel with ferns in the lobby and a European elevator. The room was in hotel olive and the bedspread was pink with crinkles.

I'm a detective, start talking, young man, oh, "thanks— There." The boy was gone before he had time to ask about Mrs. Cope.

He sat in the room most of the afternoon, feeling quite apathetic and not at all sure what to do next. He didn't know where to begin looking or who to question—everything was closed on a Sunday anyway, better start tomorrow; he was too torpid to move. Meanwhile the drama of everyday life went pounding along outside, and now he found he couldn't stop observing it: but just in these dismal waves of awareness. The decimated Sunday life of the city. A woman walking her dog, terrier, was it? he didn't know much about dogs. A car (Buick) trying to park in front of the hotel; the doorman snarling like a bulldog, protecting his master's frontage. The car stayed and a fat man got out. The doorman dipped under the awning, with defeated shoulders. The fat man went into the flower shop, opening the door with a key on a key ring.

There was nothing to read except the Bible. He picked that up several times, without thinking, and put it down again with irritation. He hadn't come here to read the Bible. Oh, no, he didn't care, but it couldn't be only twenty past two. His watch must have stopped. He held it to his ear; it gave a loud derisive tick. He lined up the shot and fired the watch at the wastebasket. Become a new man with these big careless gestures. It hit the tin with a clunk and went on ticking, with a metallic echo. Maybe he should drown it instead. Tick blub tick at the bottom of the tub, there was no way of destroying it, it was a closed system. He plunged it deep in the suitcase and went back to the window.

He managed a kind of time-destroying trance at last. Two Armenians were arguing, they looked as if they might run rival health-food stores, and the next thing he knew the lights were on across the street and the Armenians were gone. He could always sleep easily, that was the other thing. Lights twinkled along the street, amazing lot of lights for a Sunday. The couple in the opposite window could have been in Bloodbury. The man had reached the book section, the woman was knitting the neck and holding the sweater against her chest for guidance. They were little clockwork people, at the hour he would strike her with his newspaper and she would bow deeply. The man stood up and unraveled the Venetian blind, and they were gone again.

A city lighting up. All these separate lives. Tiny dramas. A woman working in her kitchen. Chunking the icebox shut and dropping the frozen peas into fizzing water. Teenagers hawking each other on a sofa. Old lady at a window—looking back at him, by George. He grinned and waved. Old lady impassive as marble.

Sweeping along the ribbon of street, the people got smaller. The lights got, well, elfin . . . *with metaphors like that, you can drain the magic from any scene.* Fairy lights, he knew from Alison that that was a secondhand image. He wasn't really thinking about fairy lights. It was just a manner of speaking. The woman in the kitchen took off her apron and doused the light. The teenagers remembered about the blind. Leaving nothing but the implacable old lady. Something a bit oppressive about the old lady.

Down the street again, pedestrians beginning to cluster and

merge, wedges of hats and hair drifting along. It wasn't that he was losing interest, but it took a real, conscious effort not to head back for his suitcase and fish out the watch.

A tug of fretted nerves at his elbow and another at the back of his neck got him away from the window at last. Separate lives, what mysteries behind the blinds, twinky winky lights, pedestrians—with a twinge of disgust, he realized that he didn't give a damn about everyday life, he disliked the stuff and wished to hell it would go away.

He phoned the desk and asked about Mrs. Cope, and they didn't know anything, so he said, "Oh." The green blank walls, the Bible, think, dream, do *something*. Boredom had, he suddenly realized, a sort of stale green flavor. It was three inches thick at the base and when it placed two fingers on top of your skull and one at each temple, you could hear a very thin humming noise. It was also much closer to fear than he had ever expected.

The next day, he quit his job. He hadn't meant to at first. He was going to ask Mr. Thurman for a leave of absence so that he could look for his wife, but the full absurdity of this hit him in midsentence, he looked up at Mr. Thurman in a fluster of dislike and embarrassment, looked at his desk with nothing on it except a toy flag and, under a confluence of impulses that he would never quite understand, said, "I quit."

For a moment he was flooded with ambiguous triumph. "*Call me a bore will you? Think I'm glued to this brainless life?*" Mr. Thurman looked gratifyingly surprised—Fred could imagine him thinking: "Cope hasn't seemed tired or depressed or extra puffy around the eyes. But I guess you have to expect these sneaky abberations in a big organization." He asked Fred if anything was wrong, and if he had any plans. "Need a change," Fred muttered, and Mr. Thurman's agitation surfaced and glowed on his fluorescent skin. He probably thought that somebody had made Fred a better offer. "Glad to have you back if you change your mind," he said stiffly. Fred could sense him sniffing for booze and turned his mouth away instinctively.

The thing was that Mr. Thurman was the kind of man who thought he ran a happy ship. Fred was mildly elated to realize he was doing something that Thurman would never understand: which automatically raised him above the Thurman class, admittedly the lowest. The recessive chin, which Fred associated for some reason with Philadelphia, trembled with surmise: his whole face was in second-rate torment. Was he dealing with an out-and-out nut, or was some company draining off his young talent? "Always a place, reconsider, happy ship," Thurman crooned. The interview was over and Fred wandered forlornly back over the thick gray carpet. What the hell had he wrought this time? *"You're getting too fat to quit your job, too fat to make a move of any kind."* O.K., I made a move of some kind, what next?

He took a subway down to Greenwich Village. He would base himself there while he looked for Alison. Good place to pick up her rhythm too, of course. Alison's friends said that the real Village had disappeared, that you had to go to First Avenue or somewhere; but he wasn't ready yet for pastrami and the roach explosion. Work his way up to it perhaps. He wasn't thinking very clearly this morning. The main thing was, you couldn't go back to Bloodbury—this evening, or next—if you didn't know where your wife was. Hard to explain, but you just couldn't.

He had never been down there in the daytime before. This obviously wasn't the picturesque part. The cross streets were mousy and looked like Philadelphia (must stop thinking about Philadelphia); Seventh Avenue was nothing but blast and rumble and sprint for the lights. He found a sort of agency on Seventh which doubled as notary public and CPA and looked as if it would fake visas for you in the back. A fat man was pumping something in triplicate through the typewriter, a writ of abortion, no doubt. A couple and child were waiting patiently: big redheaded man, colored girl, sleeping child. Fred did a slow double take—were they *married?*

Of course, of course, and a good thing too. He sat on his thoughts and waited. He felt liverish and slightly hungover. The fat man yanked out the wedge of documents and began to roll up some more. There was no way of telling whether he'd seen his clients. The couple looked like the people you see in Greyhound terminals, waiting for hopelessly lost baggage.

"You looking for an apartment?" the redhead asked Fred.

"Yes, that's right."

"My wife and I've been looking all over town."

"The rents are always too high," said the girl.

"The rooms are too small," said the man.

"No parks for the child. We thought maybe down here . . ."

The redhead scrupulously didn't mention his main difficulty. It was like Archie the Manager explaining why two-headed Bruskin couldn't get into the Army—flat feet or something. Didn't these people *know?* Or had they decided the only sane way was to ignore it?

Well, down here it might be all right. "With you folks in a minute," said the fat man. "I just got out of the Navy," the redhead explained. "We were married overseas."

"You just got back, you mean? You never had to look for a place before?"

"That's it, just got back."

"O.K.," said the fat man, "which of you people's first?"

There wasn't much choice among his brochures and little pink cards. The new beehives were much too expensive, and anyway inadequate to Fred's aesthetic needs. He might as well go back to Bloodbury for that kind of thing. The only other possibility was a rent-controlled walkup on Charles Street. Several other people were interested: the owner would choose the least messy tenant sometime that afternoon.

They filled out the forms, and it occurred to Fred that he was a pretty desirable fellow real-estate-wise: no children, no cats, solid references. He felt the ghost of a qualm as he watched the redhead damning himself: he was probably out of work and kept a bloodhound. At least there was no question on the form about race. Possibly illegal. The point was, Fred would never get an apartment if he gave in to his feelings every time. He put down Thurman as a reference, and Ernie Peabody too, before he had had time to think it through.

The fat man turned out to be tiny when he stood up. Perhaps he had been standing all along. He locked up his store and walked them over to Charles Street. The girl carried the baby patiently and it slept all the way as if it was already worn out from fencing with these damn agents.

The apartment was up four flights, and darkened through and through by a warehouse with a blank rust-colored back, a brick wall without windows, which leaned wearily against the apartment house's rear. The building was shabby respectable, not at all picturesque.

It was a mockery, being shown round a place so small. Even pausing to flush the toilet's sinuses and run the faucets, the survey took only three and a half minutes. There were technically

three rooms, but you were no sooner in one than you were halfway out of it. The walls were pink and gunmetal gray and peel-
ing. Was this what the world had come to, then: the world's
greatest city . . .

"You have to provide your own sheets and towels," said the
agent. "Otherwise it goes as a furnished apartment."

He didn't bother to make it sound attractive. People were
fighting for their lives to get it. The armchair with the sunken
bottom, the bed with the spinal curve, were furniture in this
rotten, stinking world.

"You can do better than this," Fred told the redhead, "for
a family."

"It's about like the others, better than some." The wife's
eyes had a dull shine almost of hope. If Fred didn't like it,
they were that much ahead.

They trundled slowly down the stone stairs, slowly because
the baby was wriggling solemnly, though its eyes were wisely
shut. Where had they met? Was she American? What did the
Navy think? These were strange waters to Fred. He had almost
wept when Marlon Brando had married the Japanese girl in the
movie, but he hadn't known about the walkup then, or the
baby that looked tired from birth. Must think this thing out
sometime.

You've all of you come to a pretty pass, said the agent's eyes,
wanting a place like this. "That's all we've got right now," he
said. "It's a nice little buy."

They arranged to get in touch with him during the afternoon,
and he went back to his shabby illegal-looking store. Fred shook
hands with the redhead and his wife, who stuck hers out under
the shawl, so that she pumped the baby as well. "I hope you get

it," said Fred. The redhead smiled. His teeth looked a hundred years old. "Good-by," he said.

Fred watched them walking very slowly toward West Fourth, resigning themselves into a sea of tight trousers and dirty hair. He went looking for a place to eat.

You could withdraw the application, but honestly, what good would it do? The redhead was so far down on the list, ten places away at least. Besides, if they weren't wanted in the neighborhood, wouldn't they be unhappy there? Fred bit into a pebble in his hamburger and loosened a tooth.

At three-thirty he went back to the agent. The fat man had the phone nestled deep into his cheek. Mustn't keep thinking of him as the fat man—that's the kind of category that drives Alison wild. His name is Marconi, initials H. W. Think of him as, say, Herbert. "I was just talking to your new landlord. He's coming right down." The contempt in Marconi's voice was stale as an old cigar: he despised people who wanted apartments. Fred felt as if he had been tossed thirty silver dollars.

"Look, I—" Marconi shuffled his papers. He didn't respond to strangled cries. "The lady's skin had nothing to do with it, had it?" asked Fred, forcing the words up his throat.

Marconi looked up, surprised at a breach of manners in a desirable tenant. "We never considered it."

"Did you show the landlord the forms? Or did you give him a verbal description?"

"He'll be right down with the keys and we can fix up the lease," said Marconi, and began typing like a dervish.

Fred felt sick. It was a rotten thing he'd done. If only he had had time to think—but that, as his wife had had occasion to observe, was the picture with squares. Their immediate responses were always wrong, she said. It took so long for them to get in touch with what they really ought to feel that by then the game was over and everybody had gone home.

It was chilly in his new house. In the gloom and hurry of moving he had forgotten to get the new sheets and blankets, so he lay under his overcoat, trying to follow the curves of the bed and huddle up warm at the same time. There was a light coming into his eyes whichever way he faced, refracted violently off the warehouse wall, and he had ripped off the shade trying to smother the glow. Outside he could hear the trucks cannonading along Houston Street, rattling his thin windows—what the hell was he doing here? What crazy game was he playing?

That couple were serious, they needed a place to live. Where were they now? In the park, or what? He didn't know what happened to homeless people after dark. They put newspaper under their trousers, but then what? Was the girl still holding the baby? he wondered. He would have put on his trousers himself and gone looking, only it was so hopeless. Nobody would ever find them again. While up here lies racist-pig Fred Cope, who drinks after breakfast and is out of work—that was too crazy even to think about—quivering with cold in an apartment he probably needed less than anyone else in the world, and trying to ward off the light and noise of a place that didn't want him and would never want him. The only consolation was that old Thurman would never understand why he was doing it. What a burner on Thurman.

His feet were cold but at least they had socks on. His fingers were almost frostbitten. He worked them up under the coat and looked at the watch. Half past eleven. He pulled his knees up through the valley of the mattress and waited for morning.

2

His decision to stay on a bit longer at Charles Street was not the clear strong thing he would have liked it to be, but a mosaic of lesser indecisions. Giving up his job—was he mad? was his first waking thought the next morning. Staying home on a Tuesday was a terrible thing to do. He walked barefoot over the bathroom tiles as a form of vaguest atonement. The roaches scurried away in organized distaste. He sat down and reached for a nonexistent magazine.

A bathroom without a magazine was a Royal Command to think.

Most people, he supposed, would know how to go about looking for their wives; it was the kind of thing one did instinctively. He could hear Alison's voice, piercing as a dog whistle now, explaining why he lacked this instinct. *Fred, you have no instincts* was what it came to.

He thought of trying cryptic personal ads in the papers, that his friends wouldn't understand, based on private jokes (but did he and Alison *have* any private jokes, besides their marriage itself?). He thought of the police, and Alison said, *Yes, you're the kind of man who would call for the police*. It sounded as if it might be one of those unthinkable things. If he tried writing to her so-called friends—or even to her care of her so-called friends—they would know he had mislaid her: I mean, "Have you seen my wife"—honestly! it was funny. Alison had always discussed his shortcomings quite gently, as if she really did want to understand him. But in memory, she had become much harsher and more vicious. Her face had sharpened like a knife. Some part of his mind must always have seen her like that, he supposed.

He was embarrassed about having behaved like a nut in front of Thurman, too. What had gotten into him? Spending the night in a hotel must have temporarily dislocated him. He had woken up on the Monday morning feeling lightheaded, had a huge breakfast—that much he could trace. Then he had stopped in a bar on the way to work, as an interesting new gesture, and look what had happened.

He tried to picture himself weaving and staggering into Thurman's office, because drunkenness was an excuse he could accept. But in fact he had had only one drink, and he knew it. His impulsive resignation alarmed him. Was he losing contact? For a moment his day-to-day style had cracked, and he could see something wild and confused within. Seal it up quick, quick. He had a sort of offer from Garden State Trust up his sleeve, *that* was why he had quit. . . .

The toilet was full of leaky, New York grievances. After a few minutes, he gave up thinking, etc., and went out and phoned Garden State, to make sure he was all right over there, at least. He was told that the offer had evaporated. (It was one of those party offers, made by a gloriously unauthorized official of the company.)

In a mood of proto-fear, he pounded back upstairs and wrote to Thurman to say that he guessed he had been feeling stale and a bit tense—we all have those days don't we, J. B.?—but seriously, maybe he *could* use a layoff, a sort of sabbatical, and come back fresh, as you, sir, had suggested.

Thurman's answer arrived two days later, bursting with relief and triumph, to say that coming back would, alas, be out of the question, but watch that health, cackle cackle— Fred was quite shaken. He had done something quite insane and Thurman's letter confirmed it; he felt hot behind the ears all morning, and came within an ace of phoning Peabody and letting his hair down.

For some reason, he didn't. He felt undressed without a job, but he didn't actually need one. *You can't face leisure,* the new Alison whistled, like a kettle. *Can't face people asking "What do you do, Fred?" and not having an answer.* An all but dead nerve of curiosity stirred in his, well, vitals, and he decided to stick it out a tiny bit longer. He had, he supposed, backed into the sort of position that even Alison would call interesting. He was out of work, displaced: did doing interesting things make you interesting, or was it vice versa? Anyway, there was absolutely no need to panic. He was dismally secure. He had enough money to stay here a few weeks or even months, major in eccentricity and think of ways of finding his wife, until the money ran out—then Ernie Peabody would take him in as a partner, manufacturing ladies' clichés, what the crap.

Let's take a look at this thing, then. Scruffy trees beginning to sprout lightly, scattered action in the window boxes, defrosting cement, constituted the flora. The old men exulted in the spring weather and bathed their bones in thin sunshine. Fred dug himself in and waited for the action to start. Eccentric Greenwich Village action (partly kidding, of course).

He hadn't thought out where the action would come from, exactly . . . people knocking on his door by mistake, maybe, real certified eccentrics standing next to him at building sites— in his Village reading, people never had any trouble meeting.

There were always lesbians, fetishists, masseurs, piled high on the doorstep: fiction, no doubt, but you'd expect at least *one* fetishist . . .

But four flights was a long way for anyone to climb by mistake. Fellow arrived the second night looking for a party, but he wasn't so much interesting as drunk, and he went roaring straight down again. Saying "zoom." An insurance salesman from Fred's own company made the trip and sat in the sunken armchair, out of place but eerily persuasive, and Fred almost bought some more insurance. Across the hall, a young Italian couple played WQXR from five in the morning to midnight. Downstairs a large Jewish family managed to live almost inaudibly in two rooms, banging on his pipes when he played his new radio too late. And so on all the way down, everyone bucking for Bloodbury.

As to the building sites—it was surprising to find that sloppy, casual people could be almost as furtive as neat, dull ones. He said, "It's a shame what they're doing to the Village" and "Is that checkmate?" and they gave him the rabbit look and the old "Mmph." There was real fear in their faces sometimes.

He walked the streets hopefully, looking into Chinese laundries, trying the different restaurants, wondering how much being Fred Cope disqualified you from real life. Everyone else was young and thin. And unhealthy and sensitive. He imagined them whispering "Here comes one of *them*. Everyone look furtive."

And he *was* one of "them," he could see it himself. Even the pockmarked bathroom mirror said, God, Cope, you're wholesome. The heavy honest line of jaw was equivalent to an Eisenhower button or a football letter. He felt simply huge as he lunged around his tiny flat, wondering why he was dull, what was the X factor? and, with the next breath, trying dutifully to think of ways of finding his wife. Hire a Pinkerton's man maybe, a wily gumshoe. It was too fantastic to contemplate.

He kept off the newspapers, not that he really took that business seriously, and bought some pocket books. There they were again, the lesbians, the junkies, the masseurs. Book people. Maybe those were the people he saw on West Fourth Street gathering every night like moths under the street lights, fluttering, transparent (Here comes Fred Cope now, open-book Fred, living yawn Cope. Don't bug us, there's a good fellow).

He went to bars, but the only people who would talk to him were the people who had always talked to him: the people who spilled their drinks and mopped at them fretfully with their handkerchiefs. The Black Cat down the street was supposed to be a hangout for mandarin beats, so he decided to make that his ace in the hole. If nothing happened there, he would just give up. Second week out, he put on his tweed coat and took off his tie and mooched along to the Cat.

He got there early, but the bar was already crowded. He gave his order over two men in cloth caps and dripped some shocked beer on them when the barman said "Thirty-five cents, please." "Thirty-five cents for a beer?" "That's right," said the barman in a gust of rage. "*Thirty-five cents.*"

"It's since the place got famous. It isn't the same," said one of the men in cloth caps.

"I'm sorry I spilled beer on you, sir," said Fred.

Very noisy though, fellow couldn't seem to hear, down there under the hat. "Nobody comes here any more, it's a tourist trap," he said.

"Is that so?" Fred boomed, brushing the beer into the cap.

"What?"

"I said, is that so?"

Fred had made a friend, but they couldn't get in touch. Fred wanted to give it another try, but the man seemed to get existential nausea when he looked up and he turned back to his friend, leaving Fred mired in an encouraging smile. The man had just wanted to say that about the place being a tourist trap.

The early crowd at the tables could have been tourists at that. Their eyes swung like raking searchlights, probing for celebrities and hoping for unforgettable action, lighting up hopefully at Fred and dismissing him over and over.

They're not really looking at me, are they? He was getting trapped between the crowd at the bar and the newcomers pounding through the door, Paranoiaville Junction. Everyone else seemed to find a niche, but Fred was stuck in the slipstream, saying "Excuse me" and "Watchit, There." They were pretty rough too, with their bony shoulders, and the girls with the thin heads and ratty faces . . . he was getting to dislike this crowd but he ordered another beer and hoped they would start to look better in a minute.

The smoke and the splintering noise and everyone looking so ugly, why did artists look so dirty and ugly? not to other artists no doubt . . . it was really quite depressing. He was too old to be upset because no one would talk to him. Or because everyone who caught his eye in the glass looked like a homosexual with designs on him. But for an old salesman, he had certainly gone all to hell poise-wise.

"Hi, Fred."

Whosat? The bar mirror teemed like a scene by the Ganges, and he felt a great swirling displacement in his area. A hand thrust through and slapped at his shoulder blade. "Fred Cope, you son of a gun." He was filled with a wild, Dale Carnegie joy. He looked cautiously back over his shoulder. It wasn't possible, Ernie Peabody, no, no, *no.* Ernie, baby.

"I thought I saw you standing over there," said Ernie. "You with somebody?

"No."

"We have a table if you'd care—"

Peabody didn't have to finish his sentences; most of them had been finished long ago by the great American consensus. . . . Laugh at Ernie, O.K., but there he was. A friend.

A well-scrubbed, shiny friend in a sea of black fingernails.

"Joe, I'd like you to meet Fred Cope. Fred, this is Joe (something that sounds like Brodsky), one of our clients. Joe's from Chicago." But the chin was made in Philadelphia. Stop saying that about Philadelphia.

"It's a wonderful atmosphere down here," said Joe.

"Joe wanted to see some of the real Village, so naturally I brought him to the Black Cat."

Joe and Ernie looked wonderfully exotic in their business suits. Across the table, when they got to it, a beard smirked at them without warning, a wet white twist of lips; a girl flopped sightless, profoundly contemptuous. Fred hoped he didn't look like Ernie, who was saying, "How come your wife let you out, Fred? Fred has a beautiful wife, you know—and intelligent, oh, boy. I'm frightened to talk to her, you know that, Fred? A genius, I bet. How is Alison, Fred?"

He wondered what kind of appearances he'd left behind. A porch overgrown with newspapers and milk, of course. A car gathering dust. A spring lawn beginning to pop and straggle. He hadn't had the nerve to go back and fix things.

Ernie was looking at him without guile. Bloodbury was not

a terribly gossipy town and anyway Ernie was above personalities. He mightn't know. This might be Fred's chance to send back a discreet message, try to plant the news in a favorable way, though with such crazy news, what could you do? "We've separated. Temporarily," he said.

"Oh, my, that's too bad," said Ernie. Joe clucked agreement. Fred was startled by their instant understanding. "I and Anne separated temporarily once. A lot of people do," Ernie said. "I think *Coronet* had an article about it."

"It was the *Digest*," said Joe.

"No, it was *Coronet*, Joe— it said marriages often improve with a separation—"

"It was the *Digest*."

Everyone in the bar had bumped into him at least once by now. That should be enough. They wore those huge duffle coats, which brushed against his face now that he was sitting down. He could tell it was raining out. Swoosh.

Aloof and radiant sat Joe and Ernie. "I'm sure it was the *Digest*." "Well, anyway." They had another round of beers, and Ernie said, "This is great beer," which it wasn't and Brodsky praised the pretzels, which were just pretzels, and with the elbows pumping and dripping onto his head, Fred began to feel kind of lousy. It wasn't his philosophy of life he was worried about any more, but the minute-to-minute discomfort. He clawed, pretty rough himself by now, to the men's room, where the customers were slowly wearing down a big chunk of ice; and when he got back, Ernie had lined up more beers.

"We'll ask Fred," said Ernie. The article was in *Playboy*. No, what was that? "Fred, Joe was talking about the last I.P.A. stock split. I thought it was" —It was a nightmare, that's what it was.

Fred had his pneumonia dream. The oxygen was going way down, and the nurses were pumping desperately, filling his mouth with smoke. The decks were jammed with people in inflated life-jackets. Girl screaming with dirty hair. Beard caked with cheap food, fanning her cheek. Back to sleep, everybody, it's better asleep.

"Fred, I'm over here." Ernie snapped his fingers.

"It was last October," he said.

"There!" said Ernie.

"It was August," said Brodsky.

They had a lot more beer, and Brodsky's eyes got like pinwheels, and somehow less civilized. They kept watch over a hot, empty pit, the Brodsky within. The tourists—how Fred despised tourists—had gotten tired of waiting for somebody else to do something and were just getting drunk. But nothing interesting would come of that. They sang "On Top of Old Smokey," for Godsake. Even Fred knew better than that.

"I was *hop*ing they'd start singing folk ballads," said Ernie.

Fred felt a spasm of meaningless rage, acidity you could cut with a knife, because they were singing the only folk song he knew. The ban*d*lity of it. He was onto Brodsky too, with that evil little face. He went to the men's room again and attacked the ice venomously. (Make believe it's Brodsky.) It was down to nothing. Good system, though.

Ernie was looking uncomfortable when he got back. Brodsky's chin was down to ward off burps. "Ask your friend," he said. "Go on."

Ernie's round face was racked. "You really want me to, huh?"

Brodsky nodded, burrowing further.

"O.K., then. Joe wanted to know if there was any place around here where we could find, you know, girls."

"What do you mean, girls?"

Brodsky shook his head briefly, as if that explained what he meant, girls. Ernie looked to Fred for understanding. You know I don't go for that stuff myself. But he's a client, and *you* know.

"I wouldn't know any place like that," Fred said sulkily. A girl for Joe—not with that damned chin. And those crazy eyes.

"Well, somebody must know," snarled Brodsky.

Peabody was all vestryman, an undone vestryman now. He was trying to wash his hands furtively of Brodsky before setting out with him. Brodsky snatched away the soap. "What's the matter, Peabody? The way you were talking earlier, I thought you were a regular guy."

"Yes, well."

"You think something's wrong with it? After the way you were talking—"

"No, there's nothing wrong with it. I guess."

"All right then, let's go."

Fred cut in. "I don't think you'll find anything." Brodsky was the kind of man who would expect to be beaten senseless with an umbrella. There weren't any girls for people like that.

"Are you *kidding?* What kind of a town is this? Sure we'll find something."

Peabody shrugged. Quaint atmosphere, show him the Village, have a few beers, and this has to happen.

"Why don't just *you* go, Brodsky," said Fred. Hopeful Peabody, vestry regained.

"Are you *kidding?* Go without my friend? Anyway, my name isn't Brodsky."

Brodsky left, head down, with a damn bad grace. Ernie followed, gesturingly holy reluctance: gave Fred's shoulder a grieving tweak. "See you, Fred." How far did Ernie's duties extend, what kind of power did Brodsky wield in Ernie's particular board room? Fred felt the swell of the beer again and the noise starting up; national morality, boy, down and down and down. Words like sewer and jungle came readily to mind. Brodsky was really a traveler in contaminated scrapple. Peabody had no god-damn values. After a couple of hours with the squares, it would be nice to make his peace with the Black Cat. But the good part of the beers had gone into the stock talk, and all he had to make peace with was stale mouth, heavy head, thick thick fingers. Would like to be a butler and throw that bearded fellow out, though.

He was happy to make the street—cool and fresh after the rain, no, it was still raining, it took him a second to feel it. Coming down quite hard, as a matter of fact. Liked fresh air. Wet sidewalks and streaks of neon, zoom along in his squad car. Was halfway up the wrong stairs before he realized his mistake and made sheepish amends.

3

Fred lived up the back staircase; a whole different lot of people lived in the front rooms. Fred got a note from one of them, next day, the first thing in his mailbox in two weeks. "Hi," it said. "Meet thy neighbors, Apt. 2A, 8 o'clock. Ruth Button and Madge Willis." He remembered dimly bumping into a girl on the front stairs last night; already the collision was bearing fruit.

That was it, then, the first overture from the people "out there." He felt exceptionally good anyway, after his night on the beer. He seldom had hangovers like other people, but only great stirrings of the juices. Even though he stepped on a sort of beetle in the shower, which meant the poison he'd bought wasn't working worth a darn, he didn't feel too bad.

A week before, he had found the kitchen pulsating with these black things, and he had felt close to the end. There was also a heavy mantle of lint in the bathtub as if a man in a dirty tweed overcoat slept there every night—it brought on an ungovernable thirst for comfort and smooth white porcelain. But now he would say to the girls, "What do you do about your black things?" and they would say "Aren't they awful"; and they would give him something to take for the sucking noise in his pipes, and maybe they would be good-looking too, hey, hey.

Supposing they were, what was his policy on that? As he waded through the inevitable, interminable black tights on West Fourth Street for his morning outing he began to have tactical doubts. What did you really talk about with girls like that?

Well, first you said, "That's quite nice, what is it, a Motherwell?"

Then you said, "Wonderful feeling of depth."

Then you said, "But I don't like it."

You certainly didn't talk about roaches.

To hell with it, watch the chess. In blotchy green shade, the men made their moves: the decisive wise guys slapping them down, the sages refusing to be rushed: steady friendship over the chess. Fred wished he knew what chess was all about.

He also wished he knew the names of trees, the brands of dogs, the derivations of words. He had a vague sense of enjoying everything this morning, but he didn't know what any of it was called. Once the antic juices had subsided, he would be left with nothing to think about, because he didn't know the words.

Washington Square looked especially good today, fringed with spring paintings, Einstein and the ballerina—Alison said they were like the stuff at the Russian trade fair. Fred liked them fine, but only because he was feeling good anyway; his aesthetic was seated in his liver.

Behind the Square were the beehive buildings: awful what they were doing to the Village. Awful, yes goddammit Cope, awful. Buildings made of cream, doormen in Kelly green, black cars purring up from the garage, chic giggles and Thank you, George; expensive knees writhing in fur—it spliced onto an old daydream of Fred's. He used to dream about big confident men in roadsters and white tuxedos, and striking blondes in white dresses dancing expertly to the one-two-three Palm Grove orchestra, then a sprint along the coast in the roadster—all his dreams were so trashy. As a grownup, he chased them away. His private screen was usually blank these days except for the odd nude. And ballerinas and heads of Einstein. Russian trade-fair head. The buildings at the bottom of the Square would never look really bad to him, even though they were undoubtedly ruining the Village.

(*Well O.K., O.K.,* improvised Alison, speaking from a bearded chess player, *build on that then. There's nothing intrinsically wrong with skyscrapers and superhighways. It's just this passive, soft . . .*)

All right, that's enough out of you, get a shave then we'll talk. The memory of Alison was irritating in a way the real thing had never been. He left her surrogate ramifying into whiskers and palm and wandered to the other end of the Square. What he really needed was an artistic education. Buy some books, sit at somebody's feet. Pity they had torn down the old Brevoort—grand place, the old Brevoort. Damn shame about the Village generally. Say it often enough and someday we'll suddenly see what it means.

At eight o'clock sharp he trotted down the back stairs and up the front, and tapped on 2A. A chubby girl in curlers and a very short green dressing gown opened the door a pinch. "Is this number 2A?" he said, looking at the number. "You must be F. Cope," she said. "Come in, F." "I must be too early. This watch—" "No, not at all." She led him among the Motherwells and said, "If you'll excuse me a moment," and disappeared into a small, steaming bathroom. "I'm Madge Willis, by the way," she shouted over a sudden roar of water.

It seemed like a long time, and he looked at the magazines, which surprised him slightly by being mainly women's fashion magazines. Dreary, bony women, dammit Alison never allowed him to get places on time like this, it was strange being in a girl's apartment again with the girl fussing in the bathroom. He was fidgeting through the corsets when another girl came in, cropped blonde, bag of food, kicking the door shut with her foot. "Hi," she said and trudged through to the kitchen. "Excuse me a minute." She clunked and rustled the grocery bag. "I'm Ruth Button. You know, 'button, button.'" He laughed and thought Alison wouldn't like that, Alison couldn't stand automatic jokes.

The water went off and he could hear things being laid on the basin—curlers, eye pencils, lipsticks. Shuffle of feet, medicine cabinet with sticky door opening with a shudder, whispering search, closing bang bang, this must be a special corset number doesn't pinch or chafe tummy bulge larger woman, wow, look at that one. How the hell did you get *into* it? "You're awfully quiet out there"—was he supposed to talk? "I'm fine," he said.

"You haven't got a drink." Ruth straggled halfway through the kitchen beads, waving a French loaf and a piece of cheese. "Madge didn't offer you a drink."

"That's all right."

She slurped some California wine from a big jug in the corner into a tooth mug. "We're short of glasses," she said. Only 8:30. He watched the burlap flapping over the fire escape. Grimy red hems. Listened to the quiet bathroom sounds, Madge dressing for two. Observe, observe. "Is that a Motherwell?" he asked. "What's that? No, it's a Gottlieb." "Ah, yes, a Gottlieb."

There was a sonorous chime and a fluster of girls. "I'll get it," get it, get it. The bathroom door opened. Madge Willis was still wearing pants and a sweater. No makeup. What the hell had she been doing in there?

It turned out to be the Italian couple from his own staircase. Whoof. The girls must have thought they'd go well with F. Cope. He'd have to wait another night for the perverts. The man looked belligerently shy. The wife was small and you could tell she was talkative. Mouth looked overworked (husband's looked unemployed). "We've seen you," she said. "What do you do, anyway?"

"I'm in insurance," came out just automatically.

"Insurance, very interesting."

"Sort of between jobs."

"I see," the wife nodded.

Ruth sashayed through the beads with a plate of cheese canapés. Madge filled a tooth mug, a jam jar and a regular glass with wine. "We're short of glasses," she said. "We keep meaning—whoops, I'm sorry." She dabbed Fred's knees.

"I was admiring your Gottlieb," he said.

"Yes, it's nice, isn't it?" They all looked at it, speechless. Always like a nice Gottlieb, thought Fred. Texture and all that. Warm? How about warm? Ruth said, "We got it at the arts-crafts shop on Tenth."

"You get a lot of good things there," said Mrs. Tosti, the Italian lady.

Tonal values? or was that only music?

"How much do you think we paid for the curtains?" said Ruth.

Density?

"Two dollars?"

Feeling for the medium? Fred, you just can't.

"Two-fifty, only two dollars and fifty cents for those curtains."

"That's remarkable. I was guessing low, of course. They really look like five dollars' value. Or more."

It was pretty flat after bracing yourself for Gottlieb and Motherwell. Having finally cracked a Sarah Lawrence-type apartment, he didn't feel like talking about a bunch of burlap curtains. He wanted to say, What's the point, old clothes, dirty fingernails—where's the kick in that? "An amazing man, Gottlieb," he thought of saying, but he was interrupted by the doorbell.

It really boomed, that doorbell, like a Cadillac horn attached to a Volkswagen, a regal boom. It came from a little dark girl and Fred was in trouble right away. He couldn't go to a party without falling for some girl, it was a mark of his superficiality (said Alison, whose voice had changed again—a trace of Charles Laughton in it, maybe).

"I'd like you to meet Austin Gold," and she sat next to Fred on the sofa, and drew in her knees, as though getting into bed and pulling up the covers. She didn't say a word, and this struck Fred as wonderfully sensible, the way things were going. They were pricing the damn carpets by now.

He got lost in the $1.99s and suddenly he saw that some drawings had been pushed at him and he couldn't imagine why anyone should be showing him pictures of dresses. He turned them over slowly, tried to catch the drift. Maybe Ruth or Madge was a model. Or a fashion designer. "I like that one," he said, holding one up at random. "That one? That one didn't quite come off," said Ruth. "I like it anyway," said Fred. "It's a good concept."

The conversation began to bifurcate. Mrs. Tosti was examining the weave of the tablecloth, and obviously wanted to make a point about that as soon as she could. Mr. Tosti listened abstractedly, nodded, ran his finger compliantly along the tablecloth. Ruth talked to Fred and Austin. "Where are you from, Fred?" "New Jersey"—the perfect squelch. Whereabouts in Jersey? I don't know if you know a town called Bloodbury. Isn't that someplace near Teaneck? To get to Ruth his words had to pass Austin Gold; she seemed to watch them like smoke rings or bubbles. They weren't funny or anything, dammit. He wanted to show off a little for Austin. But Ruth had him in a box.

"Where are *you* from, Ruth?"

"I'm from the Middle West, Iowa."

Snigger at the Middle West, no, better not, some people could get away with it, but not him. Austin obviously approved of silence anyway. Show off that way, then, join her under the invisible covers.

Ruth fought to create a conversation, making up her own questions. "We lived on a small farm. God, it was dreary. Have you ever heard farmers talk? Mother was an isolationist." Austin and Fred smiled and nodded: "I can imagine," "You must have been glad to get away." Ruth kept going, but began to frost over slightly. "I went to the state university and Daddy was just furious. He thought that girls . . ." Fred had caught Austin's large, possibly humorous eye, and smiled straight into it. To hell with what father thought. Ruth stood up and said icily, "Would anyone like some coffee?"

The Tostis had to leave early. Tom Tosti got up at five every morning to take the tube to Jersey. "Fancy commuting to Jersey," said Hilda Tosti. "Whenever we offer people coffee they say they have to go," said Madge. "I guess we should never offer people coffee." Hilda smiled slightly. "No, we really had to go." "That's a switch, commuting to Jersey," said Fred.

"Well, now." Madge clapped her hands, as if the party could really start swinging with the Tostis gone. "Well, now."

"They're awfully nice," said Ruth.

"He's very quiet," said Madge.

"But nice," said Ruth.

Fred knew he was being an awful bore. But he was launched on a policy. He didn't expect to get anywhere with Austin, but he did want to make one of those fleeting impressions. Keeping quiet was a funny way of doing it, but Austin seemed to call for that, and he couldn't think of any other way of pleasing her.

(Iowa State, eh? What does *she* know about art? He felt an Alison-like superiority over his hostesses.)

Ruth took away the canapés. The beads gave a tart swish and the water came on with a horrible sucking sigh. "Your pipes make that noise too," said Fred. "Can I help you, Ruth?" said Austin. "No, there's really nothing, only these few things. Madge, why don't you put on some records?"

Austin was a bit like Alison, she made perfectly reasonable re-
marks sound brassy and obvious—Madge said, "We have Carl
Sandburg reading his own poems." "I really ought to go," Austin said. Not a word wasted, you notice? thought Fred. Just the
way that crack about Sandburg should be treated. "I'll see you
home," he volunteered swiftly.

Ruth and Madge made no objection. There was bright frost
in the air. Ruth came through the beads wiping her hands and
smiling coldly. "It's been fun," said Fred dismally. "Good, you
must come again," if you have a warrant, that is. Madge didn't
know quite what had gone wrong: she was still animated from
the Tostis. But Ruth was terribly, silently angry.

He had begun to wonder what Austin was doing here in the
first place since she kept so still. But now that she was about to
leave she kissed both girls like an old friend and talked to them
in a low voice about next Wednesday. You notice they don't
say anything to Fred Cope about next Wednesday, he told
himself.

She lived on the East Side, and they began the long hike in
their by now characteristic silence; Fred chewed over various
openings, and they just seemed duller and duller. Her silence
seemed so much more pregnant than his. Dark head bobbing
rhythmically, patiently, next to his shoulder.

They passed Julius's bar, and he croaked, "How about a
beer?" and she said, "I really must be getting home."

Along Waverley in silence.

Past Washington Square in silence.

Into dark, warehouse territory: trucks growling like watch-
dogs. In silence.

"What do you do?" he asked miserably. A talkative man,
pushed to his limit.

"I give piano lessons."

"Oh." What sort of piano lessons? Really, Cope, how many sorts are there? Trudged on.

"You don't talk much, do you?" she said.

"Who me?" he asked in the empty street.

"You're a very strange man."

Who me?

"I'm afraid to say anything, you look so severe."

I do?

"You made Ruth very nervous. Nothing seemed good enough for you."

He laughed, and said, "Where are you from, Austin? I should have asked."

"I was born right here in New York. I've never been anywhere else."

"Imagine."

She stopped in front of an old house in a disorganized part of town. "Here's where I live," she said.

"You don't meet many people who were born in New York."

"I know."

Her face was pale and small, in street light as soft as gaslight. Piano lessons. Impulsively he leaned forward and kissed her. To his surprise, she kissed back, thirstily yawpish. He hadn't meant anything like that.

She must have felt reserve in his mouth and his back muscles, for she drew back quickly and glistened at him. What had he done to bring this on? Whatever it was, he ought to patent it.

"Austin, I'm married."

"Yes, I know."

"Oh, yes, I have a ring, don't I?"

She was one step up, which made her just the right height.

He had to think fast, with the big, sad eyes. Needed five minutes or so to work it out. Dammit, if he was going to live like this, this was part of it. He couldn't live like a monk. Boyish lust struggled briefly with the reflex of fidelity. Alison wouldn't expect it. Austin's lips were looking better and better, but he kissed her quickly on the cheek, which settled nothing, and said, "When will I see you again?"

She shrugged, already quite bewildered. He couldn't blame her: he didn't know what the hell he was doing either.

"How about dinner tomorrow night, then?"

"I don't know."

"What do you mean, you don't know?"

"I don't know."

He kicked the step and said, "Well, then." She didn't move, but waited in pale confusion. "What about the next night?"

It sounded like a compromise, and she said, "O.K.," and ran right up the stairs and into her house.

He looked at the door. It said 432-4, in chipped gilt lettering. Austin Gold, 432-4 something street. He had known in the back of his mind (the part that he never used) that this would arise eventually. He must have supposed, in the back of his mind, that his instincts would tell him what to do.

His instincts! His instincts couldn't even tell him what part of town he was in or how to get back to his, how you call it, pad. He started back hopefully, and in a few minutes was outrageously lost.

4

It didn't matter about being out late, because there was nothing to do the next morning. He had thought of looking for picturesque work, but they didn't need anybody at the Circle in the Square, and he couldn't see himself as an espresso waiter. He had a feeling he was getting like Fran Wilkins, eccentric without being interesting. He didn't need the money, anyway. His last bank statement said $4,302.12, and that didn't include the stocks his mother had left him, which were so bloody safe, or his father's unemphatic nest egg—and how could you go looking for picturesque work with all that in back of you? He lay in bed as long as he could every day: this wholesomeness could be licked, dammit—by inertia, if nothing else.

His businessman's pot had begun to swell, right off, and now sat between him and his knees as if it wanted to get onto his lap. Everyone else got scrawnier down there, but not Fred Cope. His walks around the Village gave him an enormous appetite, and he plunged into the Italian restaurants and gorged himself on pasta; after which he usually felt sleepy, and the long hours in bed that followed gave the food time to settle in quietly and take over.

He was doing something wrong. He still worried, but it made no lines in his face. Greenwich Village wasn't changing him at all. He felt less and less like looking for Alison every day as his new life took on a pleasant regularity. He was already hooked on the *Village Voice*, which wasn't a regular newspaper, and he couldn't wait for it to come out each week. He looked forward to his scrambled eggs and his afternoon walk.

Was that why he decided to go ahead with Austin? He needed something like that to get some of the weight off. No, not really, but some human interchange did seem to be called for before the lint in his navel took over completely and began to ruin his life.

This was the kind of self-parody that he had always resorted to in moments of distress and that was already beginning to grow more vicious and less funny. But in fact, he also had not one but two dreams about Austin, and his astral self was not so easy to parody. Stripped of his cumbersome cruising style, he became in dreams lithe as a panther, and serious. He courted Austin two nights running, and she yielded to him with stunning sweetness. The second time he forgot to take off his armor but it didn't matter. He woke drenched in sweetness, a serious man for a few minutes, and rang Austin before the mood had quite evaporated.

The first dinner was unpromising enough. He discovered it was one thing to be strange and deep with a girl who talked a lot, like Alison, but another with a girl who was even more silent than yourself. Fred's main deepness trick was looking thoughtful, and you couldn't do that in a vacuum.

"Don't you do anything, Fred?" Austin said over the crème caramel.

"Nothing. Absolutely nothing."

"No, really. You must do something."

"I have never found anything worth doing. Beating your brains out from nine to five in some office? So that some Mr. Big—" he wasn't any good at it. He could feel her wincing.

"I'd die if I didn't do something."

"I've been thinking of taking up painting," he said lamely.

"That would be nice."

He found her house with no trouble this time. She looked depressed through and through. Mr. Big indeed! Taking up painting actually . . . He was the most synthetic bohemian in history. He gave her an apologetic dark-hearted peck, and again she sprang to life, substituting her mouth for her cheek with a convulsive swivel. Poor kid he thought, must be desperate.

She stood back looking at him questioningly. "Next Tuesday?" he said. She nodded and shot up the stairs.

He had never done so well with a girl before. He was the type fellow who had to wear them down slowly, and listen to their ideals endlessly, to get even modest results. "I just don't think of you that way," said Rose Newton in the back of the car, and he could have had the words inscribed on his shield. (Just above "Why, *Fred!*" and "Let's not spoil it.")

So now for only the third or fourth time in his life he found himself forced to make decisions in a field where decisions had usually been made for him. After Tuesday's dinner, they stood on the steps for a long time making hesitant sounds, watching each other like wrestlers. Fred didn't want to upset her with any of his old moves: she looked so likely to cry. But then again, maybe she would cry if he didn't. And vanity, the old man with rouged cheeks . . . Then he thought that was a hell of a way of reaching a moral decision, and he kept out of range, and finally marched off somewhat stiffly, hip two three: he really must do some hard thinking about this thing. By next week at the latest.

To cut short the next awkward silent meal he thought of getting the *Times* to find out about musical events, but decided he'd better not start on papers again. Instead he went uptown to Carnegie Hall and City Center and got some tickets for Friday evening, glancing at the billboard on the way out: an evening of some wop, he meant Italian, violinist. He hoped it was all right.

"I've got tickets for Friday's concert"—small problem was that she might ask what they were playing and he didn't know how to pronounce the guy's name, but she just said "Swell" in a flat voice and rang off. With Alison he had always taken the trouble to learn the names. Real love, that was.

They had dinner near the Hall, and the service was slow and Fred got unusually harassed. An evening of music always took it out of him. There were people bulging against the chain waiting for tables, and the waiters were embattled and rude. The patrons were shouting and banging their spoons. Fred gazed around with a slight edge of irritation: he didn't mind shouting himself, but he knew that Austin wouldn't shout back. "How's the fish—now that you've finally got it?" he bellowed. Her lips moved. "We'll have to hurry," but she didn't seem to hear.

Fat men shouldn't eat snails, then. And they shouldn't go out with girls like that. A hell of a way to live, you know that? Charming little French restaurant was what they called this pig sty. Waiters green, bursting from liver trouble, where the hell is ours? Customers dried out with grievance. How did fat men ever get hold of girls like that? Getting fat yourself, Cope. But it hasn't reached the hands yet; don't eat snails like that, yet.

His steak arrived at last, and he had fifteen minutes to get through it. So he could listen to some unpronounceable crap on the violin. He poured a disgusted finger of wine, and realized that the bottle was nearly empty. Austin looked up unsteadily; there was fuzz on her eyes. "You think I'm such a bore," she said defiantly—all that wine just to say that?

"What the hell?"

"I know you think that," she said. "And I am."

It had honestly never occurred to him. The spoons beat a

dirge. "We won't have time for dessert," he shouted, and she nodded: not quite straight. "We've only got five minutes." She nodded N.E.S.W. "If you really want to go."

They headed through the snarling roar to the cashier, who was grotesquely jovial and said, "You mus' coll again"—curly red straw, powdered flab, you're getting angry over nothing again, Fred—"You and your p'tit ami, com' an' see us real soon, hein?"

The cold little eyes stabbed them, leaving little punctures on their spines. Fred had bolted his meal belligerently, and everyone looked just awful. The concierge obviously kept a fifteen-year old lover—kid from the Levant, with a peculiar sense of humor. The lights were too bright, and all the people had cruel-glittering eyes.

"We've got to—"

"I don't want to go to it," said Austin.

"You don't? But—it's a concert."

"I know. I just don't feel like a concert right now."

"Oh." Taxis churned past, circling the theaters. "Would you like to take a taxi somewhere? I mean, would you like what? What would you like?" His dinner knifed at his chest.

"Let's go to a bar," she said.

Great! He really did want to increase his music appreciation, but perhaps some other time. With Austin there he would have to look so intense—no goofing off—and say something afterwards. All in all, a bar sounded much better.

They found a big, tomblike one with three well-scattered customers quietly a-guzzle in the dark. Austin wanted to sit at the bar, so they made for the two stools furthest from the twin television sets and haunched up on them. It looked like the Yankee game, dammit, and Fred couldn't keep from squinting over her shoulder at it. Geez, sets at both ends of the bar, what could you do?

She asked for a stinger and put it down in swift silence, and asked for another. Fred wanted to concentrate on her and not the game, but she gave him so little to work on, and by his second beer with the score two all—Ugly game baseball, when they did it on television. You lost all the grace, all the speed. Be nice to talk about this with someone, but heavens, not with Austin. Not baseball with Austin.

The sound track was down, so he couldn't hear the commercial. It looked really demented, you know? Simpering over some stupid cigarette. What about the kids watching, too? "Can I have another of these?" said Austin. Why had she brought him to a bar anyway? He had imagined she wanted to say something, but surely she would have said it by now. "Same again," he told the waiter. An anonymous batter in a shiny hat stepped up to the plate. The new helmets protected your head, but what if you got hit in the ear? What—

"I'm not even as interesting as an old ball game."

Fred sat up, or at least meshed his vertebrae. He had been here before. It was always his "old" ball game. The accusation rang in his head. "I wasn't really watching," he said.

"I know I'm dull. I can't seem to talk to people I like. And when I do talk, it doesn't seem worth saying."

"I wouldn't say that," said Fred.

"And you're so interesting. I mean, with your attitude to work and nine to five jobs—I've never met anyone like you."

Fred was dismayed. "I wouldn't say that."

"And you're so aloof about small talk and everything, and it's the only kind of talk I know, and I don't do even that very well. And you"—the dark bar was hell, and the other customers were the damned, and there was Dante behind the bar, in a flick of neon, preparing the ice for the worst sin of imposture ever recorded. "Look—"

"I don't know what you see in me—there, that's a cliché right there, and I have lots more. And you, you—" The stingers were getting at her vulnerable eyes and making the lashes twitch. He couldn't bear it. He put his hand, warm as a soap opera, over hers and looked into the fitful eyes, and whispered, "Never mind, Austin, I know this sounds silly, but I'm dull too."

His astral self was not the least discouraged. He dreamed about Austin for the third time that night, and she was more dazzling than ever. Fred was vaguely aware even as he dreamed that the real situation was not quite keeping pace with the dream. But in the transfigured softness of his bedsheets he thought: so much the worse for the real situation, baby. And the next morning, for several minutes, he thought the reality had somehow improved during the night after all, and that he was on the verge of something extraordinary.

They took the Staten Island ferry that afternoon and she said she didn't really like night clubs or parties or jazzing around. She said she was going to spend Easter with her nephew on Long Island . . . Fred stared into the gray waters and the words lapped against his ears. A nice soft voice, gentle, good with children. So this was what it all came to.

He had found the mailbox stuffed that very morning with Bloodbury mail. By some mysterious chain of inquiry they had run him to ground, and there they all were: two phone bills, two gas bills, appeal for the community chest, the inevitable heart fund, cancer, blindness, Sears Roebuck, bank statement —all crushed and wheezing in the box. And lined up against the

wall, six copies of *Time*, six copies of *Life:* despair in a handful
of mail. The Wilkinses wanted him to come to "a sort of land-
locked clambake," they called it. Ernie Peabody's card said
"Let's have lunch," and, "oh, P.S., my friend passed out as soon
as we got in the cab." So that was all right.

Peabody was behind the whole thing.

"My brother—that's my younger brother, Leo—took violin
lessons for years and years, but I guess it wasn't to be. His fingers were the wrong shape or something." Austin shook her
head.

The worst part was that he *liked* mail. It was torture taking
the magazines down to the corner and dumping them. It left
him strung like Leo's violin. Who the hell was Leo anyway?

"My sister never wanted to do anything except get married
and settle down. But the funny thing is, I don't think she's as
happy as Leo, who didn't want to get married at all. That's
funny, isn't it?"

Lack of attention was one of the symptoms. If he was reading
it in a newspaper, and Leo was Arthur Miller or somebody, he
could have followed it. But he had to say, "I'm sorry, I didn't
catch that." And then the whistle blew and both their voices
were lost as the boat drifted in on ohwell Staten Island.

5

Nothing much to do on Staten Island either. Have a soda. Examine your conscience. Wait for the next ferry. The Wilkinses'
clambake was on tonight ("we know this is short notice") and
he still hated to miss a party. "We used to come here for pic-
nics," said Austin, "my scout group."

Staten Island was a place you could set out for (especially if you were a scout group) with a high heart because of the bracing ferry ride and the escape. But somewhere on the way it got lost. He was too old to be having an ice cream soda, was part of it. Austin was a sweet girl, but, well, he'd done sweet girls already. Sitting on a high stool grinding at twin straws. Soda jerk saying, "You pay at the desk, buddy."

Every wind brought soot from somewhere, and all the green was a little bit gray. They walked a ways into the country, but it was only country up to a point. Fred was trying to think what a gentleman would do next; and when that didn't work, what a rogue would do next. Austin was sad about having to go back to the city. She had lived there so long, she didn't know how people ever got out. "You have to stay in New York to make enough money to stay in New York," she said, and he knew she'd said it many times before.

They turned back towards the ferry and she put her arm forlornly through his. She was like a sparrow or something, who lived in a cage. Fairy lights and sparrows, what a poet. Getting to Staten Island wasn't getting out of New York: it just reminded you of how far in you were. The coincidence of twilight and return made it seem awfully poignant, and he grasped the hand that came under his sleeve and tried to give it hope.

"What do you plan to do eventually?" he asked.

"I don't know. I'll never become a great pianist, I guess. I don't seem to have the spark."

"Oh, don't say that, I'm sure you have the spark. All you need is the luck."

"You think that?"

"Sure I do. It's the same with everything. It's not what you know it's who"—a pang of remorse, no bigger than a man's hand—"I mean, I know some people in the business and they're always looking for talent."

Don't do that, screamed Alison. Don't go around claiming you know people who can help people. Who do you know in the concert business? Joe Garms, of course, but he's hardly in the concert business. Orchestrating TV commercials isn't the concert business. And then, you don't really know him, do you? He's more a friend of a friend. Why do you do it, Fred? Because the kid needs encouragement? Or just salesman's swank, showing you're in every know there is?

"Are they really?" she said. He didn't know whether she was conspiring in fantasy or really believed him. He had done this once to a young man who wanted to write. Well, Fred really *did* think he knew some people in publishing: it was only when Alison began analyzing the list that he realized how many of them were more on the production end, or mainly in textbooks. (The boy phoned back the day after the party and asked for introductions. What a mess *that* was.)

"Oh, yes, they're looking for talent all right," he said quickly, "all the time. But suppose, just suppose, you don't make it as a concert pianist (I know you will), what will you do then?"

"I guess I'll just go on, teaching. Some place out of New York, though." She couldn't say she wanted to marry and settle down because that would bring up the question of whom; it would sound pushy. So she said, "I really like teaching. I can't think of a finer calling," in a stiff little voice.

The water just looked damp on the way back. New York's second-best skyline, the Wall Street range, could twinkle all it liked: it was still prison walls for people like Austin. "I hope you make it," he said, and she squeezed his arm, and he squeezed back, though he knew that all this squeezing was just making it worse. The evening got chilly, and the wind seemed to whip them together, and they were the only people left on deck and finally, it just couldn't be helped, he kissed her salty lips, and tasted the failure, past, present and future: failure that no amount of breaks could touch, and now his own lips were literally rubbing salt into it.

In a trance of compassion, he agreed to have supper at her place. Silently they bought the potato salad, cole slaw, cold meat. Gad, the poignance. Trudged with it up the stairs, shabby genteel stairs like his, and into her apartment, which he had never seen before: frail upright piano, family pictures on top, pictures of the trapped sparrows. Mr. Gold, kind, wistful, Mrs. Gold, blurred—in any photo she would look blurred, Leo whose fingers were the wrong shape (rickets, you know, poor little mite . . .).

Austin pattered with quiet pluck in and out of the kitchen as if she was afraid of disturbing someone. She carefully laid some tinny-looking knives and forks on the bright checks; arranged the cold meat in circular design around the potato salad; said, "Well, I guess we can sit down."

Sentimentality, said Alison, is unforgivable in your particular case. So be it.

They ate quickly, and Fred just hoped that his trance would either last forever or go away immediately. The checks on the tablecloth were pathetically gay. "I forgot, would you like candles?" said Austin. Candles! Oh, no!

"I'll do the dishes later," she said, and came to him on the Castro convertible. They embraced, and she was even smaller than he expected without her spring coat on. She wore a black shirt of soft cotton, which purred against his hand.

With the lights out, he could see only the wrong Austin. Not the shadowy Austin who writhed and clung like an Amazon, but the Austin who couldn't talk because she was afraid even of Fred; the Austin who wanted to teach piano in the country because it was a wonderful calling. You couldn't make love to someone you felt so sorry for; it was obscene, you needed an equal.

He wondered what she really wanted. Was she serious or was she following a crazy long shot that would take her out of New York? ("*The dingy suspicions of the square mind,*" said Alison.) He stalled and stalled, and asked Austin how old she was, and she said twenty-eight, which brought new waves of gloom. If only he knew something about people. When in doubt, follow the old code, he supposed. But perhaps he should have thought of that sooner. Could he pretend she was Alison, old non-pitiful Alison? The idea disgusted him and rendered him suddenly useless.

He wished he could see her face; but he did at last sense her patience slipping. And felt her voice almost before he heard it: "When lonely people find each other . . ." she whispered.

That did it, the clarifying formula. He had made another of his enormous blunders. Austin was no part of his stupid experiment. He wasn't lonely, in her sense, at all.

Gently he disengaged himself, and when he switched on the light he saw that she was more of an equal than he had thought. Her face was white, and wilder than he would have guessed possible. The hair came across in zany strands. He didn't know her at all. "I'm sorry," he said. (No use asking her to turn out the light and start again?)

She didn't answer, but looked at him with wild, blank eyes. No use, either, asking if she was doing this with marriage in mind —although it might have helped to know.

"You're a wonderful girl," (at least he hadn't said "great kid") "and if only we'd met years ago. Before—"

She just nodded. She stood up, not too disarranged, and said, "You didn't have a coat?"

"No. Austin—"

No response: would wait patiently for him to have his say, then let him go. Tears nowhere in sight. At twenty-eight you knew better perhaps.

"Good-by, Austin."

"Good-by."

Wait a moment. The day couldn't end like this. All that on the ferry. The closeness. The talk about plans. He felt cheated.

He tried a small, you-know-how-it-is smile. No response. "Well, good luck." And feeling clumsy and absolutely huge, the dullest man in Bloodbury, possibly the world, backed through the door and made off down the stairs.

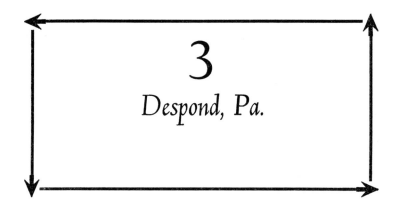

3
Despond, Pa.

1

The car furrowed between toasted lawns and tumescent summer trees and neo-Colonial houses; from there to bare lawns and scruffy trees and neo-Depression houses; and finally into Stapleton itself, a small town patiently sweating out another scorcher, worst July fifteenth since eighteen eighty something, opinions differed. The disadvantage of being a certain kind of blonde was that you didn't share the community glow: Mr. Perkins at the bank and Mr. Willard at Sears would say, "How do you manage to keep so cool?" She wasn't the least bit cool.

Alison Cope thought she saw a parking space near the firehouse, backed in quickly and clunked a man trying to get out. She watched him mouthing into her rearview mirror. A fireman sitting on a crate cackled soundlessly. It made the heat seem much worse; Stapleton was like a warehouse that had been locked up for years.

"I'm awfully sorry," she said.

"Hey, aren't you Alison Willoughby?" The driver got out of

his car and came up. "I'm George Pyke, remember me?" He could have been anybody, with that face, but she remembered the Pyke part. "In the sixth grade," she said and, of course, all the other grades. "Keerect," he said.

"I'm sorry about hitting your car."

"S'all right. Only a dent." he rested a pink forearm on her window sill. "So, how you been keeping?"

"Fine."

"I see you got a Jersey license."

"That's right."

"You just down on a visit?"

"That's right."

"Well, that's fine." He edged off. "I hope I'll be seeing you, Alison."

She hadn't meant to be rude, but there were so many George Pykes. At first she tried to take them all on separately, but it wasn't easy. They had had a hundred faces when they were kids; they only had one face now. The Stapleton face. They were all in the construction business, had three, four kids—and that was where you stopped, they couldn't describe their lives one inch further. "How about you, Alison?" they asked, and she suddenly felt like the worst kind of vamp, having to say she was sort of separated. It was too hot for her separation today.

"See you, George." She got out and looked at his car. She had crinkled the fender all right. He swung it hurriedly away.

The shopping list was even longer than usual today because her aunt and uncle were coming to tea. Aunt Matilda and Aunt Matilda's brother, Uncle Henry, liked their tea in the afternoon. They sat there very solemn and Quaker and you thought nothing was happening, and suddenly you realized that two plates of cakes were gone and a dish of hot biscuits. Real charac-

ters. Alison took a deep hot breath, and headed for the supermarket.

She had come back to Stapleton because there was nowhere
else she could afford to live, but only as a temporary step. She
had kept a separate bank account, as a gesture, and it was pretty
emaciated by now. A lot of it had gone into buying a car. She
assumed that Fred would try Stapleton right away and that his
attitude would determine her next move. She had never expected
a whole sweltering summer of it, shopping lists and joyless teas
and "Aren't you Alison"—

Her parents had taken her back without reproach or enthusi-
asm. They were lapsed Quakers, and the inner light had gone
out some years ago. But she was glad to get back in a way. This
was the real country out here, not the suburbs; these were real
people—in a way. She had her old room again, musty and un-
comfortably small, but a crow's-nest for watching people come
and go. Used to have parties up there and watch for her parents
to come home: scuttle down the back stairs, destroy the candy
wrappers and into bed in a twinkling.

She thought her old friends would like to remember about
the parties and things. They came up and said, "Hi, Alison,"
and she didn't recognize them at first because of the Stapleton
face, mild, unresponsive, a little dead around the eyes. Rimless
glasses, rimless faces. She hoped that old memories would ani-
mate them and give them back their old expressions. She talked
urgently of the past, trying to bring it to life in them, like blow-
ing on a fire; and they flickered for her sake. But nostalgia wasn't
really within their range: that was an artificial indoor emotion
that they had no need for.

Real people, all right—but why did they have to be so plain?
as if some vital part of their faces had dropped out. The features

were regular enough, but they weren't pulled together right. Handsomeness seemed to be a sin out here. She must say she was disappointed about that.

But it was only one side of things, and she knew it was her fault for expecting the wrong things. She thought they would be glad to see her, but really there was no reason why they should be. They had been burrowing into their own lives, raising children, worrying about money and furniture; they hadn't been waiting all agog for Alison to come back and talk about the old days. And she had expected them to look interesting—as if that mattered.

What hadn't let her down was the countryside. The town was nibbling along and had already consumed her parents' house, which used to have the whole block to itself, and was teetering on the edge of Brookdale Creek. But beyond that there was violent loveliness, the snarled woodland she and her friends used to play in before everyone got so dull; and Brookdale Park where Washington probably encamped and made some key decisions: and the silver Pequod River, sinuous between lanes of pines and a few honest-to-God cypresses.

She would like to get out again this afternoon and do some sketching but for this profoundly unnecessary tea party. Saturday afternoons had always been ruined by these uncles and aunts. They sat in the dark living room while the sun was foiled outside in a smother of grim branches. Aunt Matilda would fan at the dead air and put down cakes behind her fan. The sicklier the better—Alison leaned over the cake counter and winnowed a batch of pink and green ones, the kind that leave your thumb a sticky shambles. Halfway down the list now straggling toward the prune juice at the bottom, she turned and bumped into George Pyke's wagon. The heck with small towns, in a way.

"I'm awfully sorry." She grinned, because technically it was funny. "I keep bumping into you."

"Hello, Alison," he said quite solemnly, rerouting his wagon. "Doing your folks' shopping?"

"That's right."

"Well, nice seeing you again, Alison."

Wonder Bread, maple syrup—it was good to have real buckwheat cakes again. Wasn't it. Oatmeal; in the middle of the summer, oatmeal. Candied fruit for Aunt Matilda gobble, gobble—her mother took it for granted that she would do the shopping, item by item during the week, and the jumbo load for Saturday. It wasn't a punishment, it was just the way it was. Uncle Ben's rice, Jello. All the stuff she used to buy in Bloodbury. Almost finished now, her wagon groaning with regional specialties, she headed down the last aisle, found they were out of veal chops so got lamb chops, wedged in six packets of frozen limas and two spinach and joined the getaway line at the front of the store.

Why was there never any mail on Saturdays. (Charity appeals from Bloodbury definitely didn't count.) If she didn't hear from Fred soon, she would have to write to him; and she had no idea how she wanted to sound. If he was ill or something, she wouldn't want to send him an angry letter. No use getting angry with Fred, anyway: it didn't do any good and besides it wasn't his fault. He was just the last flowering of some dreadful system.

She was still quite clear about Fred, anyway. He was the sort of fellow who went to sleep while you were criticizing him. How could he ever learn anything? Every insult, every attempt to understand just led to more "Yes, dear," "Oh, I don't know about that, dear," "You may be right, dear," and from that quite logically to snores.

I'm going away for a few days to think things over. Did you hear that Fred?" An aborted grunt in the dark and "Yes, dear." *"Now listen carefully: I'm going to the Delphi hotel until Friday to think things over, then maybe I'll go down to Stapleton for a few days. You can write me or phone me there. Is that clear?"* Behind the pillow, Fred said, "S'clear."

Nothing very significant in the RFD box. The Stapleton *Gazette*—check up on old friends, to Betty, a son, to Beulah, a daughter, R.I.P. John Pontifex. The Bloodbury *Chronicle* came on Fridays. She wondered if Fred was forwarding her stuff; it didn't look like his handwriting. You couldn't be sure with those Palmer-method people, though. (Typical of Fred to write with the Palmer method.) Fran Wilkins invites you to a pajama party, oh, no! Not so funny, because she could just see Fred, looking hearty in his pajamas. Why didn't he write? It was making her feel a little foolish. Cerebral palsy, poor little chap, but nothing to send them this year.

She stuffed the mail into her purse and got back in the car.

Aunt Matilda and Uncle Henry had to drive twenty-five miles in their old Chevy to get to tea. It was a chore because Matilda drove slowly, and on Saturdays there was always remorseless honking in back. (Sometimes Alison went for little drives with Aunt Matilda in the old days and she still remembered kneeling on the seat, reading the faces in the cars behind, with dumb agony; fat men swearing, boys with shaved heads sniggering. Matilda's face would be set firm against the honkers and the car would seem to go even slower.) Matilda was old and cautious then; what must the journey be like now, with Matilda even older and the other cars faster?

She showed no signs of any ordeal when she turned up at four; no signs of erosion, either. Changeless, Quaker mask. She had written to say she was dying to see her niece again, but she played her pleasure way down. "Hello, Alison," she said, and shook hands firmly. Uncle Henry shook hands too, and said, "How do you do," as if he wasn't sure who it was he'd been brought to see.

Nobody seemed pleased to see anybody. And yet they had gone to so much trouble, they really must be pleased a little bit. They sat like stuffed owls on the hard chairs, and it was another dead Saturday with life fading remorselessly in the old room, grownups sitting with their shoulders back and their knees together. Waiting for someone to die in the next room. She remembered the whole sequence: *"Come inside, Alison"—panting around the house in an old pinafore to see who it was. Oh, them again—"Guess who's come to see us." Then the dead, dead talk, about people she didn't know, the slow slurping of tea, only a faint hint through the drawn blinds that another unused afternoon was pulling out of Stapleton. "Jim Phipps had another boy"—all right, let's hear about that—"His mother died, you know"—all right, his mother—"Betty Friend got married" —oh, to heck with it. They weren't even interested themselves. They wouldn't let themselves get into anything.*

The intolerance of youth. It was only after she was safely away from Stapleton that she began to wonder whether she might have missed something there. In their passionless way Matilda and Henry did have a broad and steady interest in people. They took the trouble to keep up. Every Christmas

Matilda sent Alison a check for one dollar. Beat that for steadiness.

Mrs. Willoughby brought in the tea, a glutinous abstract of pinks and greens and yellows. Aunt Matilda turned lusterless, unexcited eyes onto it—give anything to feel her pulse, though —and Uncle Henry pulled gently at his cuffs. They really liked their food.

"Now let me see, you take milk and no sugar," said Mrs. Willoughby, "am I right?"

"You're down here for a bit then, are you?" Uncle Henry asked Alison.

"Yes, that's right."

"I'm afraid you're not seeing us at our best. It's awfully hot, isn't it?"

"Yes. I suppose the Pequod is all dried up again."

He seemed perplexed. "Yes, as a matter of fact it is."

"It always dried up in hot summers."

"Yes, that's right." He looked seriously puzzled at how a stranger could know this, but happy that the cakes had arrived.

"I hear," said Matilda, "that Jane Forbes has gone to live in San Francisco."

"Yes, her brother was posted out there, and she's gone to join him."

"Who's Jane Forbes?" asked Alison.

"You know, she used to live in the Mill Cottage. Before the Murgatroyds moved in."

"Oh, yes."

"Edith Murgatroyd's been quite poorly."

"I'm not surprised. That house is just terrible for rheumatism."

"It must be awfully old," said Alison.

"She's had a whole new system put in, so age isn't important," said Matilda, flaring up slightly, meaninglessly. "Anyway, it wasn't rheumatism. It was sciatica."

"I thought it was rheumatism."

"No, it was sciatica." Matilda took a swig of tea. "Emily was the one with rheumatism."

You mustn't expect fireworks, thought Alison. It wasn't what these people said, it was what they were. Uncle Henry's great-grandparents had built a homestead near Lancaster and held it against the Indians and the British and so on. His grandparents and parents had farmed it steadily, keeping close to the soil and drawing their strength from that. You didn't go to them looking for bright chatter, but for roots, for steadiness and sober experience.

No, she really meant it.

Nothing in the room had stirred since she was a fidgety child. The tassels hung as still as drapes in a mosque. The lace tablecloth was hiked up in the same place. Aunt Matilda in her gray dress, Henry in his collar, roots with tassels on. Her father had the same half smile that made people think he was so nice, only it wasn't really a smile at all if you looked at it closely.

"Alison has taken up ceramics," Mrs. Willoughby said.

"Is that so?"

"Yes, she has a little workshop up in the attic, and she makes some of the prettiest things. She made a lovely little ashtray, didn't you, dear?"

What they probably meant was, It's excellent therapy for the poor dear. She can still lead quite a useful life with her little pots and things. Using her fingers and everything. Still, O.K. She could handle pity.

"There's a lot of money in pottery," Uncle Henry burst out suddenly.

"Indeed there is," said Matilda. "Henry has a sister who opened a little shop"—she made a small gesture—"just off the turnpike. She's done quite well, I believe. Hasn't she, dear, hasn't Agnes done well?"

"Oh yes, Agnes . . ."

"Does anybody mind if I open the window?"

They looked at each other with wild surmise, "I don't." "No, I don't." "It's right behind Aunt Matilda's neck, Alison. It'll blow on her neck." "No, that's all right," Matilda said. "Some fresh air would be quite nice." She raised her shawl.

The window was stuck in paint-sweat and plaster. Alison tugged and tugged at it—must get it open. The blind had gone up all right, with a dry snap, but the curtains kept closing on her. She pushed them off with her elbow and they closed against her cheek. Oh, come on!

She gave an almighty yank, and the pane went tumbling into the street.

2

The event of the season. Alison was momentarily exhilarated by the splinter and tinkle, but the others just watched. The phlegm that had built the homestead was not to be tricked by some broken glass. There were no Indians outside. "I'll have Wilbur fix it when he brings the new skylight," said Mr. Willoughby.

There was something unearthly about their calmness. Four grandfather clocks. Alison's attention came loose, the four faces ticked and chimed and she stumbled past them, excuse me excuse me into the back row of the Stapleton Paramount. Ticker tape, Armistice—no, she didn't remember that. Crash,

Wall Street, getting warmer now. Depression, Mr. Willoughby calm. He lost his real estate job and had to hack around for a bit—sorting mail, repairing fuses, she believed. Then Mrs. Willoughby lost a child, the one after Alison. But she kept calm. And then the war, and their son Pierce getting killed by the Japanese. Alison was old enough by then to gauge the effect of that nicely. She felt in her own bones a gloomy, trembling excitement (so little happened around here), and looked forward to an orgy of sorrow; but she didn't get so much as a quivering chin out of her parents. They showed no emotion at all over Pierce's death.

They weren't like Christian Scientists. They didn't try to out-stare the event. Mrs. Willoughby talked more than sufficient about it, wondering what to do with Pierce's things in the attic, wondering whether the body would be shipped home: both parents bending the steel back as far as it would go.

Alison was indignant, but worse than that frightened, that no one would shed a tear for Pierce. (Supposing *she* died?) She shed some noisy ones herself, partly with her own funeral in mind, and hoped that they could be heard downstairs. If her mother would just come up and sit quietly with her, that would be fine: she wouldn't have to fling herself on the floor or anything. But she never came, and Alison knew her parents had passed their stiffest calmness test, and would not be troubled again. (She hoped it had been a test.)

In a way, she admired them for it now. They would not allow themselves the pleasures of sorrow; by contrast she saw that she had taken a very complicated relish in her brother's death. An odd reaction: perhaps if you found that you were excited by disasters, it was better to make yourself feel nothing as they did.

But the relish turned out to be only hysteria, more orthodox sorrow followed, and she mourned Pierce's death for several years.

The only way her parents showed the death was that suddenly they began to leave her alone. As long as she was quiet and neat and didn't fidget when guests came, they let her go to hell in her own way. It seemed as if the interior bleeding over Pierce and the nameless child before that had sapped some of their attention. They wanted to avoid fuss, anyway. They asked no questions. She could always whisper up the stairs in her socks, wash the lipstick off and look forward to an understated breakfast. They had been quite harsh when she was a child, but seemed suddenly to have given up on her.

It wasn't quite a spoiling, because their lack of approval was awfully oppressive, and she took it for judgment and was somehow restrained by it. Her late nights were often just lonely, brimming walks to the Pequod banks: she expected to see other children of lapsed Quakers dancing and crying along the way, but never did. She had a little friend called Hazel, who was briefly moved by her moon-and-star talk and agreed to go out with her one night; but Hazel got frightened and began to whimper-giggle; and some boys who were checking their beaver traps heard her and began making noises in the woods. That was the end of Hazel—Mr. Willoughby, with his superficially kindly face, seemed to be smiling at her now. As if he shared the memory and wanted her to go on with it. Aunt Matilda was still checking off names in her endless personal directory. Uncle Henry had glazed over completely: what succulent ice-pink fantasy had he made his getaway to?

All right, then. The lipstick nights were mostly dances and weenie roasts and ice skating-cum-sleigh rides. They sang songs around the fire to Felix Pontifex's guitar, and she felt exalted and wanted everyone to stop thinking about trade school and pledge they would go on like this forever. Some of the boys sang pretty well, in harmony, and she wanted them to form a group and do something, but they lost interest and probably never sang at all now. That's the way it went, and goes: the drive to dullness was universal, and much stonger than sex.

Uncle Henry and Aunt Matilda were leaving at last no they weren't. Just shifting their thin bones. She wanted them, the boys that is, to sing folk songs, not just pop stuff, and they did try to learn a few, because the boys around there were pretty malleable, but there was in every sense no future in them. Stuart Trimble got a job nights, and the other fellows just lacked the drive: pity, because they sang so beautifully, she could hear it still, just like the Weavers or the Squirmers . . .

"We must be getting back," said Matilda. "The traffic gets heavy towards evening, and you just have to *crawl*." There wasn't a cake to be seen. Yet Matilda and Henry were both very thin. It had something to do with attitude, she supposed. Fred, for instance, was quite fat.

"Good-by, Alison, you must come and see us."

"I'd love to. And see the old house."

"You'll find it changed. We have a television now, you know."

"Oh, really?"

"Yes—Henry loves to watch. Don't you, Henry?"

The answer to "don't you" was "yes," so Henry said "yes."

"They haven't changed a bit, have they?" Alison said, after the Chevy had chuffed out of sight.

"He's getting a bit vague," said Mr. Willoughby in a detached way.

"I thought she was looking a bit older," said Mrs. Willoughby. "She's had a very trying winter."

"How's that?"

"You know, her grandnephew, cousin Wandsworth, Wandey, didn't I tell you about him?"

"Tell me what?"

"Well, you knew he was a bit queer, didn't you?"

"No."

"Well, anyway, he embezzled some money and left the country . . ."

Good old Wandsworth, she thought flatly, nothing queer about escaping from the Woodside Trust Bank with a stash of complacent deposits. Such a colorless, toneless fellow, Wandsworth, living with his uncle and aunt: nobody ever called him queer before he did this, she bet, at least not in her mother's sense. That was the real interest of a place like Stapleton. You had a boy with the mind of a ninety year-old man and he wound up robbing a bank. You mustn't give up on Stapleton.

She could hear the downstairs phone ringing through the gash of broken glass, and they went back in the house. That was one change, an up and a downstairs phone. The one downstairs was bright yellow. It must have taken some salesman.

"Hello, who's this, who?" Mrs. Willoughby frowned and handed the phone to Alison, "It's for you. George Somebody."

Alison's first personal call in two months. She took the yellow receiver. Voices sounded funny over the telephone, didn't they. "This is George Pyke," it said, "I saw you today in town."

"Oh, yes, George."

"Listen, Alison—I thought it might be fun to get together sometime and talk about old times and stuff. Alison?"

"Yes."

"Oh, good. Listen. It was real great seeing you again in town today, and I wondered if you were doing anything tonight, for instance."

"Well, nothing special."

"Could I drop by and pick you up? Around eight?"

George Pyke. Well, he might be all right. He was quite funny once. He told jokes with a Swedish accent. And played the harmonica. Find out what had happened to old George, then. "Alison?"

"That'd be fine," she said.

"All right. I'll be round at eight, and listen, it'll be grand to talk about old times."

She saw no reason not to go out with other men—but with little George Pyke? That was just silly. George more than anybody was frozen in the sixth grade. You couldn't go out with someone in the sixth grade.

"I'll be out tonight, Mother. After supper."

"Oh?"

She knew what the "Oh" meant, because she felt a bit of it herself. It was one thing to decide to go out with other men, but another actually to sit in front of the mirror, combing your hair, blocking your lipstick, waiting for doorbells. "It's just George Pyke," she said. "I used to know him in sixth grade."

"Oh?"—what difference does that make? There's right and there's wrong; that's all I know.

"You don't know what happened to him, do you? Whether he went to college, got engaged, or what?"

"I don't remember any George Pyke."

"Don't you? He was kind of stocky, dark hair, teeth . . ."

Her mother turned away with a tray of skittering tea things.

These silent people had ways of saying it. This is different, dates and things; but perhaps your father and I are old-fashioned. She felt the crushing weight of their disapproval, and yet caught no flicker of skin or lash to confirm it. Conscience spoke to conscience, and Alison remembered that she herself was a Quaker only twice removed, and didn't have to strain to feel guilty.

Still, it was only George Pyke.

Her room in the attic was separated by just a cardboard wall from Pierce's old room, which she used for her potentially profitable pots. (Henry's sister sitting by the turnpike with no legs and a handful of pots.) She thought about Pierce a lot up here. She hadn't known him terribly well in life because of the age difference, six years and a bit, and just had a spectral admiration for the sounds next door. But after his death he took on real substance; she felt him move into the room next door in earnest, a companion who got closer and closer to her own age, and then kept pace forever: setting the standards for both of them. Setting the standards by which she had finally left Fred —in a way.

Pierce had licked the game. He would never get the Stapleton face now. At twenty-one he was over the hump, and she remembered his vivid, seeing eyes right up to the last visit. Pierce was aliver right now than anyone else in Stapleton. He was still trying to learn ventriloquism on his last visit, at an age when most Stapleton boys had long given up learning funny things.

Before that it was yodeling, a strange night-noise that brought on a beating, and a muffled discussion with her father which scared her in half sleep next door; and before that, he corresponded with Charles Atlas, and she heard him grunting his way to strength through the partition; and oh, he kept bugs in a box and pictures of the Pittsburgh Pirates and finally a diary which was mailed back from the Pacific and which she eventually got hold of and which fleshed her dream. Fellow with so many interests could be bouncy and superficial, she knew, but not Pierce. He had enough life for each of them, and they were not interests but passions.

Well, enough of that. She didn't want to get sentimental and spoil it. Pierce was made of nervous energy, like Captain Marvel. Melancholy chased him away. It was time to get on with something else. Like choosing a dress for her date with George oh no Pyke. (Never would have thought it would come to this, dating George Pyke.)

Dinner was quieter than ever. Mr. Willoughby always said he came to the table to eat, not talk (Pierce used to wonder where he *did* go to talk). The lima beans were burnt, which was no better than a scarlet woman deserved. "What time is your young man coming?" her mother asked. "I told you, mother, eight o'clock." "Oh, yes." It was impossible to feel grownup. "Be sure to lock the door. You know how it works? First the top bolt, *then* the catch, then the bottom bolt." "Yes, Mother."

After all that, George Pyke looked much bigger than she expected, with a heavy man's jowl and wide hands with hair on them. Her mother was right, she was going out with sort of another man, after all. After his telephone bumblings, she was looking for something smaller and more diffident. But he greeted her parents with big man's assurance, and flicked her into her wrap and out the door with the ease of an industrial process.

"I feel awfully guilty about that fender," she said. But the dent was already gone. The car was sleek and long and waxy. George Pyke was a whole new thing after dark.

"I thought we'd go to the Pomfret Inn to start with. All right with you?"

Dark blue suit, little white corner of handkerchief, but I know you, George.

"That's a nightclub, isn't it?"

"Well, they have a band, I guess. And a singer."

Nothing very wicked about that, but what she knew about George Pyke, a memory lost forever if he hadn't just said Pomfret Inn, was that once upon a time he had a frantic devotion to the game of post office. This was in the *seventh* grade, and he was quite a little grinning pest about it—they brought him along for his harmonica playing, and he wanted to play post office.

Silly to hold that against him now, and she didn't really, but the other half of the memory concerned the Pomfret Inn itself. It had always been a glamorous place for the Stapleton kids because rumor had it that you could get drinks there under age, and drinking had a high moral charge around Stapleton.

One night when she was still in grade school the Inn was raided—not the kind of huffing puffing keystone-kops raid that failed twice a year (on the same exact dates) to unearth anything, but an efficient deadly raid. Pierce was found there drinking beer with some classmates. He still had three months to go for his eighteenth birthday, and there was a lot of fuss around the house which she couldn't follow, and another scene with her father which she couldn't quite make out through the partition, and soon after that Pierce went into the Army.

It wasn't till years later, after she had completed her own Pomfret Inn phase, that she saw Pierce's diary, and found that he died believing that his father was behind the raid. Mr. Willoughby must have known the graduating class was planning a sortie. He often talked about having the Inn raided. "And when I said 'Well, did you?' he just stood there." Alison felt at first nothing but white, blind rage at a man who would call the cops on his own son, and she left home as soon after reading the diary as convenient (two years later, actually). Piecing things together she saw that Mr. Willoughby had probably lost control of his boy anyway; the last attempted beating had just ended in a shouting and maybe retreat as well. The bad years had left him a bit weak and indecisive, and he didn't have the moral courage to stand up to Pierce again; but he must have felt he had to teach him a lesson somehow, before even that was too late. That might almost excuse the raid.

So there was plenty against the Pomfret Inn, besides George Pyke's sticky kissing games. She said truthfully, "I can't talk when there's music going on. And I really would like to talk about old times."

"O.K. with me, Alison. Any other suggestions?"

A banana split at Howard Johnson's was hardly the thing, although it was just what she wanted. "Is the Bear still open?"

"Well, yes . . ."

"All right, let's go to the Bear."

"O.K.," said George doubtfully. "The Bear it is."

3

She'd forgotten about the Bear. It really was pretty ratty. You might have thought Stapleton didn't have any bums (she bet a lot of Stapletonians did think that) until you got to the Bear. But there they all were, ranged along the bar or trying desperately to play shuffleboard. They probably slept upstairs and never went outside at all. Maybe there was a civic ordinance about it: bums out of sight.

Alison was a little taken aback at finding them here, although they had never bothered her in New York. For a short time she had done relief work there, and had seen them from the domestic angle. A nice man when he's not drinking: some sweetness preserved in his children anyway. Here they were hostile, rootless. Or was it that her own timidity level was lower in Stapleton? "I haven't been here in a long time." said George, "but I heard it had gone down. You want to try another place?"

"No, this is fine."

He was amusingly embarrassed and took her to a dark booth away from the bar. All right then, George Pyke, let's see what you're made of now. Is it just the face, or did they flatten you out all over?

"So," he said, "how've you been, Alison? What've you been doing all these years? Oh—what would you like to drink?"

"I'll have a beer, I guess." Didn't really want a drink, but if she was ever to find out what gave with George Pyke, she would have to make concessions. No use taking notes over a ginger ale.

"So, you left town and went to Jersey, right?"

"No, I went to New York first and *then* to Jersey."

"I see. You went to New York first. What did you do there?"

"Well"—better get it over with—"among other things, I met my husband."

"I see. So you married. And *then* you moved to Jersey?"

"Yes, then we moved to Jersey."

The beers arrived, distastefully served by the bartender himself. Table service was meant to be for people who wanted cold mutton sandwiches with their beer.

"What part of Jersey?"

"Near New York."

"That's convenient, huh."

"Yes."

"Do you like New York?"

"Yes, I love it."

"So, how long have you been married and living in Jersey?"

Well, at least he was fluent.

"Do you still play the harmonica, George?" she interrupted.

"The harmonica? Oh, that. No, I don't get much time for that."

"Pity."

"I might take it up again."

Results of the first round, not very promising. He ordered another, pointing out that they were small glasses. As soon as they were poured, he trotted up to the bar to intercept them from the bartender.

"What was I saying?"

"About the Army and Korea."

"Oh yes. Well, I was in for two years and—"

"What was it like?"

"Like? Well, you know the Army."

"I don't, as a matter of fact. I was hoping you'd tell me."

He smiled shyly. "Oh, you know."

If she didn't get to the real George soon, she was going to scream.

"All right, you don't like to talk about it. The pain of the old wounds, as my uproarious husband would say."

"It's not that. There just isn't anything to tell. Was your husband in the Army?"

"You bet he was. One hundred per cent."

"Well, then."

"Well then, what?"

"Well then, you know all about it. It was the same for every-body."

"All right, then, back to dear old Stapleton. No Korean war bride, I take it. Stapleton girls are the best in the world."

"I wouldn't say that," he said with a boyish grin, left over from post office days like light from a dead star.

"How come you never married, George?" she asked.

"I did."

"Oh. I'm sorry."

It was rather shocking. The point about people like George was that they didn't say things like that. She changed the subject, but her mind dragged behind. Dull people had no business getting divorced. No fair calling George dull yet, give him another five minutes; but how could someone whose mind never left the same trolley tracks care which girl he was married to?

She watched his mouth (she was a mouth watcher anyway) for clues. Was there anything in George sufficient to generate the necessary distress for a divorce? Pierce's divorce ruling was unequivocal: Never give up on another human being as long as he's alive and changing; but once he's stopped breathing, get out. The dead and the living should cleave to their own, that's why she'd left Fred. All Pierce's doing, in a way.

But now, take George, was his death established? Used to be a lively fellow once, give him another shake.

"Would you like to dance?" she asked.

"What—here?"

"Certainly here." There was an old juke box near the door which seemed to have been overlooked from a happier time. She went to it and saw old songs that nobody else had any more,

"The Breeze and I," "Skylark," "Orchids in the Moonlight." Once upon a time, people had danced at the Bear. The floors had been clean and so had the barman's coat. Oh, years and years ago.

The first real emotion she had seen on George turned out to be monumental resignation. He held out his hands like a method actor surrendering to fate, and she speculated from that that he might have an inner life and was probably all right.

He danced very well, even while he was still stiff with embarrassment; and once it was clear that nobody gave a damn, he really went, gliding over the cruddy floor and navigating the shuffleboard like a master. George Pyke at dancing school, of course of course, the first boy to say "I don't care if it *is* sissy." George Pyke, who was going to take up taps.

They danced the whole set, and a man at the bar gave a small clap at the end: the others hadn't noticed a thing. They danced off to "The Jersey Bounce" and laughed and laughed, and she went spinning into his hands. He held her shoulders, and just like that, his laugh went calculating: it said, "Aren't we having fun together." The music had stopped, and George had lost his spontaneity as sure as Cinderella. Or was it she who had woken up and lost some innocence? She pulled away from his hands, a bit dizzy and chilled, but still laughing from momentum and they had another beer and nothing was seriously wrong.

"I haven't danced for a long time," said George. "It's fun. It gets you out of yourself."

"Yes, a good place to be sometimes."

"What's that?"

They panted and drank the beer and he proposed the Pomfret again, for more dancing. "Not tonight," she said. "I'm out of training too." "Well, how about next week?" She had no time to think, between breaths, but had a notion she'd made a small mistake and had to go through with it. "Yes, all right." "It won't be just these old tunes at the Pomfret." If he'd said *that* a moment sooner— "Isn't there any place but the Pomfret Inn?" she asked. "Oh, sure, there's the Water Wheel and Herman's, but the Pomfret's easily best."

In the car going back she kept right over by the door. It was just lack of practice and jitters, but she sensed something in him now like a smell. Through the smart blue suit. The beer and dancing had shaken this thing loose in him and any minute he would be wanting to play post office again. . . . Fancy George being divorced. Divorce had arrived, all right. The cautious people were getting on to it too. Driving so carefully, after his three beers.

"It's been swell, Alison. Seeing you again."

"Yes. Thank you."

"It's good to see old friends and talk about the past."

George Pyke, always joking. "Did you ever take up tap dancing?" she asked.

"No." He laughed. "Why tap dancing?"

He came round and opened her door. She braced herself, but he made no move. She sensed something moving under the blue suit; but he was nothing but very polite and sincere.

"I hope you had as much fun as I did." He did look so dreadfully sincere that she said, "Oh yes, I had a wonderful time." She hated conventional lying and felt flustered as he said good night Alison see you next week same time swell. He knew all about how to behave on a first date. Why on earth had she let herself in for a second, though?

The house was as still as it always had been. She took off her shoes and gave in to the old stealth. Boards creaked this summer that had never creaked before. One of them went off with a bang outside the door of her parents' room, but she didn't see the dreaded nightshirt in the doorway. For years she had feared it at just this point. But after the death of Pierce, they never appeared at night.

The attic room was dark and stuffy, even with Pierce's door and window open. The bed light was smothered in moths, which dropped in a fluster onto the pillow and onto the face on the pillow. All the same she left it on until the moths were like an aviary, and turned the stiff, lined pages slowly. Apparently her parents had never even bothered to read the diary. They would never have let her see it if they had. Pierce hated his parents; and it stood out sharply because he hated nothing else on earth. They stood between him and the light, he said pompously. The light got through anyhow, but he would hate them in hell anyway, he said. Pretentiously. It wasn't fair, she felt herself protesting, every time she came to one of those very occasional and uncharacteristic entries: just because they don't know how to show their feelings doesn't mean they haven't got any. . . .

If they did have any, they would have been put to a fresh test by the arrival of the diary. Fancy getting a thing like that in the mail. From a dead son.

But she was sure they hadn't read it.

4

"Did you have a nice time with your young man?" her mother asked.

"It was all right."

"He seemed very nice."

"Yes, he's all right."

Sometimes it happened like this: just when she stopped talking her mother started.

"I never thought you'd marry a Stapleton boy. I always felt you were more ambitious than that."

"What do you mean, more ambitious?"

"I don't know." Mrs. Willoughby's eyes went glassy and she began to make more buckwheat cakes. She hated discussions where people made contact.

Alison was still full of her brother's diary. She had read it all the way through again to counteract George. And it said what it always said: not to give up on people like George, to wrench them out of their social context and try again. Pretend it was just you and George removing the fuse from a bomb. Pretend it was . . . God knows, she'd tried—tried removing fuses with Fred, tried it with Fred's friends, and now with George, and sometimes it worked, but sometimes she just didn't see how Pierce kept it up.

"You know, this is beautiful countryside," she said to her mother, who answered absently, "Yes, it surely is."

"I'm surprised more artists don't come and live out here."

"Have some more buckwheat cakes."

"No, thanks. Or do they? Artists live out here?"

"Not that I know of. Except for Maurice Stebbing, of course. He's done some beautiful things. We used to get his calendars."

"That's all?"

"That's all I know of."

She knew Stebbing's stuff. Calendars and magazine covers: landscapes that could have been either Vermont or Oregon or Scotland for all their personality. He was the kind of fellow who still thought it worthwhile to paint Wolfe taking Quebec. Funny him doing it all in Stapleton; maybe he was born blind, though.

"Where does he live?"

"You know the big white house on Witecka Hill? Behind the river? He lives up there."

Her mother wasn't often so talkative. Her prune juice must have done a job this morning, thought Alison. Mrs. Willoughby hardly knew how to cope with her relief; she spoke awkwardly. But it was nice to hear her talk at all. Maybe they could break twenty years of ice this morning and then start chipping away together at her father? Alison sat in the kitchen a long time, chatting about who lived in what houses. Her mother's thin face had seams of character that worked attractively when she was animated. Important to keep her talking.

"This fellow Stebbing, what is he like?"

"Well, like most artists, I suppose. He wears a beret and corduroy trousers."

"Oh dear, he does?"

"You'd think people here would resent that kind of man, but they don't at all. He's very well received."

"Yes, I suppose he would be."

"He's very eccentric, but in good taste, if you know what I mean."

"Yes."

Why couldn't Pierce pretend he was fixing a bomb with his mother? He had a whole different set of rules for her. "People like M. shouldn't have children at all," he wrote. "I'm not prepared to argue about that." It sounded like an imitation: the handwriting looked smaller and quicker. He didn't want an argument, even though it could only have been with himself, in his own diary. Alison liked her mother, especially on her loose days.

"As for F." . . . she winced at her own decline in attention span. Her mother went off to the bathroom, leaving Alison to finish the thought. Her father never seemed as grim as her mother, probably because his insides were more flexible. But over the years you came to see that he never actually did kindness to anyone; he smiled and chatted amiably, but he never actually spoke well of anyone, either absent or present, and of course it wasn't really a smile. He was so equable that other people assumed he was good-natured: but there was no connection between the two things. Pierce went further: "F. doesn't often get angry, but when he does, it seems completely *right* for him: he seems to be himself, to have come home . . ."

A cold man, for his own good reasons, and there wasn't much you could do about him. But with Mrs. Willoughby, you sometimes got a feeling you could help. Once a month or so she was briefly dispensed from her constitutional dourness, and was apt to come floundering after companionship, like this; then, on heaven knew what compulsion, a signal from conscience perhaps, or a drying up of the juices, her stomach would begin to bind again; dourness would crawl back into her mouth and eyes, like a new ice age. Nothing could be done, except more prune juice. Why hadn't Pierce realized that? It was Alison's one serious quarrel with him.

Mrs. Willoughby stayed in the bathroom (there were enough old magazines to last a month), so Alison finished her coffee and stood up.

There was nothing much to do today, just pick up some

funny-looking underwear at the laundry. Uncle Henry and Aunt Matilda had blunted her taste for ceramics or anything else constructive. She didn't feel like reclaiming the bums at the Bear. So she took a useless walk in the very heavy warmth of the woods. Witecka Hill was just beyond the Pequod River; it looked as if the frightful Stebbing might even have planted the cypresses. He had a big property running lushly downhill to the river. Must be a pretty cynical fellow, with his beret and all that. Must have given it a lot of thought, deciding whether to be a country gentleman "who just happens to paint" or a typical artist "who turns out to be a hell of a good guy."

Since he was on her mind this morning, she was tempted to keep going, up the hill and then right into Stebbing's front gate (his house sided onto the river). It wasn't much of a temptation, but she didn't feel like sitting down and she didn't feel like turning back, so she went along with it. She could pull his whiskers anyway and tell him to get out of Stapleton.

The door was opened by a pretty, dark girl in slacks. She would have been a model, only you didn't need that kind of model for Wolfe taking Quebec. "I'm Mrs. Stebbing," she defined herself swiftly. People around here usually squinted over their door chains and said "What do you want?" when you called on them.

"Hello. I'm Alison Cope, a sort of neighbor."

"Well—come in."

Mrs. Stebbing led her vaguely into the interior. Unless Stapleton had suddenly gone all tolerant, Mrs. Stebbing ought to do something about that walk. "Maurice, Maurice—we have a visitor. I'm sorry, I've forgotten your name." Maurice popped out as if he was waiting: an upstairs door opened, and he came trotting down the curved staircase with a hand in his pocket and a small smile on a wide mouth. Arty and homespun, whichever you preferred.

"I'm Alison Cope."

"I know. I've seen you sketching our river."

"Oh, yes."

"It's lovely, isn't it?"

Would he kiss her hand, or break into a square dance? Impossible to tell at this stage. His eyes were much busier than she'd expected, considering his blind drawings. "Sit down, and have some coffee with us. Or a little Pernod." Well, he was preposterous all right. His accent had a slight suggestion of foreign, which he could lean on a little if the play went that way (happy days at the Sorbonne); his hair was gray and curled at the back—you know how it is with us artists; his pink shirt was, was, she groped for a phrase about that. (Fred used to say how can you be so catty about people and still say you love them? Fred, who wasn't catty and didn't love.)

"It's a marvelous house," she said. "How long have you lived here?"

"A very long time. It must be thirty years."

"I never knew that."

"Well, we're practically hermits, of course."

"Maurice finds it wonderful country for painting," said Mrs. Stebbing. "Just the greatest."

And where do *you* come in, thought Alison; old Hermit Stebbing must have done some foraging outside Stapleton—that was a good question of Fred's about catty. Stebbing turned his hands over at mention of his painting: a gesture of delicious modesty. "I traveled a good deal as a young man, but I always had my eye on Stapleton."

"Your eye?"

"Yes, I was born here, you know."

It was like one of those "he said gently" anecdotes, where the last line is " 'But you see, I *am* Mrs. Roosevelt,' she said gently." Born in Stapleton, by George.

"Maurice says the countryside here is just the most—"

Oh, you again! but she really was interested in Stebbing. He might be just about the biggest cynic of all time. At any rate, he looked as if he might be intelligent enough to talk to. There seemed to be an unusual amount of glass in the living room: full-length mirrors, a wide wide mirror over a sideboard full of cut glass decanters and sherry glasses; French windows. It made her feel nervous to have every gesture reproduced to infinity.

"How did you get started on painting?" she asked. Stebbing pressed his fingertips and looked at his wife as if giving a signal. "Maurice always wanted to paint," she said, "from earliest boyhood. . . ." Maurice shut his eyes, and his wife said, "Maurice decided that his subject would be nothing less than America itself."

Alison had always wondered what kind of people did those terrible calendars: now she knew. Cynics in glass houses. She looked around at acres of shivering glass. Stebbing looked modest, modest, modest, in all the mirrors at once, while his wife intoned his biography. "Until he was nineteen, Maurice had never been more than fifteen miles outside Stapleton. However, later he went to Paris and studied under the masters"—to cut a long hand-out short, Alison gathered that you can't really take Stapleton out of the boy; you can dress him like Toulouse-Lautrec, and cut off his ears and so on but— "For years, Mr. Stebbing lived in different foreign countries, but he was restless. He couldn't paint America from the shores of Lake Como, or the side of the Matterhorn." Well hardly. But it wasn't all waste, averred Mrs. Stebbing. "The years abroad taught Maurice something very important. They taught him America. Maurice went on to develop a style that was to appeal to people who usually cared nothing for art—a universal style . . ." Alison couldn't believe it, just couldn't. Not in somebody's *house*.

The speech must have been memorized: it came out in a flat little-girl voice; take it or leave it, this is what we tell the people who come here. "Stapleton took Maurice to its bosom. As one farmer humorously put it, 'He didn't let his head swell in those foreign countries.'" The chandelier dilated incredulously. "It wasn't just a great man condescending to come home. Maurice Stebbing saw things the way Stapleton people saw them. He had the genius to re-create the common vision." Not even what was there, but what the Stapleton people thought they saw, what they thought of as "art." No wonder he kept his eyes shut. If they had betrayed him into that.

What made the thing so almost admirable was that *nobody* could be taken in by this spiel; it was an insult to the most unsophisticated guest; there wasn't a single honest phrase in it. He must be a very cynical man indeed, to teach his wife a routine like that and make her perform it like a circus puppy. All that remained now was to take the squirming guest on an ironic tour of the galleries.

He opened his eyes and they were busy as ever. If you're going to be a fraud, go all the way, they said. And she couldn't help feeling a little sneaky approval of that. (If Fred, for instance, was ever a fraud, it was only by accident, or out of blind panic.) Without referring at all to his wife's patter, Stebbing said, "I knew your brother Pierce quite well. He used to come out here on Saturday afternoons. I liked him, of course."

5

The change of subject made her feel dizzy and a little bit sick. "I knew that Pierce's sister had come back," he said, "and of course you look just like him except for the hair."

"How did you know?"

"Everyone was talking about it. You know how it is in a small town: 'Alison Willoughby is back, tell two friends.' " He smiled charmingly and his face seemed to go flat.

Mrs. Stebbing got up abruptly and left, since it wasn't going to be that sort of visit. She must have a hard time keeping this house going on top of being press secretary. They were still sitting in the lobby, under a complex of chandelier—just dusting that would take a lot of ingenuity—and Alison wondered how many other rooms they used. He must be pretty rich. (Also, was he *really* interesting, and if so, could he become interested in her?)

"Were you close to your brother, Mrs. Cope?"

"Oh, yes." Why didn't he deck the place up as a Parisian garret? This Versailles business was way out of character.

"It's funny, he hardly mentioned you."

It was true, but surprisingly painful. "He was about eight years older," she said.

"Yes, of course."

"But we were close. Quite close."

He nodded and didn't say anything. She felt as if she would have to pass some delicate kind of test before he would talk to her about Pierce. Which was annoying, since she was chief proprietor of Pierce's memory, and he was just a fraud.

"What did you talk about with him?" she asked sharply.

"All kinds of things. Pierce was a boy of wide interests."

"Yes, I know."

"He even did a little painting. He believed in living twenty-four hours a day, you know. We had a lot in common, Pierce and I."

"He didn't put it quite like that, did he? Twenty-four hours—"

"Pierce was quite a promising young dauber—warm, unpretentious . . ."

She looked round wildly. Everything seemed swirling, suddenly wonderlandish. She could see the white ceiling of the second floor through the swirling bowl of the staircase. If you weren't used to it, the height made everything seem the wrong size. Stebbing's head was in scale, but the rest of him was too small. She hadn't expected to have her view of Pierce threatened like this. Stebbing was joking, in the depths of his slyness, saying the things that would hurt her most. Living twenty-four hours a day indeed! Pierce had never used a cliché in his life.

"Living is the chief art, don't you think? Living every minute of the day, grasping the moment—"

Please, Mr. Stebbing.

"And you—you got married? What happened to that?"

"I left him."

"Oh, dear, I'm sorry."

"I don't think so."

"Marriage is a sacred thing, a beautiful thing," he said solemnly.

Please, Mr. Stebbing. I've just seen your wife, remember?

This was the first person she'd met in Stapleton who could possibly understand what she'd done. An artist, even a bad one, would understand cutting away dead flesh like Fred. And he was fending her off with this crazy early-American pose. And worse still, implicating Pierce in it.

He shrugged enormously, little pointed shoulders up up and away. He was the Red Queen, that's who he was, and they were sitting in the middle of the board; they should be over by the French windows. She was quite dizzy and sick, a midday nervousness that she used to have years ago.

"What are your plans now?"

"I haven't any."

"No plans?"

"No. I don't think plans are so important."

Stebbing shook his head, faking disapproval with rather disconcerting authenticity. He *was* a fraud, wasn't he? "Pierce always had plans," he said irrelevantly.

"Well, that was Pierce."

"What do you do with yourself every day then?"

"Ceramics, sketching . . ."

"How many hours a week, do you suppose?"

"It depends."

"Depends on what?"

"On how I damn well feel."

He had intelligent eyes. He was just having her on. She was exhausted with his subtleties. Why did he pretend to disapprove of her if he was a friend of Pierce's? Why did he live in this house? She was, unusual for her, sweating slightly.

"I apologize for asking so many questions," he said. "I was curious about Pierce's little sister."

She realized she was also scowling horribly, and on the brink of nervous tears; Stebbing was making fun of her in some peculiar way. He was a clever man who refused to take her seriously. He was made of plastic, which was difficult to deal with when you were used to wood. If she shut her eyes now, his ectoplastic face would stretch up the stairwell and snap together again like bubble gum. And he would laugh with a great gurgling roar.

"Pierce did mention you once or twice, Alison, and I wondered how you'd turned out."

"Not very well, I'm afraid."

He waved his hand. "You mustn't give up on yourself, Alison. If you don't love yourself, nobody else will"—as if she'd *really* meant that she hadn't turned out well. Oh, dear. He was making such a fool of her.

"It's been nice meeting you, Mr. Stebbing," she said abruptly.

She could see tapering black slacks in a downcast mirror. Mrs. Stebbing was standing in one of the doorways, holding an imaginary coat.

He was still spouting homilies like a geyser as Alison backed away. Perhaps he'd fallen into the habit of talking like that, and it wasn't *just* to annoy her.

She looked at him from further back—perhaps that was the right distance for him. From fifty feet she saw that he had the Stapleton face almost as badly as George Pyke had it. It could come, couldn't it, with a big mouth or a small one, most any kind of nose and eyes; preferably set close, but you could do it with wide ones. Stebbing's face broke all the rules (even the stupidity rule), but it was a Stapleton face all the same.

"You must call again, we're such hermits," said Mrs. Stebbing. Maurice was smiling like George Pyke from the center of the room, and Pierce was standing next to him, smiling like George Pyke, and . . .

Alison glanced in the last mirror on the way out. But of course, the wearer never saw it.

She imagined the Stebbings laughing for five solid minutes after her exit. Alison had had too much of Pierce too and suddenly felt quite sick of him. He became briefly linked in her mind with Stebbing, two vivacious country philosophers playing checkers at the post office. "Life is worth living is what I always say," "It's what you put into it, bunky." She could see Pierce whistling up Witecka Hill every Saturday, turning in at Stebbing's door, drenching the house with his dreadful bored-child vivacity. Trading aphorisms: "A woman is like a blank check, a violin, a game of something."

It wasn't fair to Pierce, there was nothing like that in his diary. Still, his friendship with Stebbing was a puzzle. Did all that vitalism in the diary really boil down to the same thing as Stebbing's dreadful country wisdom? Would Pierce have wound up a dreadful old sage? She could just picture Pierce winking at Stebbing, "Here comes Alison," and the two of them swapping their truisms and laughing to themselves. This was the kind of humor she just didn't understand, and it left her a little defenseless.

She made an effort to change the subject. Why hadn't Fred written? She would lose face completely if she wrote to Fred first. She had told him quite clearly where she was going. And even if he had been answering in his sleep, which was possible, surely he would have tried Stapleton just on the off chance? She felt strangely indecisive now, without a sounding board. Her only friend was her dead brother, and he had just come back to rather unattractive life. Was it possible that he too would have disapproved of her behind a stern old Stapleton face? Or laughed at her? (*Laughed* at her?) He melted into Stebbing again in the blinding heat of midday, as she came out of the woods, onto the road, with sneakers dragging.

Alison was not religious, but raising the dead surely was: she felt ritually impure, as well as hot and sweaty as she trudged the last hundred yards over gritty asphalt. She would take a cold shower as soon as she got home to scour away unclean thoughts. She was no necrophile, she didn't *worship* Pierce, or hate him, either. She hadn't even known him, Stebbing was right; she probably wouldn't even have liked him.

The diary was on her bed table where her mother could easily see it. Didn't want to make a production, but that was careless; she began burrowing into clothes for a hiding place. Burrowing rather frantically. Her mother seldom got as far as the bottom drawers because it hurt her back to bend, so Alison knelt down to rummage: reburying the dead, interring him in underwear with shaky ceremony . . .

But Pierce wouldn't go away now. In this dreadful, lonely house he stuck to her like a clammy younger brother. With a new, fiendish facetiousness, worse than anything he had ever shown in real life: "You sent for me, master, yo ho ho" the voice on *Inner Sanctum*. She went downstairs: the attic was haunted with childish laughter. Never, never raise the dead, she thought; make a memo on that, Miss Willoughby. Something happens to them when they die, they change into something dreadful. "I'll be waiting, master, yuh yuh, yuk"—Pierce loved horror programs. The radio was always going in his old room. She could hear it now. Lived twenty-four hours a day, what a terrible thing to do. Resurrect a friend and he turns into a jeering little boy.

A pinched look of resignation and cryptic I-told-you-so

waited for her downstairs. Her mother was sitting in the living room, darkening slowly after the morning's excitement. "Hello, dear. Lunch isn't ready yet."

"Mother, I'd like to change my room."

"All right, dear," as if she understood perfectly; as if all the guests complained about that room. "It's awfully stuffy up there, isn't it?"

She even understood the need to hurry, and Alison had to unbury her relic and find a new niche for it: in the room she had refused earlier, the room next to her parents.

Her mother looked blank again. The morning's friendship had been a mistake, a misunderstanding. Prune juice plays funny tricks. Alison shut her new door and lay down, still shaking.

6

She went to bed again after lunch and dozed Pierce away. She used to have these tense, dizzy bouts sometimes as a girl, but she thought she had outgrown them. It was disconcerting to re-discover them in your old room. She was sorry now to have left the attic. A silly kind of panic that she shouldn't have given in to. Someone else had climbed inside her skin, some-one noisy with atrocious manners, who said, So you despise compulsive behavior, do you? We'll see about that! She lazed on her bed now and let the morning flow into the past, made no effort to analyze it; let Stebbing flow, and his crazy house and Pierce, out to sea in a ball, a beach ball of orange and black with pictures of your screen favorites on the spinning panels. The heat became a friend, conspiring to dopiness, and dopiness was the very best of friends because it passed the time beautifully. And so on. She couldn't remember what Stebbing looked like, and she couldn't ask for more than that.

(At four-thirty she thought: Those big stupid people like Fred can be quite crafty, at business, etc. That was why he hadn't written, it was all a trick. Beat him at his own game. Lie quite still and drive him crazy.)

The rest of the week was a lot of nothing. She meant to join the local Democratic club but didn't (Stapleton was 90 percent Republican, so it would have meant licking stamps for a lost cause). Saturday rolled up on a wave of vacuity. The date with George Pyke was a focal point, the way dates used to be. In the flat rhythm of Stapleton, Saturday night always had a slight extra throb. Excitement if not joy. Something to iron your dress for. To the tinny beat of a kitchen clock.

Every shapeless week of your life, you threw away six days —she pressed the iron between the pleats—and hung on for Saturday. It was never that good, but you had to pretend it was after wasting the six days. Pierce said: "All the killing of time in Stapleton, town full of dead time." Pierce with only minutes to live, perhaps, sorrowing over dead minutes. He was back in proportion now, whimsical, unobsessive. But she didn't want to stir him up again. She didn't want him saying, "Where's your sense of humor, Alison?" She held up the dress, dark blue taffeta. Left over from the Fred era. Fred liked Saturday nights too, the sneak. She used to say, let's sit home tonight and go out next *Thursday*, and he would say all right in that hollow voice, thinking of the Peabodys and the Wilkinses who were going out at the proper time; pretending to agree with her, but looking so forlorn in front of his insipid Saturday night programs.

We'll think about a separation, right, Fred?" Aborted snore again behind the pillow, and then in quite a loud voice "Right!"

"You agree it's hopeless?" "Right!" That was the last she remembered of Fred, a withering, grinding, invulnerable snore, a snore that said it all.

She wasn't looking forward to George Pyke as such. Nor did she especially like going out in the evenings. But life at home had already taken on a slight Fred-like dullness that she hated to admit to. She had sworn she would never get bored again after leaving Fred, but she hadn't counted on the sheer emptiness of the old house. Making pots wasn't any fun; you could hear yourself doing it in the creaky attic: and when you were done, you had another gray object—for people to turn over in gray hands . . . Sketching, reading, walking, all led back to the blank Willoughby faces, which didn't care what she did as long as she turned out the light when she was through; to the blankness they had given their house.

So she was back to ironing a dress for Saturday night, and letting a little time get killed by the kitchen clock, whatever Pierce said.

George arrived punctually in a brand-new suit, and greeted her parents like old friends. They responded with rather repulsive smiles, as if they had suddenly decided to approve of him. In what context was hard to imagine. He gave her the same conveyor belt treatment, through door and into car—you knew what was happening when Fred took you out, but with George the wheels were invisible. Fred wasn't clumsy exactly, but you had to pull your knees in quick and then wait while he looked for the right key.

The car nosed through the sober festivities of Stapleton; crowds spilling out of the soda fountains and gurgling into the movie house. Girls trying to cross the street without looking. There seemed to be a few more lights, and now and then you heard somebody laugh. Saturday night. It was uphill work, finding those "basic values" in Stapleton.

The Pomfret Inn was out along the pike and she noticed how the pike had filled up since she was a girl. The traffic pounded along breathlessly and came to dispirited halts because something had gone wrong in the unseen distance. George didn't talk about his driving problems as Fred did; he didn't say, "Did you see that guy? Geez," but he said they had a nice band at the Pomfret, and you could get a steak there now; they had a new man in the kitchen. George knew what to do on a second date as well.

The inn hadn't shrunk, as things were supposed to, but grown. It had several bars separated by glass panels with nymphs and things on them, a matter-of-fact dining room and another darker one behind it that was just opening up for the evening. "There seems to be an awful lot of it," she said to George, who explained about the new wings. A national magazine had done a piece on it, "Pennsylvania's Friendliest Inn," and copies of the article were mounted on most of the walls. "It was quite a spread," said George. "They had pictures of all the fine old copperware."

There was some copperware at that. She hadn't remembered anything like that. She remembered a dim little place where you slunk around the floor trying to look twenty-one, where you looked off in the distance and said, "Oh, just make mine a rye and Coca-Cola." George had already found a big bonhomous chap at the bar and was saying, "Al, I'd like you to meet Alison. Al is the owner here." Politician-type fellow, smile bang through you to the far wall, friendliest man in Pennsylvania. "Al bought this place two years ago and really made it go. Didn't you, Al?" "That's right, we had a lot of luck with the article." "Yes, that was a break getting the article." "Look, I'll see you, George"—his foxy eyes pounced on an invisible duty; but he touched George on the elbow to show he held a special place anyway. Fred knew a lot of owners, too, and they always went off like that. A small smile, a touch.

George wanted to go into the dark dancing room right away, but she got him to linger a while in the bright bar. Dark rooms always dismayed her a little at first, with the smoke and whispers. She even preferred places like Schrafft's to really dark bars. "So, what have you been doing with yourself?" said George.

"Well, I saw a man called Stebbing."

"Maurice Stebbing? The painter?"

"Yes. You know him?"

"Uh-huh. He's quite a character, isn't he?"

"I suppose."

"We had the contract on his house, you know, to put in the deep freeze unit. We thought he was going to be, you know, queer, but he turned out to be a real nice fellow."

"Yes."

"I guess artists have to look that way. For business reasons." He gave a hopeful I'll-laugh-if-you-will chuckle. He must have thought things over since last week, perhaps even remembered something (although Stapleton's faceless days and weeks made remembering difficult), and decided that Alison Willoughby meant laughs. He was very jovial about Stebbing. "People become painters so they can look at nudes," he said, watching her. "I used to think that."

"I'm glad you got over it."

Well, Alison *did* mean laughs, didn't she? It wasn't healthy for a Stapleton man to plunge back into the gray past like this; but sometimes it had to be done.

"Anyway, he's the local character. I guess there's one in every community."

"Yes."

"What's the matter, Alison? You're not talking much tonight," he said a few minutes later.

"No."

"Well, sometimes I like just to sit and think too. It shouldn't be necessary to talk all the time."

She couldn't help smiling, and said she was willing to dance now. You couldn't mind going into the dark with someone who liked to sit and think.

They weren't able to dance right away. The supper show was just beginning and there he was, the comedian who turned up at all these places: the short man who rolled up his trousers and pulled his hat out of shape and did the imitations. George was looking at her, she could tell. He was like Fred who always wanted permission before laughing at the rough stuff. The comedian puffed his dinner jacket into a bosom: she didn't know where you began to laugh at this. But they had a ringside table, and the comedian looked like the kind who could make brutal fun of a solemn customer. Thrust the microphone at you, the way the fellow had wherewasit—she remembered Fred caught between embarrassment and giggles, her own face hopelessly frozen—only tears would dissolve it; meanwhile the cold microphone picking up every indecisive breath. . . . She smiled at the bosom.

George smiled too, and shook his head slightly as if to say: Oh, really, but you can't help smiling a little. He knew he hadn't been given any green light. Rather a clever fellow, George, in his subverbal way. Suppose he got a good table here because his firm handled the fluorescent light contract. She tried to think of something funny so she could laugh in time with the comedian. It went on and on, and she got so she could laugh anyway, just surrendering to the comedian's bounciness. They were "having a good time" now, and George put his hand lightly on hers. He must have timed it. A real pro. She shrugged it away, and it was so light that nothing had really happened.

The comedian introduced, with a few tasteless words, a blonde torch singer. "It's usually better," said George. "We had Jerry Lewis last year."

The singer writhed around the room in gold spangles, and Alison thought, If one wasn't a woman, one wouldn't have to go out with people like George, one wouldn't have to marry people like Fred. She was only here because of a million years of suppression.

Even at that, one had to pretend that marrying someone like Fred was a mature decision. One had to say, He's really sensitive deep down; and anyway, I need somebody who's solid, what with being so sensitive myself. Being twenty-five had nothing to do with it of course; rooming with a girl she didn't like, social work getting to her nerves, had nothing to do with it. Sam Chester's departure—irrelevant (Sam the sensitive, a bit *too* sensitive, jilted her for a fellow called Howie.) It was winter and the heat wasn't working. Mavis was spiraling into worse and worse tantrums. Twenty-five. Very mature decision.

Fred had only had to act a little bit aware, just keep quiet at the Museum of Modern Art and awake at the concerts, and she said "I'll take it." He had a sort of cloudy expression which might have meant he was thinking. And big fluttery jaws. And thoughtful eyebrows. Pierce's diary said "Some of the biggest idiots I've met out here have turned out to be very *sensitive* idiots"—lucky Pierce died so young. He would have made a dreadful marriage. "Thank you," breathed the girl, "and now by popular request, I'd like to sing my own rendition of 'Stardust.'" An elderly couple by the wall clapped. George ordered another drink. The gold spangles began to quiver. Pierce thought it was pompous not to like nightclubs, but honestly.

"You've been a wonderful audience," but the applause was thin, and when the lights went up, it all seemed to be coming from the same table. A party of middle-aged women, looked like a reunion of some kind. Bryn Mawr '27 about. She could make out the word "girls" and gusts of crazed laughter. They applauded until the stage was cleared, but their palms were small and birdlike and they didn't make much noise.

She rather didn't want to dance with George now. She had the jitters about him again. George obviously did a lot of this kind of thing. He proceeded by metronome and egg timer to his goal. His goal wasn't her goal.

But he danced so well and made her so comfortable that her nerves slowly unwrinkled: it was like being in the hands of a good masseur. There was a physical side to things and it came out with a rush. She hated to admit it, but really, she was attracted by men like George and Fred. Very much attracted right now. (The interesting ones usually looked dreadful.) George's egg timer was working just right, for when he touched cheeks, her reflex of caution only stirred slightly and rolled over.

"It's sad what happens to children," she said, hoping he would understand a little. "Such a mess they grow up to make."

He said nothing, but held her tight, presumably signifying passionate concurrence. "What happened to you?" she whispered. "Where did you foul up?"

He went slightly embarrassed against her cheek and said gruffly, "What do you mean, Alison? Foul up?"

"Your divorce. How did it happen?" Was she up to her old mistake—thinking that because they felt good, they knew what it was all about?

He loosened his hold and began to shrink and cool. "Didn't you know? Didn't I tell you about that?"

"About what?"

"I haven't got a divorce. I'm still living with my wife."

"Oh, no."

He didn't understand the "oh, no," of course, and began saying something stupid about the sake of the children (children?) and Susan understood and was a swell girl, and incompatible the greatest biggest stupidest word and they agreed to give each other their freedom, like two squirrels in the same cage, very generous; Susan might even turn up here tonight and they could all have a drink together, grand! He didn't see that the "Oh, no" meant "not in Stapleton, not to George Pyke; not modern living for George Pyke."

Stolid children in striped T-shirts: this half-witted arrangement was for *their* sake, would make all the difference in stolid later life.

There was no point talking about it. She said, "Let's go home." He explained some more on the way out, and more again on the way home, about how Susan didn't mind—how would you know whether Susan minded or not you big, oh what's the use? "I hope you're not mad at me, Alison."

She shrugged with a sour kind of relief. One thing you could say for Fred—

"I'd hate to feel—"

"Good night, George."

Smoothness all gone, rumpled from within. "I'm sorry," he said humbly, still trying.

At least Fred had more class than *that*.

7

The next week she met another old friend in the supermarket, Hazel Withers, now Hazel Robinson. Again Alison was slow to see through the new face (was it just that all the features got larger and spread the expression thinner? was that what maturity mean in Stapleton?).

Hazel had become quite plump since school. She had a baby perched on her push cart and two more swirling at her knees. She smiled at Alison and, surprisingly, looked quite a bit like her old self. She said she lived nearby, on Maplehurst, and invited Alison to come over for a cup of coffee and a piece of cake. And it seemed like an extremely pleasant plan.

Hazel was the girl that Alison had taken to the woods years ago: and there was still some of that compliant, eager quality about her that had made it seem like a good idea. She was the kind of girl you shared your discoveries with, to get maximum mileage out of them—although you could be disappointed, of course.

"Who is Mr. Robinson?" asked Alison.

"*Dr.* Robinson, he's a doctor."

They walked to her house and into a kitchen where everything was at eye level and the air conditioning worked. Alison felt comfortable with her old friend, more so than she had felt in a long time. Hazel, with plump back turned, seemed quite tremendously receptive. "Who is Mr. Cope, then?" Hazel said over her shoulder.

"He's just Mr. Cope. He's a professional bore."

A bit catty, but Hazel gave a friendly giggle, and Alison went on in rather schoolgirl style. "We're separated sort of. I just couldn't take him any longer. Such a, you know, goop."

"Are you legally separated, or divorced, or what?"

"I haven't decided yet. In fact, I don't even know where he is."

Hazel giggled again, rather irritatingly this time.

"I mean, I assume he's still at home, boring the neighbors—I really couldn't care less, until I've decided my next move . . . "

"It sounds like a funny arrangement. You take cream and sugar?"

"Just black, please. Well, I suppose it is from a conventional point of view. But since I haven't decided what I want, it seems to me to make sense. There are no children involved."

"What does *he* want?"

"I haven't the faintest . . . to be left alone, I guess. I know I demanded too much from him."

Hazel sat down at the kitchen table. At one moment she looked like her old self, at the next she didn't quite. A glaze of premature middle age came and went. "That's always a mistake," she said judiciously, "demanding too much."

"I don't happen to think so," said Alison.

"You don't?"

"No."

"Well—and so how did you happen to marry him if he's so boring?" She said "boring" like a foreign word, hesitating slightly and self-consciously. The word was a little exotic and pretentious for Stapleton.

"God knows. Loneliness, panic. He's not stupid, you know. He can talk intelligently for several minutes at a time—in a derivative sort of way. But, I don't know, he just isn't *interested* in anything."

"Thank heavens Dr. Robinson has interests."

"Dr. Robinson? Yes, well anyway, I married Fred at a bad time. He wasn't himself. I mean, he was in love, I guess, and that gave him a kind of sparkle he can't usually manage. It's his cruising speed you have to watch out for."

"Doctor, that is, Tim, has many, many interests."

"Fred has interests, but he isn't really interested in them, if you know what I mean."

"I guess so. I mean, he sounds very peculiar."

"No, very normal."

Hazel gave up, the way she had given up in the woods. She isn't stupid, she knows what I'm talking about, thought Alison, but at the sound of danger, strange sounds in the dark, Hazel always made herself go stupid, plunging into a possumlike trance.

"Oh, there were other things," said Alison, "of course."

Hazel snapped to. "Of course, I knew there must be. It's difficult to talk about, isn't it?"

"I'm not quite sure what to do next, to tell you the truth. I have to decide what my life is all about, don't I? I mean, separation for *what*, is the question."

She had an eerie feeling that Hazel was going to go to sleep, like Fred, if she went on talking abstractly. So she said, "If I write to him, what should I say?"

"Tell him, well, that you're sorry, but it's just no go; I mean, tell him he's a fine man and all that. But when two people—"

"Why, that's fascinating, Hazel. Where did you learn to talk like that?"

"What? What did I say?"

"Nothing—I'm sorry, I really am, but to get back to the other thing for a moment . . . Do you think I ought to write to Fred at all, maybe? or wait for him to write?"

Hazel looked startled. "Well, definitely, I'd write."

"You would?"

"Definitely."

"Oh."

There was no point in pursuing it. Hazel was obviously right. It was crazy not to send a letter.

"Hazel, it's been grand."

"You too, Alison." Boola, boola.

She went home with every intention; but for some reason or other she didn't write the letter that afternoon, but just went for another walk.

The citizens of Bloodbury were fundamentally no brighter than Hazel, but you could sometimes coax or trick them into appearing so. Living so close to New York, they absorbed sophistication along with the diesel fumes, and you could con them into using it . . . Of course, like Tolstoy, she would gladly trade them all in for one clear-eyed peasant—but Hazel wasn't precisely that either. Stapleton had just begun the long painful evolution into Bloodbury. George Pyke, for instance, was proto-Peabody; Hazel was Fran Wilkins without the annual trip to the theater. When the hot weather let up, she would have to leave Stapleton and try something else. This was simply impossible.

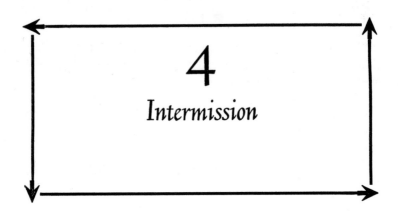

4

Intermission

"Bob says it's the hottest summer since nineteen something."

"At least I haven't heard anyone say is it hot enough for you," said Ernie, who was just catching up with the anti-cliché cliché.

"Which was that other hot summer?" Fran ran it down. "Nineteen fifty-one, was it? We were living in New York, I know that, and honestly, we couldn't breathe. Every night Bob had the mattresses out on the fire escape. Nineteen fifty-two—what was it?"

Fran Wilkins had given up and was just having a regular party. "Bob thinks we have too many parties, but I say you can't have too many parties."

Gagging on the stuffy air and sucking on the customary drinks, the gang was killing another summer by inches. The McIntyres had been fighting sand flies at Cape May for the last two weeks and looked red and frantic by the fire. Bert Flax was the only one with any winter paleness left, and he and Betty were off to Cape Cod on Monday. Duckworth Miller always made a big thing of being tired and overworked—but his face was dark from hours of sun. Only Bert had any real phosphorescence.

"Here's to absent friends," said Fran.

"Who's absent?" asked Bert, who had just come back from the hospital or somewhere. "Everyone seems to be just where I left them."

They laughed encouragingly. Bert had hardly said a word so far. Betty whispered something to him, and he nodded without interest. Fran came over to them and said, "I had a letter from Alison." She looked at Bert to see how much sensation he could take.

"You *did?*" said Betty. "What did she say?"

"Well, she said—she's down with her parents, you know. She didn't say it was hot or what it was, you know how Alison was about small talk—" She kept looking at Bert, but he was just paying poilte attention, not listening or anything, "She said would I or Bob or someone please tell Fred to write to her. It was a funny kind of letter. Why couldn't she tell Fred herself?"

Bert said "Huh" quite loudly.

"It was a tragedy about those two," Fran went on. "Two of my favorite people . . . "

"Maybe she can't find him," said Betty. "I mean, *we* can't, can we?"

"Somehow I don't see Alison Cope in such a crazy situation, losing her husband and all. She was always so serious and on top of things, wasn't she?"

Bert suddenly looked interested. "You mean Fred just disappeared?"

"Well—yes, in a way."

"I didn't think that was possible these days."

Fran didn't know what to say. It was so difficult to talk to somebody who had been—unwell. Suppose Bert was planning to disappear himself?

"Oh, heavens," said Betty, "it's easy. People do it all the time. I was reading an article that said that at least ten thousand people disappear every year. Or was it a hundred thousand?"

"I read that article. It was in *This Week*." Ernie Peabody had come up through the dark. "But was it every year or every month that they disappeared?"

"Anyway, it was a lot," said Betty.

"Huh," said Bert.

"We were just talking about Fred and Alison," said Fran.

Ernie gave a sort of sigh. "A tragedy," he said. "If ever two people . . ."

"You were the one who ran him down before, weren't you?" asked Betty.

"No, that was Duckworth. A fellow he knows tried to sell Fred some insurance—can you imagine, trying to sell Fred *insurance*? No, I was the one who heard where *Alison* was. Fellow I knew in the construction business—well, I won't go into that, but anyway, I saw Fred a few weeks after he left home and I could have sworn from the way he acted that it was just a temporary thing. A lot of people break up like that, you know, and then they think it over"—he stopped and looked at Bert. Suppose Bert had been worried about his marriage, and that was why . . . You couldn't be too careful these days—"and I'm sure that they *will* get together, too. Nobody can make me believe . . ."

"Definitely," said Fran, who might have been thinking along the same lines. Bert was looking at his hands with an empty expression. But it was too dark to be sure. It didn't seem possible that people could have nervous trouble in Bloodbury. Yet Bob Wilkins was awfully jumpy. And even Ernie Peabody had behaved very strangely one summer. *Very* strangely.

"So meanwhile, where's he got to?" said Betty impatiently.

"I wish I knew. He left his place in the Village and he didn't tell anyone where he was going. I went around and his apartment was taken by a girl called Osborne who didn't know a thing."

"All those people disappearing," said Bert, and Betty touched his hand and smiled.

"It may have been Shelley. Shelley or Osborne."

Fran moved off to pollinate another group. After a moment, Ernie followed. "Here's the man who knows the most," said Duckworth Miller. "What do you think happened to Fred, Ernie?"

"I honestly don't know, Duckworth. His box was full of mail, and I tried to make out the postmarks, but you know how it is with those little boxes. I asked some people in his building, and most of them couldn't even remember ever seeing him. That's big cities for you—people don't know their own neighbors, as they say. Just this one girl remembered him. Stocky kid. She said 'You his friend?' and I said 'Yes,' and she said, 'Well, I don't know what happened to him.' Why do people in New York always sound so angry?"

Duckworth shook his head.

"Anyway, that was all the trace he left. Big cities are terrible, lonely places, as the fellow says . . ."

"Ernie says the grocer thought he could remember him," Fran said to the McIntyres. "That was all."

Bloodbury wasn't gossipy, partly because the taboos of this

particular subclass said "no gossip," and partly because there wasn't too much to gossip about. People lived carefully, following the hundred great rules of the West; the houses were big and set back from the road; and the longer people stayed here, becoming known, the better they knew how to protect themselves. What Fred had done stood out in isolated grandeur and was clearly in the public domain, too. "He left his affairs in an awful mess," Ernie confided. "I had to talk to Mr. Willard at the real estate place and square things at Sears . . . " It conjured a world of wonder: disorganized finances were to Bloodbury roughly what drunkenness was to Stapleton.

"Do you think he was dis*turbed?*" whispered Fran.

In another corner of the lawn, behind a screen of fireflies, Bert and Betty Flax sat quietly, holding hands. Betty hated to join in the orgy of tactfulness that made life so prickly for a nerve case; but she took just a peep into her husband's eyes, to make sure.

He was looking almost hysterically uninterested. A healthy reaction in the circumstances. Bloodbury gossip was so restricted in scope and so puritanical in method (you mustn't show honest pleasure in it; concern for the parties must always be uppermost) that she was getting a little hysterical herself.

5

La Feria de Vanidades

1

The colors were harsh white for houses; black for dresses, and perpetual mourning; yellow for ground; brown for faces; seamless blue for sky. The only change was in the water, which turned muddy, green and charcoal gray, as the sand, seaweed and tar swirled under the surface. (Fred supposed that these were the major influences. If there was one thing he didn't know about, it was sea water.)

Lined along the wall, the men with the slashed and withered faces laid out dominoes and drank water or coffee or mostly nothing, and talked with unlikely animation. (Wonder where the idea of strong silent men came from, certainly not from here.) It was more than beautiful; it was painful. Everything shimmering in the same dull glare; a troop of flies trying to climb into the mouth of a sleeping dog, tumbling out again in confusion. I should be at work, I should be at work, What am I doing here?

Count the beards go by for a while. Abortive fluff on the new arrivals, lush vines on the older settlers; three abreast, new faces, if you could call them faces; wife in tights, lugging two babies, husband staring around vaguely. "Hey, Fred"—a friend, Pete Glasser; coming over for chat; beard will probably grow in better when he gets to be more successful.

"Hi, Pete. What are you drinking?" Fred reflexively reached for his own chin and began to rub it.

"Oh, God. Drinking," said Pete.

"Another rough night?"

Glasser shook his head. "Wound up at the Merluza of all god damn places. Drinking anis, for Godsake. O.K., I'll have a beer."

Glasser stroked the whiskers and stared off into space. He was Fred's first writer-friend, and Fred was mildly surprised that he didn't talk much, or brilliantly. He said, "Look at the goddamn *estranjeros*. Christ," and drank his beer; his wife Marilyn brushed the flies off the babies and said, "It's a bloody shame, what they're doing to this coast." Never mind, they would say something interesting in a moment.

"You coming to Jeff's party tonight?" Glasser wiped his mouth with a small, nonabsorbent napkin.

"No, what party is that?"

"Jeff's giving a party for Linda. She's going to Africa for two weeks."

"Does it make any difference that I wasn't invited?"

"Nah. Jeff prolly meant to invite you and didn't get around to it."

"Which one is Jeff?"

"Don't you know Jeff? I thought you knew Jeff."

"No."

"You'll like him," said Marilyn. "He's exhibited."

"No, it was Jack that exhibited. I made a mistake."

"I thought it was Jeff."

"No, I made a mistake."

They sat in feverish silence. Marilyn had to go home after a while and feed the kids; Pete stayed on, having another beer and watching the dog and the flies. "The way they treat dogs around here, Christ," he said.

"You do any work today?" asked Fred.

"You kidding? After a night on the anis? I'm lucky to be alive."

"You're an indifferent caretaker of your talent, Glasser," said Fred. "Which one is Linda, then?"

"Don't you know Linda? Christ, Fred."

The church clock didn't work, but the bell inside did, and it couldn't promise anything better than twelve o'clock. Lunch at the pension wasn't till two-thirty, even if you were lucky. Fred's pink and white Penguin on the table had a marker in it at page twenty-five: that was as far as he could get with Camus. (You could see Camus was good, of course.) His towel and trunks were drying out on the next chair, making a dank stain on the slats; he couldn't very well take another swim before lunch. Endure, endure.

"You think it'll be a good party?"

Glasser shrugged. "You know the parties around here."

"Yes."

He had been to two, and they had seemed rather flat. But afterwards everybody said, "These damn parties . . ." Their eyes were glassy and their faces were waxy and they said, "I've got to cut out these damn parties."

Pete went across the street and came back with a copy of the Paris *Tribune*, which he proceeded to read in disgusted spasms. Something about Berlin, it looked like, something about Al-

geria. Fred decoded upside down, DeGaulle looked funny upside down, as who did not, weather in Paris 21 centigrade.
Weather in New York, 96. Brother. He could just see them
glittering in the elevator, hear them talking weather.

It had just been hotting up when he left, as a matter of fact.
Clammy breathless night at the Black Cat where he went to get
drunk after that thing with the girl. First he had tried taking
long walks and saying to himself "I certainly learned my lesson," but to his surprise, that failed to disperse the embarrassment. He tried getting drunk. Humid weather was terrible
weather to feel embarrassed in, the Village was wet and steamy,
Fred knew he'd had it after the thing with the girl. Better to
phone up Thurman and eat dirt; get some of his job back somehow, scuttle to Bloodbury and forget the whole thing.

He drove back the embarrassment with beer after beer; and
because he was really desperate and clumsy and randomly lung-
ing, people seemed to find him authentic, the people who came
to watch were watching *him*. He must have begun to sing at
some point, because a boy grabbed a tray and beat it next to
him, and a girl started to writhe just like that, and the tourists
clapped their hands and Fred beat his big foot and began to
sing in earnest—power with restraint, a bit like Paul Robeson
this time.

This was what art was all about then, not affectation and
how-do-you-like-my-Motherwell, but crudeness and spontaneity;
the out-of-towners shouted "Go man," and he went: "Swing
low, sweet chariot," "Ol' man river"—he had them in the
palm of his hand: he could modulate and play with them or
rock back and let them have it between the eyes. But the focus
swung off him at "scared of living" and, no, hold it, *tired* of

living, and a more professional group took over. The girl transferred her writhing to a different drum. Fred's voice wasn't as big as he thought; he tried to compete, but his bass notes got lost in the swell until he could barely hear them himself.

Still he had had five pretty good minutes, he was king in there for a while. He went up to some people at the bar who had been clapping and presumed on that. They were strangely cold and private now. Try somebody else. The boy with the tray was whooping it up for the new singers and looked a little peeved at Fred's off-harmonies. Fred stumbled about unrecognized and unwanted; but before he could get angry about it and hit the little bastard with his own tray, a friendly small man with an Irish brogue came up and offered him a beer and steered him to a table.

The group at the table didn't ask him to sing, although he was more than willing to. He supposed they had asked him over because he looked amusing, so he banged and shouted a little, hey, hey and heckled the boy with the tray. They watched him, chuckled once or twice, and then forgot him and went on talking to each other. Fred couldn't think of anything funny to do except pound the table and roar, and he could see that that wasn't enough. *"You're not really very interesting, Fred. Take away the eyebrows and what have you got?"* Alison sapped his confidence so that he didn't even make a good primitive any more.

They bought him more beer and didn't show any particular disappointment with him. He remembered the Irishman and a man with a mustache and could it have been a sailor?—polite hands in the dark, holding out mugs, quiet voices. One of them had just come off a ship. They had a dry, detached way of taking their fun. "But it's not what it was," said Voice A (Irish sailor with a mustache?); "it's become very what's the word predictable."

"These so-called beatniks," confirmed a second Roman citizen.

"Where should you go?" Fred suddenly wailed. "Where is it still fun?"

They talked about that for a while, about places they'd been, most of which washed over Fred—Zanzibar, Rio (by the sea-o, sang Fred forlornly), don't go to Liverpool, but he did hear somebody say something good about Spain, and when the tide receded and when he was thrown out on the sidewalk for incorrigible singing, he couldn't stop thinking about Spain.

What he saw so clearly out on the sidewalk was this, that the moral fiber in America was all shot to hell anyway, look at that girl for instance, where was freshness and joy by God? The terrible drunken rhetoric seized him and led him muttering into this strange territory. If you stayed in America, it was just one dismal defeat after another. Throwing a man out of a bar for singing! In Spain or somewhere you danced in the sun, rubbing your backside with a colored scarf, and squirting wine out of goatskins: and put your arm around a girl, innocently, lots of moral fiber. But here—they didn't throw out the homosexuals, you notice, just the singers. Well, wasn't that symbolic, eh? It had just been humming, at first. But the people at the table went on and on in their low voices and he got bored and no one was paying the least attention, so he began to sing "In Spain, they say *sí, sí*," a bit like Frankie Laine, he thought, but what was all right at midnight was not so good at three. And besides, Frankie Laine . . . It was blistering early-morning hot and muggy on the sidewalk and he decided to go straight to the Spanish Embassy and wait on the steps till they opened. *Mañana,* cha cha cha.

When he got up next day he felt pretty sheepish; he never let himself get out of hand like that. He remembered the people with the low voices watching his indignant retreat, smiling; his collar was sticking up when he got home. (He went home to look up the Spanish Embassy address, and sure enough there was the phone book. Open at Philmore.) To make it seem not quite so bad, he tried pretending that he had made a serious decision about Spain. It certainly beat going back to Bloodbury. There was really a lot to be said for it. Not peasants dancing in the sun, not that this morning, but something vaguely interest- to offer Alison, supposing he ever ran into her again. He thought about Alison a lot that morning; the beer had made the sap rise as usual, and after the thing with the girl, he supposed it had to be with Alison . . . he could just see himself saying "Oh, yes, spent the year in Spain." He imagined that Alison would be living by now with an intensely witty Chinese sculptor—tiny, fascinating man. He would need a feat or two to match that. He found some Spanish addresses in his pocket. One of his friends at the Black Cat must have put them there. (Later it was to turn out that all the addresses had been long vacated.) He was free to go, dammit. Live like a rajah on $3,000, someone had told him. So why not? Duller people than he had gone to Europe. Ernie Peabody had gone to Europe.

Before leaving, he did get in touch with two of Alison's friends to find out if they'd seen her. He hated admitting that he didn't know where she was; but he wanted it on the record that he had tried to find her. They knew nothing and their letters sounded slightly amused. To hell with it. For a wild moment, he even considered writing to her parents in Stapleton, Pa. But he remembered Mrs. Willoughby's thin face and invisible lips (he rather liked *Mr.* Willoughby), and he knew that he couldn't let them in on his problem. They might even come up and investigate.

And anyway, if there was one thing sure about Alison, it was that she hated Stapleton. Talk, talk into the night about its values; he was always so sleepy he hardly knew what was supposed to be wrong with Stapleton's values. She had (he certainly remembered that part) a very annoying brother called Pierce, a real horse's neck, and sometimes she used to quote his jerky sayings until Fred was fast asleep. (If only Fred hadn't been so sleepy, none of this would have happened.) But deep down, as far down as he went, well, you know—finding Alison. Great idea and all that. But can't it wait? If she walked in at this particular minute with her Chinese friend . . . outside of brainless hungover lust (which she could always detect) what would you have to offer, F. Cope?

Going abroad would postpone the problem neatly and make him as fascinating as any Chinese sculptor. Anyway, it was either that or go back to work. His bumbling old colonel of a conscience probably wouldn't let him stay in New York much longer without working. But travel was permitted. So he went and got a ticket on an Italian ship, added a thin coat of pasta to his face and middle, and waddled off at Algeciras; took a bus along the coast; got out at the town near Torremolinos where most of his bogus addresses were; found a pension where the walls shook from the donkeys and motor bikes; and had progressed as far as reading the Paris *Tribune* upside down and waiting for lunch.

"Shit, more trouble in Algeria," said Glasser.

"Oh?"

"Yeah. Christ!"

Pete Glasser from the Bronx. Writer and shit-sayer extraordinary. The most wistful beard in town, and the youngest eyes—second always to mine, Fred supposed. (Am. men nev. g. up, Alison's college cheer.)

All that Fred knew about American writers was that they said things like "I had a beautiful talent, baby" and "I went five rounds with Stendhal." He could hear Pete Glasser talking like that someday.

Meanwhile, Pete said, "You wanna go to the bullfight Sunday?"

"Sure."

"I'll get tickets. Hey listen, I gotta go."

"O.K."

Peter Glasser got up. "See you tonight, heh. José Antonio. The big house."

Fred watched him shambling thin-shanked off. You write close to the horns, baby. It comes with the *cojones*. The flies were still working on the dog. The men shuffled their bleached dominoes. Fred took his hand down from his chin because no one was watching. A man's got to live with himself, baby. Fred had just the beginnings of a beard, and had never felt so stupid about anything in his life.

2

Waiting for lunch at the Pension Ferdinand was all hot bleakness and panic. You sat in your room smoking black cigarettes and feeling the emptiness from your mouth to your groin.

Breakfast was a long since exgurgitated roll and butter. Since then, Fred had swum and talked, and even tried cheating the clock by thinking. Now he just listened, in shuttered twilight, to the shriek of children, the asthmatic gasping of mules, and the stutter of motor bikes, which marked the drag of time.

At 2:25 he hit the dining room, with the usual American optimism. There was no sign of life there. The tables were covered with dessicated oilcloth, and flies. No cutlery even. The beads to the kitchen hung in dead strands. Fred took some letters out of his pocket and put them back. The flies came at his eyes and tickled his hands. One of them got into his nose. He ought to be at work, not fidgeting his life away in empty dining rooms.

There were some smart hotels around, but they were full of rich women with dogs and lobbies you could roller skate in. Very gross and attractive, but if you were going to do Spain right . . . Fred got a soggy napkin out of the corner cabinet and began flailing the flies. He was glad there was a party tonight, that was one thing. Most nights, he crowned the day's emptiness by just sitting around waiting for the late dinner to go down; there really wasn't much else to do.

At quarter to three a stocky maid came sashaying through the beads with a plate of hard rolls. She gave one to Fred and went out again. The whole dining room was done in early French movie; he could just picture, who was it?—Jean Gabin munching on one of these rolls. A Spanish couple came in at 2:50 and bowed to him. Then a huge family from Morocco, and at 3 o'clock some honest to God food.

He was so hungry by then that he ate too much and had indigestion. The afternoon stretched out from that as long as the morning had. He walked, very grim and uncomfortable, to the beach, and watched the fishermen mending their nets.

His body was on fire with saffron and hot sausage, and the fishermen looked dark and full of menace. He wanted to talk to them about their work, but indigestion made him diffident; and when you came right down to it, he had had indigestion on and off since he got here, so he hadn't really talked to anybody.

It was just another afternoon and it burned itself out slowly. It hurt too much to think: Alison took on a black, twisted face in his mind. He remembered sitting on a beach with her, some beach someplace, which should have been a nice memory, but she suddenly began to swell all over and blotch and he had to send her away. She said that she didn't want children, and that seemed a terrible, terrible thing. She said it meant buying things that don't pinch or chafe "baby"; it meant planning a future for *him* with Mutual Life; he couldn't remember what it all meant, but he was pretty damn horrified. There was something wrong with Alison, there really was. He woke with a jerk and shook the sand out of his hair.

It was like solitary confinement under the sharp blue arch of sky and behind the blinding white walls, and Fred began seriously to think he might be cracking up: he had never had this chaos in his head before. . . . Alison had never said those things, either: he was investing her with demonic qualities. But lunch went down at last, and a breeze came hesitating up, and the features of the fishermen softened a bit. And Fred went back to the café for a beer.

Indigestion again. Dinner wasn't till nine something, by which time he was raving hungry. (With nothing else to do, you got hungry just from thinking about the pretty colors: pimiento, shrimp-pink, pea-green, saffron-yellow.) He hoped he wouldn't wind up spending another night in the bathroom, wondering where he had gone wrong. The tiles were fleur-de-lis and there were seventeen of them from where you sat to the diagonal corner—eighteen if you moved your feet. The smell was IRT men's room—maybe just a hint of BMT. The wash basin was a fake, it didn't have a waste pipe. My, that was depressing, watching the water drip through the basin into the bucket, clunk pause clunk.

The biggest mistake you could make was to go to bed too early. The long wait and the big meal made you sleepy, and whoof— Nowadays, he flogged himself awake every night, inching through Camus by dim electricity (the bulb in his room flickered like a candle) and taking suffocating walks, until he was more or less settled. Tonight there was this party, and his only problem when he got there was to remember to sit up straight and not slump back on the sofa, folding up his pipes and tubes. . . . Even with the pipes upright, the cognac ignited everything it touched; but the really insane thing was that he was getting hungry again.

There were twelve beards at the party, make it twelve and a half, and twenty-seven pairs of pants. (Fred had always had a weakness for statistics.) There was one suit, his—he thought that since the party was *for* somebody, you wore a suit, wrong again. Squinting down on all sides were Jeff's nudes, with their green skin and conical breasts. "I like that one," he said to Jeff's mistress. "It has a lot of life." She grunted noncommittally. Perhaps she was feuding with Jeff. He really didn't know what to say about the damn paintings. Last week at Harry Siedlitz's party he tried "You seem to like orange"—orange skin and sagging breasts were the order of the day at Harry's—and Harry had said angrily, "I utilize all the colors, not just orange."

Fred wasn't really with this crowd yet. He got to the parties because Pete Glasser invited him. But wherever he sat seemed to become at once the outermost rim of the group. If he sat in the middle of the room, he clove it in two. Which was where he was tonight, taking in scraps of two conversations at once. Jeff's mistress was twisted towards the fireplace. Pete Glasser, on the right end of the sofa, was curved the other way, like a second bookend. If Fred wanted to wedge into either conversation, his voice would have to carry a little farther, be a little louder than anyone else's: and he could think of nothing worth saying in a loud voice.

"The green is amazingly vivid," he said to Janet, but she didn't hear.

"So what's new?" he said to Pete Glasser, his only friend. Pete looked round with runny-eyed irritation: that was a funny thing about Pete. As soon as he got you to these parties, he acted as if he didn't know you. "Nothin's new," he said. Please don't interrupt me again, leave a message with the clerk if it's something really important.

Oh, what the hell, the only problem was to look occupied. Member of one group notices you, look as if you belong to the other group. Laugh, slap your knee, lean forward thoughtfully; sit back and examine cigarette; put finger to chin and squint back at nudes. Why he bothered he didn't know. Manners, he supposed.

"I hear you write," said a girl with hair down to her waist.

"Who me?"

She had been watching him for several minutes, forcing him to keep leaning into Pete's group—then lean back when he began to look like a hanger-on there, and puff and squint, and it was a relief when she finally came over and said, "May I sit down, my name is Frieda, I hear you write."

"Well, sort of."

"Are you published?"

"Well, no."

"I like to talk to writers," she said. "What do you write?"

"Novels, mostly."

This wasn't really Fred's idea. Pete Glasser had said, "Everybody down here is a painter or a writer, it doesn't mean anything, go on, say you're a writer." This was at Morrie LaCoste's party, and it seemed like a funny idea at 2 A.M. in a strange house. So when Mimi LaCoste had asked "What do you do, paint or write?" he had squinted at the middle distance and said, "A bit of both, write, paint, all that kind of thing . . ." It never occurred to him that he would see these people again and again, and always thereafter as Fred Cope the writer-painter.

"You look so aloof and stern," said the girl called Frieda, "as if you were taking us all down for future use."

"Oh, no, it's not like that at all."

"The creative process is funny, isn't it? How do *you* do it, inspiration or plain hard work?"

"Well, you know"—he spread his hands, was going to say a little of each, but she narrowed the choice for him. "I don't believe in inspiration," she said. "I don't believe there's any such thing as inspiration. What do you think?"

"Well"—the die was cast—"there's no substitute for hard work, is there?"

"I quite agree," she said. "That's what none of these people down here realize. They're all failures, you know. But I think you're going to be a success. You *look* like a success."

"Thank you," he said awkwardly. She had squeezed in between him and Janet, and although she had the usual baggy sweater and stringy hair, and looked ridiculous from a few feet away, she had presence at this range. He didn't want to start all that again, and he was about to tell her it was all a silly joke about the writing; but she kept rushing him into positions. "A lot of them don't even write at all," she said. "They just say they write because that way they don't have to produce any canvases or anything."

"Yes, well," he began. She managed to get her bosom onto his forearm, an arresting move that silenced him again.

"Morrie LaCoste hasn't written a word for two years. Pete Glasser, well, it's really a shame about Pete. He's only twenty-one, you know, and he's sort of given up too. This damn cesspool. I asked if I could see some of Pete's stuff, and he said he didn't have anything in shape right now. That's what they always say. You'll despise them, honestly you will. You come to crave for an out-and-out businessman or something, after watching these crumbs for a while."

Her face, what he could see of it, seemed to be drawn tight with sudden fury. He forgot what he wanted to say. "Don't you like it down here?" he said instead.

"—ing right, I don't like it down here. This —ing cesspool." Fred refused to believe that women used those words. He winced every time Glasser swore in front of his wife—although, as usual, he had no very clear reasons: it was just messy and wrong. He left the words virginally blank in his mind. She had said, "Right, this cesspool." What next?

"Why don't you leave, then?" he asked her.

"Wouldn't I love to, though, oh, ——, ——, ——." She whisper-wailed and shook out her hair; Fred was having a hard time erasing all the —s.

Her rage had come up so suddenly. It always took Fred hours to get mad, and he couldn't handle the swift stuff. Suppose she was going to have a fit or something; both groups would wheel round and Fred would be caught with a weeping woman.

"You see that big idiot over there?" She pointed at three shaggy men on the daybed. Their eyes were turned up to the ceiling like three Russian mystics; they held their cigarettes out in a kind of paralysis. "Which one do you mean?" he asked.

"The one on the left. The *big* idiot."

The one on the left had vinous hair running down both cheekbones. He swiveled a lonely eye down on them—more a mirror than an eye—and up again. It vanished into a spider's web in the corner. "That's my husband," she said. "The biggest slob in the whole slobby town. His name is Mortimer and he hasn't written a line in three —ing years. Now, if you'll excuse me, I'm going to be sick."

3

She was, too, which was funny, since she didn't seem to have been drinking. As she stiff-legged her way to the bathroom, he noticed an extra looseness in the hang of her sweater. An awfully thick, droopy sweater for such a hot night— Hey Cope, you're getting pretty observant, just give the boy time.

With Frieda gone and gagging faintly in the distance—Mortimer didn't blink, so he supposed it must be all right—he was back in no man's land with no one to talk to. Stern, aloof Fred, taking it all down; merciless recorder of the human comedy.

It was a funny sort of party. Instead of getting louder, it seemed to be getting quieter. He could hardly make out what Glasser's group was talking about. They had stopped yakking about agents and "making it." He watched Harry's mouth move for a minute but wasn't sure that Harry was actually speaking. Pete Glasser vibrated gently in answer. If only he could make it out, this was probably inside talk. "What was that, what did you just say?" he said desperately to Pete. Glasser's eyes swam around and around. There was a tape of Thelonious Monk going, and the talk seemed to be strangely entwined with that. No, they had stopped talking and were just looking at him; furry chins and faraway eyes. Glasser shrugged: what does it matter what I just said? It was part of the music, was all.

What Fred said was never part of the music. Get a new score, man. Play it with a little feeling. Glasser could say all that without even coming into focus. Fred swung back to the other mob, the girls by the dead fireplace.

"Where did you get those lovely curtains, Janet?"

"I got them in Mijas, Málaga, Marbella, Madrid; I got the beads in Saragossa, Segovia, Seville; I got the rugs in Bilbao, Barcelona . . ." That was how the girls by the fireplace talked. Even here there was a hip and a square community. He seemed to have drifted slightly away from squares, without quite reaching the hips. Fred felt the boredom explode in his chest. This was the slowest party he's ever been to, almost preternaturally slow. And yet tomorrow, he knew they would say, "Man, these parties . . . I don't know." Pete Glasser would shake his head, "I can't keep this up much longer."

He went out on the patio, which was soaked in simple moonlight. There was a warm breeze off the sea, and Fred said to himself don't worry your head about all that crap. Frig them, basically. The sky was clear, the sea was, well, mysterious, the feel of the ground, hold this feeling, these are the verities, man. He tried, and it was like swimming under water; a rush of trivial thoughts—why is Frieda wearing a sweater, what do these people use for money—drummed in his mouth. If he could just feel the sky and the sea and nothing else, then he could afford to sneer. But he kept peeking back furtively through the archway at the silent movements. Frieda had come back and was bent over her husband, whose knees flopped foolishly to each side of her. The saxaphone diddled around, a small sound out here in the rich night, but still it was the one that drew him. He couldn't keep his mind on the sky and sea or the night silence; they were obviously important, but he couldn't get the juice out of them. The party was obviously unimportant, but he made for it like a moth.

"We're going," said Frieda.

"Hell you say," said Mortimer.

"Can we give you a lift anyplace?" Frieda turned to Fred.

"I guess you can. I'm at the Pension Ferdinand."

"That dump, hey." said a voice from the dark. "Did you hear that, the poor bastard's staying at the Ferdinand."

"We're not going, baby. Relax," said Mort.

"Hey, Fred, you want a house?" said one of the girls by the fireplace.

There was a sudden flurry of interest even in Glasser's group. "I know about a house. You want a house?"

The mooch through empty rooms, the long evenings—"No, I guess not. Not right now."

Attention sagged again. He'd noticed it before. The only possible way he could interest these people was to want a house. Several of them scavenged a living agenting and promoting around. Harry Steidlitz decorated, with bullfight murals. One way or another, everybody had a stake in it.

Frieda and Mortimer were still working out their travel plans. "Look, we're not going. Sooner you get that in your

⌐ing head, the happier we'll be." Fred erased quickly: a hell of a way to talk to your wife.

"Come on, Mort, let's get the —— out of here." Fred gave up his erasing. The fucks dinned like rain on a roof, losing all meaning, all suggestion. Nobody but Fred was listening anyway. Mortimer was just barely listening and just barely talking. "I like it here, you know that?" he said, "the beauties of the night. Shadows, I saw a man die once and his ass turned bright green—I like that."

"Give me the fucking keys."

"You're going to Africa, is that right, Linda? Remember your old pal Mort, huh?" The mystic eyes looked through, around and over his wife, without moving.

Linda, anonymous by the fireside, nodded cautiously. There was a clatter of broken sentences as everyone stopped to listen.

"Bring back some grass for your old buddy."

"Hey, Jeff," said Pete Glasser, coming to the surface with a rush, "that's a great recording, you know that?" Fred sensed that something indecent had finally been said, even by this group's standards.

"Yeah, I got it in," "bought the mats in"—the sentences were picked up viciously, leaving Mort just smiling to himself over what he had just said; nodding slightly, beating time with a finger. Frieda yanked the keys out of his hip pocket. "Come on, I'll drive you."

Fred went over to Pete Glasser and said "I'm going. With Frieda."

"So?"

Pete had plunged back into apathy. "See you, then," he said. Some of the others nodded randomly. Jeff, the host, didn't stand up but sent a swift startled glance halfway up Fred's suit.

"Glad you could come." His eyes were like loose buttons. Fred stood indecisively over him: you couldn't leave a party just like that, could you?

"Have a nice time in Africa, Linda," he shouted.

"Thanks, Fred," she said vivaciously, "I will."

"I'm sorry, I wasn't invited," he said to Jeff, the host. "It was awfully nice of you."

"That's all right," said Jeff, "perfectly O.K."

"Well, good night."

"Good night."

Look, I'm leaving, pay attention. O.K., forget it. He and Frieda stumbled out through thick, vaporous darkness, a long, dank corridor, probably full of wooden spears and stuffed birds if you could see a little better. "Christ," Frieda greeted the night.

He squeezed into the Volkswagen. She swore at the motor for a while and then remembered to put it in neutral. It grunted teutonically to life.

"*My* husband," she said sarcastically.

Racketing over cobblestones, bouncing the ever-tender stomach like a jai-alai ball against the rib cage: Fred could still see the faces, very pale for high summer, each of them wearing an expression quite irrelevant to what Fred took to be the situation.

She said, "I suppose Mort had talent once, I don't know. That was the understanding. He talked a great game about the artistic life."

Fred must have nodded; the Volkswagen made you nod like an idiot.

"You agree, the real artist just gets on with it, doesn't he, to hell with the artistic life. That's what I like about you, Fred— you don't look like an artist at all."

"No, I guess not." They shot rattling around the corner into his street. He tipped against Frieda and apologized. There was no doubt about it, she was well pregnant. Did people like her have babies then? raise them, send them to school? Have group photographs taken?

"You look like money in the bank, I like that. You're going to make it someday. You're going to get *published*."

The wonder of it! Fred just sat there. They had reached his door and Frieda had snapped off the engine. Her face was shining.

"But Mortimer just goes to these stinking parties and smokes pot, and dreams it all away," she wound up.

"*What* does he do?"

"Smokes pot. Don't tell me you didn't notice? The daffy look?"

"No!"

"The crazy smell? Haven't you ever smelt marijuana before?"

"Not that I know of."

"Christ, you *are* dedicated. Yeah, every one of those great talents was smoking pot tonight. Personally, I can't stand it, it makes me sick. As you saw."

It occurred to Fred that he was being more stupid than absolutely necessary. Of course there was a funny smell, his nose was still full of it. A little remembering, and there it was again, the same smell at Harry Steidlitz's place. He must have supposed it came off the damp walls, a typical Spanish smell.

"They bring it up from Tangier."

"Everybody does?"

"No, just this group, the imitation beatnik group. At these rents, we can't afford real beatniks, you know. Haven't the guts for heroin, of course. But you—if you went in for something, you'd go all the way, wouldn't you? . . ."

If he saw someone as stupid as himself in a movie he'd say, Oh, cut it out. People must be stupider in practice than they were in theory. In a movie he'd have known something was up when he saw all those crazy eyes; he'd have known the director was telling him something. But in a hot, smoky room, and you're worried because you're not invited and because the girl next to you thinks your name is Bob, your brain just gets paralyzed.

Frieda was still talking her heart out in the next seat, but he hardly listened, he was so fed up with himself. He wasn't getting anywhere at all, just discovering new layers of subcutaneous fog. No wonder nothing very exciting ever happened to him—he had to be told what it was, or, far as he was concerned, it just didn't happen.

"And you're such a good listener. Mortimer never listens at all." He gathered she was still using him as a flail against Mortimer.

"I'm afraid you've got the wrong impression, Frieda. I'm not a very good listener . . ."

Neither was Frieda. "This stinking coast anyway," she said, "second-rate people, second-rate talents. I'm sick of the very word art. I used to paint myself, you know. But these people make it foul. I come from Idaho, you know, and all you want to do when you come from Idaho is to get the hell out and live beautifully; and then you find that living beautifully means being sick in a toilet that doesn't work, and sleeping in dirty sheets." She was getting worked up again and Fred was doubtless being stupid again, but he couldn't make out why she kept whipping herself into these states. Of course, if she was expecting a baby, that meant she was stuck with Mort, and Mort didn't inspire all that much confidence; but—and this was certainly very callous and stupid of him—there seemed to be something a bit stagey about these rhythmic tantrums, something you could set your watch by. He yawned and probed for the door handle.

He said, "It doesn't help to keep thinking about it," and she said, "Oh, I know that. But there are so few people you can talk to. And you seemed so kind . . ."

Trouble with trying to be understanding was that you could only take so much of it. The sticky ooze of compliments was beginning to run down his neck. Kind, good listener bushwa! Those were just the things you said to anyone who was big and slow.

"Well, thanks for the ride," he said sharply.

"Not at all. You must come over some evening and see us."

He jerked the door open and reclaimed his knees from the dashboard. She gave him a sprightly three-finger wave, and he suddenly knew who she was: she was the town bore, the person who went up to strangers because the people she knew were turned to stone by her footsteps and the look of her house and the sound of her ringing on the phone. ("I suppose we've got to have Frieda" and "Oh, God, here comes Frieda.")

He should have known better than to suppose anybody else would come up to him at a party here. He was catnip to Friedas, though. He had a roommate at school who was sort of a Frieda. Pete Webber was his name, and he used to say, "I'll bet you'd be good at bowling" or "I'll bet you could beat up just about anyone in the class. With your size"—increasingly wild compliments, that bored him and made him nervous at the same time. Once the charm of novelty had worn off, he had really come to fear Webber's compliments; argued with them, tried not to hear them. Finally, he had his room changed, as most of Webber's roommates did.

Frieda couldn't be dumb enough to think he was going to be a successful writer. That was Cope-type dumbness, unique of its kind. On the other hand, it wouldn't have helped if he'd denied the writing altogether; she would have bounced back with something else just as silly. She had to manufacture enough flattery, no matter how poor the quality, to keep him listening to her.

Something rather touching about that little wave of the hand. Damn plucky. He felt sorry for her, but knew that he was destined to be crueler and crueler to her until he had shaken her off; and she would float loose again at parties, and abuse her husband, and swear, and wait for more strangers. And tell them how Fred Cope lost his talent, along with the others.

Sad, but he couldn't help feeling pleased with himself for spotting it so soon. He mightn't know much about pot-smoking, but as soon as self-pity showed its tiresome little face, he was on to it in a flash. It was the one good thing he had received from his mother (not the kind of mother from whom you expected good things ordinarily). "Who pities self de dum dee dum."

Fred did feel pleased with himself and stood on the sidewalk a minute longer: looking at the moon, and trying to pretend he was enjoying *that*, and not simply his idiot euphoria, which was off on another fatuous round after the evening's agitation. Feel good, Fred, feel bad, go to sleep, Fred, smile—Christ, what a *sheep*.

Swearing was so goddamned contagious. The inside of his head was beginning to feel like an Army novel. Shit yes. It didn't mean a thing any more.

4

Next day they were all at the café except for Frieda, drinking beer and talking houses. Mortimer especially was a changed man by sunlight. He talked crisply of putting in new bathrooms and game rooms. "He building a house?" Fred whispered to Glasser. "Don't you know Mort Frihoff?" said Pete. "He builds *all* the houses around here. Jones, Frihoff and Santiago, you gotta have a Spaniard."

"I thought he was a writer."

"Yeah, he's a writer. Tim Jones is a painter. Santiago's a bum. That's how it goes down here."

"The living room is six by four and a half," said Mort.

"Gee-sus," said Marilyn Glasser.

"Gee-sus?" said Mort.

"I don't know," Marilyn shook her head. "Six by four and a half, Pete, what's that in feet?"

So—they were building a house for Pete Glasser. It seemed fantastic. Pete couldn't be much more than twenty. He only had the one undershirt. And here they were planning what sounded like a palace for him, halfway up the mountain behind town.

It sounded as though Harry Steidlitz was going to decorate it. Morrie LaCoste was planning to do a mural. The two other mystics from last night, whom Fred hadn't sorted out yet, were talking about trellises on the patio.

Fred dearly wanted to ask where the money was coming from, but his whole training was against it. Ernie Peabody used to ask people where the money was coming from, and the question always stood out like a horrible red inflammation. Money was the acid test of sensitiveness, and everyone passed it but Peabody.

All the same, Fred was tempted to ask. They sat clustered discreetly around Pete, as if he were a Greek shipowner or a Guggenheim fellow: "What you need is a picture window; what you need is a sunken driveway." And there was Pete slumped deprecatingly, so that you hardly would have guessed he was the focus; leaving it to his wife Marilyn to handle the details.

"Look, the wall comes out to here, right?" she said.

"Right."

"And the fireplace will be over here, right?"

"Right."

"So where are we going to fit the—"

"Ah ha! Look" . . . "That's what I was coming to" . . . "Be nice in the winter, too." It was all too abstract: Fred couldn't remember where they'd put the fireplace. By the time they got out to the patio, he couldn't find the bathroom.

Marilyn seemed incapable of thinking in square meters, and everything sounded wrong to her at first. Mort was very patient. "Five meters isn't small, it's really quite big, Marilyn." Pause. Then, contritely, "Yes, it is, isn't it? I keep forgetting."

Glasser looked uncomfortable, as though he were to blame for his wife's slowness. Fred knew the look because Alison used to give it to him sometimes. It said: "I know nothing about this. He (or she) seemed all right when we got married; later, just to annoy me, he or she began to get stupid . . ." Glasser was probably pretty bright; he was inarticulate on policy, but you could tell he was thinking. His occasional glance at Mort was sheepishly apologetic: "Look, even though I'm not to blame for my wife, I'm sorry, all right?" But Mort didn't seem to mind; he enjoyed teaching, savoring the fundamentals; Marilyn couldn't be stupid enough for his taste.

Fred tried to ease things for Glasser by bringing up something new. "What's it like smoking marijuana, Pete?"

"Well, man, I'll tell you . . ." Pete paused and smiled thinly: Come *on* man. Questions like that!

"Do you smoke it around here?"

"Yeah, some of the guys."

"You?"

"Yeah, I've had it."

"But you don't want to talk about it?"

"I don't mind talking about it." His attitude was obligingly limp; it was like trying to move a sleeping man.

"Well, what's it like, then?"

Pete gestured. "Oh, *you* know."

He still seemed embarrassed about his wife and gave her a for-God's-sake-try-once-more look; she was probably playing up a bit to Mort's weakness for demonstration. The metric system wasn't that difficult to grasp.

"What about my workroom?" he said to Mort.

"What about it?"

"How's it coming?"

"O.K."

"Good. It's important."

Pete swigged the last warm trickle of beer and said, "You going home, Marilyn?"

She shook her head.

"What about the kids? Isn't it about time for their lunch?"

"Juanita knows what to give them."

So little to do around here, the people argued about

whether to go home now or to wait a while and then go home. To do nothing here or someplace else. Pete said, "I better be going," but he didn't move. The mystics tried to corner him about the trellis again. "Yeah, well it sounds nice, I'll think it over." Eventually, Morrie LaCoste pulled out and was replaced by Hans Pfeister, the German painter. Harry Steidlitz ("I got to see a man") was replaced by Wilhelmina van didn'tcatchit, the Dutch painter. Seemed her Swedish friend—"Yoohoo, Ingrid"—was looking for a house: chairs scraped forward with interest, a house somebody looking for a house? The sun was high, driving like an ax into Fred's brain. He was out of place in the Village because he didn't know about art; he was out of place here because he didn't know about houses. He couldn't adapt to conditions anywhere.

"How do I get into housing?" he asked Pete.

"I don't know. Buy some land . . . start building."

"I see."

"I bought some land a year ago. Value's gone up oh seven, eight, times on it."

"Could I do that?"

"I don't know. This was special land. Mort told me about it."

"Oh."

"And last year was better."

"I should have guessed."

"This English guy wrote an article, I forget where it came out, said you could live here for ten dollars a month or some such wild-eyed crap. People came down with their life savings, Christ what a mess, people with fifty dollars wrapped up in a napkin, old ladies with rheumatism, old deaf guys who wouldn't listen when Mort told them to go home. Hung up all along the coast, the poor old bastards, and all because some jerk wanted to juice up his copy and said you could live in this sunny paradise on ten a month; all the dregs of Europe started coming down, and all the clowns from Kenya and Rhodesia came up, and to top everything, it rained all bloody winter."

"But you had your land already."

"Damn right."

That was a lot of talking for Pete Glasser, but it didn't lead to more. He said to Marilyn, "Hey, you wanna go home yet?" And she said, "*You* go home, if you like," and he just sat there, an irresolute sprawl of old clothes: ripening his talent in the sun. You'd think boredom would drive them to work eventually, thought Fred. He was half crazy from inactivity himself, and got up suddenly to go. "Where are you going?" Mort asked courteously. "No place, just going." Mort nodded. "See you, then."

What was it—were they talking in code? These people were artists, there must be more to them than he heard, psychic overtones. Sitting on a slatted chair until the base of his spine ached, and all he got was "fireplace here, closet there. Cover it with a rug, and no one will ever know." It was like joining a secret society and finding there wasn't any secret.

He was halfway down the block and staring vacantly into the electricity shop: at the television set covered with flower pots and ferns, at the bedside lamps that didn't work. A transparent figure shimmered wistfully along the glass and stopped next to him: his friend Pete Glasser again. "Hey, man," he said, "you serious just now?"

"What? When?"

"When you asked about pot."

"Well, I guess so, sure."

"You want to know what it's like, right?"

"Yeah, I guess."

"I'll see if I can fix it up for you."

They stood looking at each other. Pete was short as well as thin, and he had a way of lowering his head and looking upwards as if what he really wanted was help. But there was a gloss of hardness too, that he was working on. "Well, thanks very much, Pete."

"O.K.," said Pete. He seemed uncertain and quasi-respectful. "O.K., then."

"I'll be seeing you, Pete."

"See you, Fred."

And Pete the writer shuffled back towards the café, lowering real estate values every step of the way; scruffy as a gypsy but without the pride.

Fred thought, and not for the first time, that it might begin to make a little more sense if he had someone to talk to about it: someone completely outside it, who could help him to define his feelings.

He thought of his father, retired in Florida. That was beginning at the wrong end. He had never discussed this kind of thing with his father: it would have been fantastically inappropriate. His father sent him newspaper clippings from Tampa about people who'd come down from New Jersey to settle, that was the kind of man his father was. (Rimless glasses, light blue suit, made a thing about haircuts.) His mother might have listened for a while, but her range of response would have been narrow—not just soap opera, but unexamined soap opera; besides which, she was dead.

Fred knew enough to hand some of the blame back to his

parents: if his life was empty, you should have seen theirs! Holding their breath during the Depression, and then through the hearty, unthink days of the war—the question of living beautifully just never came up. Hanging on in Montclair with a fairly crisis-proof job, they were always just outside events, like people sitting on a roof during a flood. They missed the "feel" of events, experienced nothing except a constant, sterile anxiety. —Mustn't rock the roof, sit tight, act as if nothing's happening. He forgot the rest of Alison's analysis. Mrs. Cope died of cancer two years ago, and he didn't want to hear any more sociology about her after that. There was nothing bourgeois about cancer.

So, who could he write to? Old sort-of friends from college and from the Army and from the ship coming over; Fred made sort-of friends easily. But not friends to write to. He had only once tried a full-blown correspondence with anyone; that was with Pvt. Larry Bedisloe, as they were both groping back to life after the Army: but it got to be more and more of an effort buying the stamps and all, and after a while he couldn't remember what Larry looked like or why he had ever started writing to him; why bother to tell Larry about your trip to Canada when there were people next door to tell it to, just the same kind of people, really. Why struggle to keep an old friendship going, with slow, lonely letter writing when there were new ones to be had all the time. . . . Something queer about men writing to each other anyway. Bedisloe apparently felt the same way, and the thing died.

(Could use Bedisloe now. Had an understanding with Bedisloe. Only queers worried about being queer, anyway.)

Who else? Couldn't very well bring Bloodbury into it, they hadn't traced him to Spain yet, and while he missed getting mail, he didn't want to give up his freedom . . . (really must get round to looking for Alison one of these days—next year at the very latest). Old girl friends, write to old girl friends and give them a thrill, Irma, Gail, Lucy—girls were for thinking: nine tenths of his few serious discussions had been with girls—but couldn't very well write to Irma, Gail or Lucy now. (Girls stood for religion, art and thinking; men stood for bowling. An epigram, but Alison wouldn't have cared for it.)

Who else? (Funny about him and intellectual girls. Irma was a Ph.D. at twenty-three.) Old faces at the mailbox. Who in hell is Fred Cope? Oh, yes, Fred Cope. And what in hell is all this about? My impressions of Spain. Maybe *you* can figure this out, dear. Fred Cope has sent us his impressions of Spain.

Nobody to write to, then.

Hey, you know who he'd like to write to? Ernie Peabody. Tap some of those possibilities in Ernie; for all he was undeniably a horse's ass, Ernie had been something of a friend at times. You could talk to him seriously (although he couldn't answer seriously, of course); you didn't feel silly afterwards, as you did with most men. His clichés were compassionate.

By the time Fred had found some paper, he saw that this was a mistake. Amazing what hunger and a little homesickness could do. Boy, he was really cracking up. You'd have to do the whole letter in pictures if Peabody was to get anything out of it. He balanced the notepaper on his knee. "Dear Ernie, My vacation, my first baseball glove, there was a great big mouse in my room called Wilbur. And one day . . ." What he *should* do was write to *her*, of course,—no, can't find her, *lost* you know, think about Stan Musial or something. He sat up sharply on the bed. Two-fifteen. Too damn early, but maybe today . . .

He stuck his big feet in the sandals and headed for the dining room.

5

After lunch there was nothing to do again so he decided to do what everyone else did and go sit with everyone else. He had bought some canvas in Málaga and he wanted some advice on the next step. It helped at the café to start out with a question.

"Hey, Mort, I been looking all over for you. What do I do about . . . ?" It gave an illusion of purpose. After the question, you could just sit.

But the café was empty, except for the Spaniards playing dominoes. Fred didn't yet know all the stops on the cyclic migration. There was an English bunch that played bridge, he knew that; and there were some Swedes who went swimming and frisking. But what his own group did in the afternoon he still hadn't discovered.

He decided to go over to Pete Glasser's apartment. Better than watching the fishermen again or the stout Swedes tugging at their bikinis. (Soggy leopard-skin briefs.) Pete and Marilyn lived in a walkup with a nice cool view of the mountains; you could sip cognac and read Pete's books, or his back numbers of *Newsweek*.

There was no downstairs buzzer at Pete's place. You just climbed the three flights and hoped that someone was at the top. Since he had all afternoon and a full belly, he rested halfway up.

For about half an hour.

This lassitude was alarming. It alternated with the bouts of fidgetiness. During the whole half hour he looked at only one thing, a dark gray stain on the ceiling. It could be either a small bear or a map of Ireland. The wall was stark gray-white. It looked like the cheap plaster in a temporary building. The kind of house that was hustled up during the war to house an inrush of something. The stain on the ceiling was like sweat, probably was sweat; the whole town was in a cold sweat.

They weren't such a bad crowd here, you know? Working for a living wasn't everything. Just a puritan reflex to think it was. Living in this wet steam, no bathtubs, of course; watching the water rising in the toilets and the plaster falling when you flushed; waiting for plumbers who never came; waiting, like Pete Glasser, for rejection slips and other bad things from America. You couldn't say they lacked character.

Tolerant, too. Nobody here knew that Fred was married, or cared. He was free to create himself. He wanted to be an author, O.K., he was an author. No proof demanded, not even intelligence. Wanted to be a painter too? Well—a bit unusual, but O.K. Sort of a Leonardo, eh? Yes, I know, but don't sell yourself short. . . . Publication would have been icing on the cake; but if you weren't published, it was because publishers were too damn timid to take a chance on you. Couple of years ago we had this fellow living here, maybe you've heard of him—Lawrence Durrell, Brendan Behan, Bertram Twilly—he's finally appeared in Penguin, sold a painting, written a musical. Nice encouraging people. That stain might just be a fur coat that somebody had thrown on the ceiling. Come along, Cope, let's move it.

On the next landing he heard laughter and soft music. Pete Glasser's one square record: Kostalanetz plays Jerome Kern. The laughter square and soft, too, Alpine bells and all that, no derision, no edge. It was sweet, made his step light on the cement stairs, an old sound of home. It wasn't until he had knocked that it occurred to him that he should have just tiptoed the hell away again.

There was silence inside, a whisper died of strangulation. They didn't want him to know they were in. He stared frozen and then began to back off quietly. But they must have realized that the record gave them away and were just using the time to compose themselves. In a moment the door opened. Fred was backing down the stairs, hard to tell which way he was going.

"Who's that?" said Marilyn. "Oh, it's you."

"I'll come back later. I didn't mean to disturb."

She just looked at him. Not a great deal of poise, she was very young, wasn't she? Hard to believe she had two children. Not that the two children had anything to do with anything—but the question kept him from moving a second longer.

Not much poise in Fred either. He stood there apologetically and began to explain that he'd come to see Pete, but that it wasn't important; he'd call again later.

What happened next he didn't quite understand. All she had to do was stand there looking confused and he would have backed all the way out to the street, and that would have been the end of Cope. But she said, "Pete's gone to Málaga for the afternoon." Kostalanetz simpered and twittered in the background. "Come on in."

"All right."

The man on the sofa was not Pete but Mort Frihoff. He was reading the back of a record album. He said "Hi, how's tricks."

There was nobody else there. But they didn't act awkward as though they'd been found out. Mort was nursing a half-empty cup of coffee with steam coming out of it. Marilyn was ironing. It was like one of those comedies where the bed shoots into the wall, Groucho is suddenly covered with shawls and the only clue to what has happened is Harpo's trouser leg sticking out from his Mother Hubbard.

Fred had no idea whether to be suspicious or not. This was a casual community; Mort was an old friend of the Glassers, why shouldn't he drop in for a chat with Marilyn and laugh like a bell with her?

Fred never knew about suspicious behavior. Before he met Alison he used to take the mechanically worldly view—man and woman alone together, well what do *you* think? Of course, it's natural; yeah, yeah, platonic—but it wasn't based on anything solid, he didn't really know. Alison had told him the attitude was contemptible, a check to spontaneous action. She once spent a night with him before they were married and when nothing happened she said, "You see?" And he did, in a way, except that he had passed a tougher night than she knew.

Mort was looking at him half amused, as if he knew all this, and thought it was no end funny; Fred, the respectable matron, trying to decide what he thought, when nobody gave a damn what he thought.

"What's new, Fred?" he said. "You want to buy a house?"

"No, thanks."

"I've got a good one, half finished, and nobody wants it. Ideal for a bachelor with fixed habits."

His expression was mainly needle-eyes and hair. But underneath the beard, Fred imagined scars, hairline furrows, parched skin. His voice was harsh and dry and the politeness hurt like a whip. His charm was overexposed. But the weird thing was that the whole thing reminded him of Pete Glasser. As if he was really standing proxy for Pete; or as if Pete practiced in front of a mirror to be like Mort.

"Build now, don't wait another year."

"That's right," said Marilyn, watching him.

"Next year will be too late."

"That's right too. Everyone says so."

"The Germans have caught on and they're coming down in platoons. The Dutch are making the scene. Even the lousy French."

"Would you like some coffee? It's Nescafé. Or maybe a drink?"

Fred still hadn't sat down and he decided he wasn't going to. He wasn't comfortable up here, there was a smell of dry rot in these cheap apartments. He didn't suspect a damn thing, but the apartment made him feel slightly sick.

"I have to write some letters."

Mort didn't move, but Marilyn made a fuss of showing him out.

"I'll tell Pete you called. It was nice of you . . ."

He sort of hoped that Mort would say "I have to go too," but he just sat there, patiently going over the record album, smiling at the jokes. Old friend of the Glassers, in for a chat, cup of coffee. Fred felt sick and was glad to get out on the bleached sidewalk.

His great-grandfather would have dropped the whole thing right there. In the days of the square ascendency, only the appearance of sin was a public matter. This was known as hypocrisy, and right now it seemed like a fine system.

As things shaped, Fred didn't know where he stood on either the appearances or the sin. In New York he knew some irregular couples, and he thought nothing of it. (In fact, when he was with them, he never stopped telling himself "I think nothing of it.") It was the usual thing—he had nothing against it. He just couldn't get it out of his mind. It was like sitting next to a Negro on a bus, pretending you didn't notice.

Between the languor of the beach and the inertia of the café, the afternoon stretched as long as yesterday's and tomorrow's. Two hours of café, and two hours of beach, and the afternoon would still be there; stuffy and motionless. He couldn't throw away his only friends on the strength of an incoherent moral scruple.

Frieda Frihoff had given him her address last night. It was on the back of an old bullfight ticket, under the inevitable Coca-Cola ad. Even the town bore was better than another afternoon of F. Cope. Calle O'Donnell 40. Shouldn't label her the town bore, not while F. Cope is around anyway.

"Señor, *por favor, donde está—*" didn't hear. "Señor, *por favor—*" O.K., I'll find it myself, you rats.

He spent a gratifying chunk of afternoon looking for Frieda's place. Jogging along identical white streets, where children with large insolent eyes stared and snickered; got in his way or ostentatiously out of it; fought, urinated, played hopscotch. The mothers crouched in the doorways, calling the plays in hard, piercing voices. Some of them said *"adios."* Not a great deal of charm, but good, no-nonsense people.

Wonder what they think of foreigners, dead drunk in leotards—Calle O'Donnell, that's it! You baby! Drunk and lazy and foul-mouthed. The sober Spaniards sat all day in their doorways and watched. Number 2, crap I'm at the wrong end. Tilt the street, somebody. Wonder what makes us think we can go where we like and make any kind of mess we like and move on. Then again, they've had the Visigoths down here, and the

Moors; we bring money, don't we? What are *you* getting so indignant about, Cope? We put on a show for them, don't we?

Now, what the—the numbers went as far as 10 and then the street changed names. Became inevitably the something José Antonio. Let's look at that little old ticket again. Four-O. The great attraction of this place was that you could knock your tail off like this to see someone you didn't even like. Back home you'd jump in the closet if you saw Frieda Frihoff coming; but here you made a lousy pilgrimage out of it . . . Wait a minute, that thing about José Antonio might have been just a plaque. Celebrating the recent unpleasantness. The numbers still going up. Whoopee, guys. Getting there, half the fun. Suppose a sniper was hiding up in the window, you'd be a dead pigeon by now. *Kerchow. Aargh.* Easy, boy.

She seemed glad to see him when he finally pulled in and slipped him a cognac right away. He could tell she'd had some herself because within five minutes she said, "The whole thing is relative, isn't it?" and he'd never heard a sober person say that.

They were talking about the foreign element; and she said, before you could really judge them, you had to know *why* they were sent down here: Mort, her husband, was a remittance man, it was a sort of public service getting him out of the country, and the others were all sick in the head and a public nuisance and some of them were half mad and some of them— Her mouth shrank sharply from the acid in it.

"You must think I'm an awful old grouch, Mr. Cope."

"Not at all. But I was going to say, one good thing you have to say about these people is that they seem to have a nice group spirit, an *élan*, you say? They say, 'You're going to make it, I just know you are.' They have faith in each other."

"You believe that?" Her voice went dismally up, and she gave a sort of pounce on the sofa. "You really believe that?"

"Sure, I've heard them. They talk about Lawrence Durrell and I don't know who else. James Joyce, wasn't he like that?"

She shook her head pityingly. "Look, Fred, let me translate for you. What they mean is, '*I'm* going to make it, not *you!*' They're talking about themselves and nobody else."

"I don't know how you can say that. You're just guessing."

"No, it's true, believe me, it's true. They despise each other. They gloat at every failure. I know them, Fred, really I do. I'm not being catty. They say, 'Had any word from your agent, old man?' and what that means is: 'Look, I know you'd tell me if you had any *good* news, I wouldn't have to ask. So permit me to rub in the kind of news you *have* been getting'—I see you don't believe me. You're a kind man and you haven't lived in this cesspool long enough to know the rules. In fact, you're the first decent—"

"Not to change the subject," he said quickly, "but I saw your husband just now."

"Oh, yes? Where was the dear boy?"

"Well, he was just walking around, I guess."

"He wasn't over at Glassers', was he?"

"Glassers'? What Glassers'?"

"He's usually over at Glassers' in the afternoon. That's the middle of town, you know, the real heart of the cesspool. Mort and Marilyn—" No, don't tell me, don't tell me. O.K., tell me: Fred surrendered quietly—"have a thing. I don't mind what he does, of course, but really, Marilyn Glasser. What is she, nineteen?"

"I didn't know, I'm sorry," he mumbled.

"Mortimer's thirty-five. It's really too silly."

What was the right sentiment in a case like that? Did you express condolences or did you sort of throw it away? He thought of "Yes, well that's happening a lot these days, more's the pity," but trapped it in time; and the result of all that soul searching was a sympathetic silence, which was probably best anyway.

"I thought it wouldn't last," she said, "knowing Mort. But it's been, let's see, quite some months now. They started in March . . ."

"But what about Pete? Does he know?" March, you say? What time in the afternoon did it start?

"Oh, Pete's just hopeless, of course he knows. You can't keep a secret in this town. Supposing Mort wanted to."

"Well, why doesn't Pete *do* something, then?"

"Like what, for instance? If you were Pete's size and temperament, what would you do?"

"I don't know. Get someone else to build my house, anyway."

She laughed. "You'd prefer to deal with a Spanish contractor? And have a house that leaks like a watering can? Anyway, Pete admires Mort, that's how it all started—"

Fred peered through the back door into the patio. A black cat, hunched on a dead flower bed, looked back at him with smarter eyes than his. He let Frieda talk, it was probably good for her. It was probably why *she* had been sent down here.

The whole story was the makings of one crazy imagination. Pete Glasser wasn't like that—nobody was like that. Nobody sacrificed his wife for the sake of a nonporous house.

Besides which, it didn't rain that much down here. How about that?

"You should get away," she said, a witch with a pipeline to doom. "It'll get you too—the idleness, the company, these people have given up on life, you know, a man like you shouldn't subject himself," etc., etc.

There was one in every town. Someone who saw evil in the treetops. He didn't know the people here very well, but from what he could see of them, they were pretty much like anybody else: they certainly didn't look like monsters—Mort was a little bit mean, perhaps, but you had to get these things in proportion.

Frieda's hysteria had set up a counterforce. He couldn't believe what she was saying, if only from the wild way she was saying it. She could probably make out a pretty good case against Idaho.

At the first decent interval he asked if he could see the house, because you always did that when you went to a new house. Together they trudged the rooms and he commented on a few items:

"That's nice, I like that."

"I'm sorry, it's a mess today," she said.

"I see you've got a fireplace."

"Yes, but no chimney." (She *would* say that.)

"But we were really very lucky to get it, really," she added quickly.

They wound up on the roof porch, looking out to sea. The Mediterranean was stainless blue today with just a dark fringe of tar tickling the beach. Farther out, bald man bobbing, innocently, beyond that two fishing boats and a white sail. The unidentified fuzz on the horizon might or might not be Africa. Then closer to hand, you had the dark gaseous possibilities of the human head. It was almost enough to make a man think.

6

He would have told her that "out there," the sky and the sea and the bald man in the water, was healthier. But it would have sounded so much like the head of some corporation recommending the simple life, and besides, he was afraid she would concur ardently and begin crowding him off the patio. He had been alone for so long now that he was prey to scalding bursts of lust; and as soon as she came within a certain range she became fantastically attractive to him.

She would say, "Yes, it's gorgeous, I love to stand out here." Good old nature, everybody's friend. You love nature too, big boy? The important thing was to get out of range before he did anything silly. Remember, Fred, you don't *like* her. That kind of thing matters.

"I really have to go . . . write letters," he said.

"Oh, yes. We've almost stopped writing letters ourselves."

"I can see how that could happen." She brushed against him as she spoke, or as he spoke, whichever it was. Gad the excitement of a hairy sweater.

She led him back into the house and told him that he was a very special friend, who must call again soon and often. She had a small pretty face, flawed only by her insane anxiety to please. Smother it with kisses, you madman. He said he would call again.

It wouldn't take much to wind up in the cesspool, as she called it. With nothing to do and no shape to your life; with no neighbors to harass you, no office fatigue to blunt you, no fret about the expense—what was to stop you? Your early training, if you could remember how that went; your inhibitions, as long as they held up. Fred was a little alarmed. He ought to be out chasing girls in his old futile way; he didn't want to be party to a neurotic seduction . . .

With Frieda's directions, he got back easily: the Pension Ferdinand was only a few blocks away. He ripped off his hot, wet clothes and took a cold shower. Self-control for its own sweet sake, he couldn't quite see it. His early training hadn't been that good. His early training just said: you get a job because—you'll see—it'll never occur to you not to, and you work hard because you can't stand the look of disappointment on people's faces; and you behave yourself because you can't stand a scene, and because you're just the necessary bit afraid of your wife; and you'll persist, you'll endure, out of apathy, timidity and because one day flows so neatly into another. But step one inch out of this system buddy boy and your early training won't be responsible for the consequences.

The shower damped down the slight glow he felt at Frieda's and left him wretchedly sober. He didn't like Frieda, he didn't respect her; theoretically, an affair with her would be the cheapest, flattest, most discouraging thing he had ever undertaken. And yet he knew that with one more cognac to cloud his cool, eighteenth-century brain, he would have yielded to the goofy warmth in his loins; he would have smashed his tiny little bit of identity: as the sort of man who doesn't do that sort of thing.

In a clean shirt and a new pair of khakis he felt he made a little more sense. He strolled into town, starting in twilight and getting there five minutes later in darkness. There was a sprinkle of cafés in the center, and tonight Fred decided he would avoid the one with the foreigners. Funny how these chaotic people clubbed together, hedging in the freedom they had come here for. There was a dowdier bar across the street, and Fred made for that. He didn't want to talk to anyone just now. For four months he had been living in a kind of trance and he was afraid he might be coming out of it. The touch of flesh made it real. The girl in New York made New York real. Here it took only the touch of a sweater. He was improving. Or getting desperate.

He hadn't slept with the girl in New York because he was sorry for her; here he had laid off so far (good phrase, laid off) because he didn't care for the available talent. Were those the kinds of things that moved him, wasn't there any more substance to his moral life than that? Boy, what *reasons*. (The women down here were really crumby, though.)

He wasn't much better at thinking than he had been in Bloodbury. It was always too hot, the sequence of thoughts got jumbled and boring, what was he just saying? Something about —you probably had to start young with moral anarchy, it was like tennis. I mean, either say, It's just a piece of tail, what difference does it make? or say, It's against my principles, and stick your hand in the fire; but don't just make up stupid excuses. For doing nothing. Look at Frieda, now, same thing. What was that? I mean look at Frieda: ladylike girl from Idaho, pigtails and sailor suit (do we have the right century with that?) coming here and learning, trying so hard to learn to say "shit" and trying to smoke marijuana without getting a nervous tummy ("tummy" was really her kind of word, not "shit"); and slowly disintegrating all the time, ceasing to be anybody at all. A square trying to be hip.

He was in pretty much the same boat, his life was every inch as dim and purposeless. The hipsters had moral standards, crumby ones perhaps; Cope had half-assed whims and ought to go home, go home to what, then? cool autumn days, copper leaves, he could still slide into that, riotous trips to Princeton and New Haven; frosty mornings, trouble starting the car, postman with earmuffs "Hi, Mr. Postman," irrepressible kids—he drank his Spanish coffee—*good* coffee, bacon for breakfast. Homesickness, should be able to manage homesickness. What is America, Mr. Woolworth? America is the laugh on the umpire's face, America is the lump in your throat as you read the insurance ad: the real case against Alison was that she had gotten him halfway out of infantilism and left him there, kicking like a lobster. He knew he wouldn't really get excited about his bacon, or the postman, when he got back. Not when he was sober, anyway. The American way of life was just a trick to get you home; a trick to make a lot of discontented people think they were living in paradise.

The people here were very derisive about America and you picked up the derision without thinking. He had no resistance to the café mythology. "Private Cope," said the plausible Chinese psychiatrist who had been assigned to brainwash him, "I'd like you to look over the following propositions": America is by and large an invention of the *Saturday Evening Post*. Old water holes and Congregational churches and so on. More Americans are going to church than ever. Check. The moral fiber is at a low ebb, however. Check. Our young people are basically good there are no atheists in foxholes but the moral fiber is down two points and everyone is on the make. Does that more or less summarize your position? Yes, Dr. Fang . . . What an intellectual history for a grown man.

He was surprised at how little he missed his country. In spite of the national aptitude for patriotic bluster, which he shared, at least when plastered, America seemed to be awfully easy to shed. The American expatriates denounced their homeland with an unreflecting ease not found in the other expatriates. And Fred couldn't for the life of him see what was wrong with the case they made.

He sipped his deplorable coffee and looked at the bright green play of light on the leaves: and suddenly wondered for no special reason what Alison was doing for money. He supposed she was planning some kind of court action eventually, but in the meantime how was she getting by? Was it possible for her to sue him for nonsupport? Nonsupport, retroactive desertion, extreme boredom and a ludicrous stab at adultery. That is where the case rests, Your Honor, Mr. Justice Fang, until Mr. Cope makes his next move.

After a while, he didn't know how long, he saw Pete Glasser's spindly legs fluttering under the light. Pete didn't see Fred because Fred was in the wrong café. Pete sat down, in the right café, under a bouquet of colored light bulbs put in for the last *feria,* and never removed. He ordered something and half crossed his legs. He looked around indecisively as if he didn't know whether he wanted to be alone or not. His beard was thin and shredded and he pulled at the different strands, leaving a disorganized clump when he put his hand down on the cognac. His face looked vague and mottled in the queer light; he seemed to be frowning and shaking his head slightly: very mild confusion, muted shock.

Fred wanted to go over and pat his back, but he had deep lethargy to contend with and mild curiosity. Glasser finished his cognac and ordered another. He frowned some more and picked at his sock. Rearranged his whiskers. Wiped his mouth. Looked around. Fred was barricaded in shadow, wondering what he expected to see. It wasn't like looking through a window at someone. Pete was right out in the open. Still, open or not, he suddenly gave a desolate shake and Fred guessed he was crying;

he wiped his nose with his cuff and you could see him trembling for control, staring at Fred's ambush like a man trying a new hiccough cure. It was quite logical that he should be doing all this. He shivered and clapped for the waiter and paid his bill and shuffled off. And that made things seem real for a little while because it was exactly the way Pete Glasser ought to behave *all* the time.

But the next week Pete gave *his* party, and Mort came along and they talked about Pete's new house, so things didn't seem so real after all. Fred decided to stay a bit longer. Having ground his way, by forced toilet readings, to page fifty-one in *The Myth of Sisyphus*, he knew that this was an absurd existential decision, made under the implacable Mediterranean sun, which holds life at once cheap and priceless, etc. But although he had picked up some of M. Camus's patter, Fred knew that deep down he was nobody's Sisyphus: he felt more like a koala bear that goes to sleep wherever you put it. Pete found him a cheap apartment in the center of town and he decided to take it. And Pete also negotiated some land for him up in the hills which promised a ripe dividend when the electricity reached it, maybe enough to pay for his whole trip. With a lease of six months in his pocket, he wouldn't have to worry about Alison until some time the following spring: by which time, he should be halfway through *Being and Nothingness*.

He had learned this much about the intellectual life: that if you had nothing to read on the john but Spanish magazines and French existentialists, you read the existentialists. (They even made a certain kind of sense at that time of night.) By spring he should know how to handle parties, too; how to stand eyeball to eyeball with himself, or slump down in fraternal stupor with

Mort Frihoff; how to talk bargains with the ladies and masonry with the gentlemen. Hipness self-taught—he had as much right to it as any other American boy. It couldn't be that difficult if you made a project of it.

. . . Unfortunately, he got used to Spanish cooking before the literary end of the project got much further. But the slouch and the lackluster eye continued to elude him by a narrower margin through the winter months. The moment he saw the point, he would have them for sure.

6

Square's wife encounters giant inertia

1

He mixed his paints quickly, reaching optimum triteness with breathtaking economy, autumn triteness by now. He left out the haze altogether and the areas of stumpy desolation; toned up the copper; vitamin-enriched the pale sky; and pretty soon you had it: November, U.S.A. With a message about hardware, and No. 311 in our series, thoughts to live by.

Maurice Stebbing took off his beret and his silver-gray hair was wet with strain. He poured two cups of coffee from his thermos and began mixing again. It was a commentary on Stapleton society that one bothered with Stebbing at all.

Eleven o'clock, time for two more before lunch if he hurried. Something about his sheer drive, his turtlenecked dedication, kept Alison from sneering openly. He was embarked on what looked like exactly the same painting, copper, yellow and blue-ue-ue. She could just see the anecdote underneath: "When Thomas Edison was a small boy, he used to tie a piece of string to his finger . . ." and a message about the McPherson reaper.

His easel had been pitched next to the frosty, brown-silver creek. In August, Stebbing had drawn a boy fishing in it (words that make men free, when Grover Cleveland was a small boy . . . shut up, Alison, before I go out of my mind) a real boy though the freckles were pure Stebbing. Beyond the creek was dead grandeur. Some of the trees were gaunt and ready for snow—she hated to think what Stebbing would do with snow (looked forward with a horrible fascination, too). This was a real professional, boy. His hands were red and scaly in the cold and his face was furrowed a hundred ways. If you didn't see the canvas first, you would swear he was the real thing.

He didn't talk while he painted, unless you counted cryptic grunts. He must be a very corrupt man, really. She watched the things that the people of Stapleton thought they saw every fall taking swift cynical shape on the canvas; compared it with the harsh, miraculous substance—these dense, inattentive people were living in heaven, but Stebbing said, No, no: *this* is what you're living in, this calendar. Isn't it charming, even under jam stains you can tell it's a Stebbing. Stinking up every kitchen in Stapleton, artificial beauty—don't look outside, don't force yourself to see, buy a Stebbing and see the world.

But she wasn't really angry any more; her disapproval was entirely a matter of principle. Let him paint what he liked, but just let him be honest with her. She needed a friend terribly, any friend.

"That'll do for today," he said. "I think I've got what I wanted."

He offered her a filtertip and took one himself. He looked at the canvas carefully, held up his thumb to it and turned away satisfied. She wondered if he would ever look at it again.

"So—you were telling me about your husband, what was his name, George?"

"No, Fred. George is somebody else. George Pyke. An absolute jerk."

"Oh, yes, George Pyke. He helped to install our cooling unit, I believe." After a flurry of artistic vagueness, it always turned out that Stebbing knew everybody and forgot nothing.

"I don't know what's to tell about Fred. He's spectacularly ordinary, and nobody seems to be able to find him. Those are the two main things." It was disloyal to talk about Fred at all, but Stebbing was so far removed from reality that it didn't seem to matter so much with him. She only saw Stebbing on her walks through the woods, and it was like confessing to some crazy old hermit who didn't really count, except in the woods.

"I wouldn't mind Fred's being ordinary, if that's all it was, because nobody's really ordinary," she said.

Stebbing laughed.

"Don't you agree?" she asked quickly.

"No."

"But Pierce used to say—"

"Pierce was very young. You'll find there are plenty of extremely ordinary people, yes. And the world is a better place for having them. Go on about your husband, though."

"I don't think I will. I'm getting cold."

"All right, another time maybe." He began packing up his things.

Maybe she'd catch him off guard one day, with his aphorisms down. Anyway, there was still nobody else to talk to. Her parents only talked in that impossible living room, and when they mentioned Fred's name at all it was with a gray-faced distaste that made her almost want to defend him. They probably thought he had done something unspeakable—the last thing Fred would do. It was no use explaining to anyone down here that she had left him because he was so dull. Dullness was no offense in Stapleton; it was hardly even a concept.

"All right, have it your way about ordinary. But let me make one thing clear. Fred wasn't the old-fashioned kind of bore you may be thinking about, the kind with integrity . . ."

Stebbing paused with his easel under his arm and his filter butt dangling. Perhaps his corruption would emerge at last, out of curiosity.

"I mean, he's not the kind of man who sees a piece of modern art and says, 'What the hell is this mess? My granddaughter could etcetera, etcetera.' He's the kind who would hem and haw and try to look thoughtful."

"You'd like him better if he said, 'What the hell is this mess?'"

She wondered what Stebbing himself would say to a piece of modern art. The baffling thing was that he seemed to understand everything one said, up to a point. Anything beyond that was ejected vigorously, of course. "Fred can fake interest in anything he likes," she said. "You might call him a triumph in technology."

"And you left him just because of that?"

"Yes, why not? He tricked me. I married him under false pretenses."

"Just because of that you'd leave a man?"

"Yes, yes, yes." She snapped a twig with her foot. "Why not? You're an artist, aren't you? Look, we're talking about a man who reads newspapers from morning to night, and isn't even interested in newspapers."

"How do you know that?" He put down his easel and opened his stool.

"Because he'll read anything, any section, as long as the paragraphs are short and full of proper nouns. He reads the Hollywood gossip columns, for heaven's sake; he reads the society pages; he reads the births and death. He doesn't know anything about society. But just let Gloria Vanderbilt get her jewels stolen and he'll sit up all night reading about it. Just let the Duchess of Windsor give a party . . ."

"Sounds like a fascinating fellow."

"That isn't funny—and he'll read the whole guest list; then if I give him an opening, he'll say, 'I see where the Duchess and Elsa Maxwell have made up their differences'—their differences, for heaven's sake. He even talks like a newspaper."

Stebbing frowned, rather impatiently. He was still doing the conventional bit, under the beret; as if he couldn't let himself understand any further; as if his image depended on never quite understanding.

"Look, I believe in marriage, working at marriage and all that, but the Duchess of Windsor—no, all right, the Duchess of Windsor. If he was really interested in the Duchess of Windsor, we might even manage to build on that. But suppose there was a lecture on the Duchess of Windsor in the next township, do you think he'd go to it? If there was a whole book about her, do you think he'd read it? Only if the names were in special print and there were lots of subheadings. . . ."

"You'd leave him because of that? Break up a marriage because of that?" Stebbing said again. "I can't believe it."

"Why not?"

"Well, Pierce thought that marriage—"

"What do you mean, Pierce? How can you plant your old opinions on Pierce? *I* know what he would have thought."

He picked up his stuff all over again and trudged off over cracking twigs. He looked, and this was grotesque, slightly shocked. And what about you and your fancy little wife, then, she wanted to shout after him, and your stupid phony house and your painting; and realized how much acid she was accumulating down here. Why she went on with Stebbing, she really didn't know. He made her wilder than anything.

When she got home, she wrote to Betty Flax. Fran's answer to her last letter had been so vague and kind and useless, but, she thought, at least you would get something solid out of Betty. She was awfully tired of this musical comedy situation with Fred. If he was such a bore, why hadn't he written? At least she had no false pride about letting her friends know she was concerned.

Her mother left lunch for her on a tray outside her door. She had gotten so tired of the silent munching downstairs that she had asked to have at least one meal a day in her room. (Her old room—next to Pierce's—she'd baffled them by going back to that.) It occurred to her that she was letting an awful lot of things get on her nerves these days. She hadn't the temperament for Pierce's total acceptance of life—Pierce's smug indifference was the other way of looking at it. ("To hell with Zen," page twenty-three; "Western man is *supposed* to be nervous.")

She ate the boiled egg with one hand and ripped open her stupid bank statement with the other; glanced quickly and crumpled it into a yellow carnation. Things to do this afternoon. Plunge into social work, ha, ha. Make dreary little pots. She spilled some tea on her letter to Betty and dabbed fretfully.

Read a good book, learn a language. The question had never come up before, but actually, what for? What would she do with a good book and a language?

The bank statement didn't even make a good carnation: it kept opening. She took it next door and casually dropped it in the toilet, flushing it out of sight; but she didn't feel so casual when it bobbed up again a moment later. Should she fish it out or flush again? Silly dilemma. She just left it there and went back to her room. It was totally unimportant. Where was she, wiping tea off a letter. Oh, honestly, start another one.

She tore up the old letter and found herself thinking fiercely about the bank statement in the toilet bowl. This was really insane. Small worries were for small people. Well, it wasn't exactly a worry; she just kept seeing it. Sitting in the water.

She started the new letter and spelled "Betty" with three *t*'s. Can't help it, must do something: she went back and flushed the bank statement again. What she had forgotten about small worries was their sheer idiot endurance. People who didn't have them said, "Look, just tell yourself this . . . put it in perspective . . . remember the old saying . . ." and you could do all those things and the anxiety would just sit there waiting for you to get finished, waiting to resume its dead man's hold on your attention. The statement bobbed up again and she fished it out and threw it in the basket.

After lunch was a bad time these days. Life contracted until nothing was too small to undo you. Spilling the tea on the letter and then trying to write over it was just about the most second-rate thing she had ever done. She got out her cloth overcoat and sailed down the stairs. Another crisp autumn walk would restore sanity.

She went out past the wooden houses, where the leaves lay

stupidly dying on the bare lawns, and the colored people stared satirically out of their windows: it was much too cold to be out walking, girl must be crazy. She moved quickly. The sky had been drained of color and was filling up with snow. Wooden houses. Old black cars. Faces at the window. This neighborhood had never seemed so ominous before, even when she was a little girl.

The bank statement was the only item in the box this morning. She hadn't opened it right away because she already knew what it was going to say. Fred had insinuated some money into her account a month ago, which meant that she could now afford to leave Stapleton if she wanted to. Of course, at any time, she could have tried for a job in New York. (But I don't know, going back to that) . . . no and anyway she was waiting to hear from Fred.

But now suddenly there was no more excuse. She could go to California if she liked or Mexico. It said it right there in last month's statement: $2,000 and probably more to come. She felt an irrational annoyance at Fred; it was a terrible thing to do, sending her money without asking. Not writing to her, as she had asked him to, not discussing the separation like a gentleman. It was just like him to—and then she saw how irrational she *was* being; her reaction was disproportionately severe. He had done something reasonably decent, for an unimaginative slob. Given her a chance that she didn't quite want at the moment.

Something about the old house, something about George Pyke—well, she had temporarily lost her nerve, that was all. She couldn't quite bring herself to leave Stapleton. Her flying visit had turned into a kind of paralysis. George's phone calls made a dismal counterpoint: whenever she felt her strength returning that voice would come out of the yellow telephone and ask for a date. She couldn't think of a master-excuse (she was in no shape to bring up his marriage) and the effort to think up minor ones unstrung her all over again.

One got so out of the way of acting independently. After Christmas she would take the plunge, her courage would come back with the spring. (She knew she had courage or she wouldn't be here in the first place.) But meanwhile, these bank statements were a plain nuisance, reminding her that she was free, that the next move was up to her. She could still see the ball of paper dripping into the basket. Really stupid trying to destroy it, no, she wasn't really trying to destroy it. Only in the house where you were once a child could you ever do anything so—I don't know, childish. Why hadn't she just thrown it in the basket in the first place? Suppose her mother found it now, all soggy and stupid?

"Well, you see, Mother, I was just trying to flush my bank statement—"

Oh, for heaven's sake, Alison, *what* difference does it make? I know, but there it is. You could take all the attitudes you wanted, prime yourself with wisdom—it didn't make any difference; a worry was blind, implacable, with a grip like a maniac's. All she wanted to do was get back and transfer the wet paper to the basket in *her* room. That was what living in Stapleton reduced you to.

She forced herself to keep going, until the sky became heavy as lead and began cautiously to disgorge itself. Clean, cold flakes, thank goodness for that. She looked at her watch. Three twenty-five. Looking at watches. She would write Fred a cool, subtle note thanking him for the money, telling him where to write, separation seems best, doesn't it? It cheered her a little, working out the tart phrases.

2

"What did you do today?" asked Mrs. Willoughby.

"Nothing. Went for a walk."

"Oh, that was nice." Mrs. Willoughby was having one of her good days and wanted to get in some talk. "Where did you go? Anywhere special?"

"No, it was just a walk."

Mrs. Willoughby put the tea bag in the saucer where it made a brown puddle.

"Well, that was nice. Walking is very good exercise."

Every time Alison looked away her mother peppered her with furtiveness. I wonder if she's getting enough exercise, I wonder if she's all right "in her mind." You felt the question marks strung along the nerves of the cheek.

The Stapleton *Gazette* lay in a dismal clump at the end of the table. It was one of those old-looking newspapers even when it arrived; and this copy had been around for three days. Mrs. Willoughby picked it up with sudden gusto.

"Let's see what's in the paper," she said.

With all deliberate speed, she hastened to the bottom of page nine.

"Hum, hum, I see the Worthingtons are selling their harmonium. That might be worth thinking about. You used to play so nicely. I wonder why they're selling it. Do you suppose Harry Worthington has lost his job?"

"I really have no idea."

"Houses to rent, houses for sale," casual as a robot, "appointments. Oh look dear, they want a secretary over at Clark's. You wouldn't be interested in that, I suppose."

"No, I wouldn't."

"I suppose it wouldn't be very interesting. What about this, receptionist at Bloomfontains."

"No."

"It says, 'Lots of scope for ambitious girl.'"

"Yes. I can imagine the girl they have in mind."

Her mother folded the paper back into a clump. Her mouth thinned out and took the "I've tried everything" position. The "girls weren't so fussy in my day" alignment.

"Look, Mother, I really think you ought to let me help out with the rent."

"I wouldn't dream of it. Your father and I . . ." etc.

Alison took her cold tea over to the sink and swished it down. If they didn't want rent, why didn't they just keep quiet about the whole thing? They thought everyone should be usefully occupied, that was why. Idleness upset them terribly; their own was so painful. Mr. Willoughby never missed a day at his dreary little office. There, processing papers or whatever he did, he was as much alive as, well, millions of people.

"I don't want to work just for the sake of working," Alison said.

"No, of course not."

"When I find something that really interests me . . ." If something interesting turned up—exotic jobs were always turning up in Stapleton, of course.

"What kind of thing do you think would be interesting?" her mother asked.

"I have no idea. When it comes, I'll recognize it, I know."
Across a crowded room.

"I see."

"I just—" Never apologize, never explain, she just left it. "I've
written to some people in New York. I may get an answer."

Her mother waited a moment.

"Well, we'll have to keep on looking, won't we?"

Alison nodded. Idleness was knitted into a motto above her
old bed. "Idleness Is Devil's Work" hissed the woolen plaque.
It was a dreadful punishment the Lord inflicted once a week.
Nobody could want more of it than that. Her parents obviously
thought she had come completely unstuck. She tried to be
coolly amused by this.

"Work isn't everything," she said.

"No, I suppose not."

"You miss a lot if you do nothing but work."

Her mother groped. "You mean nature?"

"Yes, that kind of thing."

"Well, I must say I've always appreciated nature," said Mrs.
Willoughby. She looked reflectively at "Autumn in Vermont."
"The changing seasons," she said, "and your father loves nature,
too."

Idleness meant sitting in straight chairs and dark rooms with
a piano covered in plants; watching Aunt Matilda eating cakes
and wiping her fingers. It meant Saturdays and gloomy, sinless
gossip and the blank evening. She was beginning to see their
point about idleness.

"What became of that fellow—George somebody," said her
mother suddenly.

Well, Alison thought she could take it, but she couldn't.

Divorce and remarriage were devil's work, but better than idleness. They would even settle for George Pyke. She left the kitchen in yet another rage.

The next Stapleton *Gazette* ran an appeal for a dentist's assistant, and she decided to apply. She found herself almost trembling as she drove over. She didn't even know what she was afraid of. Dry rot in the house. No friends to laugh at it with.

A job, any job—she couldn't face another kitchen conference; or another offhand reference to George Pyke and Harry Worthington's harmonium.

Before casually picking up the paper that day and casually turning to page nine, Mrs. Willoughby had asked slyly how the ceramics were going.

"I've given it, them, up."

"Oh, you have."

"Well, I haven't exactly given it up—" Alison's throat knotted itself around the lie, the slick whine of extenuation. "What have they got today, then?" she almost croaked.

"Doctor Parish wants a receptionist. That wouldn't suit you, I suppose."

It wasn't exactly the job of the century she'd been waiting for. Saying, "The dentist will see you now," and then compiling cement cupcakes for their obscene cavities.

"I'll take it."

She could still remember Dr. Parish's dull, efficient hands foraging in her own mouth—pink hands covered in spit. She drove over by herself. At the end of Dr. Parish's little gravel drive she met her predecessor, a chubby girl in a white uniform who smelled ominously of mouth.

"You see, I'm getting married," explained the girl.

Dr. Parish had the same big face and thin gray hair and rimless glasses. Dentists probably never got any older.

"I'm Alison Cope, Alison Willoughby," she said. "I used to come here."

He remembered, but didn't seem especially elated.

"How are you, Alison?"

Now came the breathless area of embarrassment, whether she was married, what was her experience—he slid past it, with his own kind of bedside manner. Alison had a sudden notion that her mother had been talking to him on the phone, greasing the way for her.

The reception room was sprucer than it used to be. There was a picture of a coaching inn on the lampshade. What expressionless eyes Dr. Parish had—glittering into your mouth, nothing personal old man; little picky instruments and soft, clean fingers to follow, *argh!* "Spit, please."

He stood by his chair with his hand on the white paper napkin that protected the headpiece. One glint of friendship and she would take the job. Enter his saliva kingdom . . .

He outlined her duties briefly, and she looked at the gray skin and thought, Leaving your husband to come to this. It made even less sense than ceramics and George Pyke. It was the admired thing, to strike out for humble independence. But this was the same chair she had writhed in as a girl; this was where the braces had gone in that had straightened the teeth, that had attracted the Fred that—

"Seventy-five dollars a week, full-time? I see—well." He obviously didn't care whether she took it or not. Old Stapleton type. "I don't think so."

Rather surprised, he shook hands and said, "It was nice seeing you again, Alison." The nurse showed her out.

"Was it the money, or what?" Her mother seemed unnecessarily shaken when she was told about it.

"I didn't like his magazines."

The downstairs meal in the evening was even more mournful than usual. Her parents were being awfully brave about her turning down the job, they kept looking at the walls and wiping their mouths carefully until it suddenly began to seem like a terrible defeat. She could just hear Dr. Parish on the phone, even colder without his cold little body. "She just turned it down, she didn't say why." Alison gone very queer, only trying to help; very good of you, Doctor. Not at all. Cold body in white paper underwear.

"I'll have my dessert upstairs."

"Very well, dear."

Her father looked up briefly: one-dimensional concern. Like a painting. People thought his face was kind and attractive, but if you went around to the back you found that it was propped up on a stick.

Their voices mumbled into her bedroom, through the floorboards and under the door. She thought she detected poor-Alison talk, but there was so little color to the sounds, it could have been anything.

It wasn't approval she wanted, she hoped she was beyond that: but she did want someone to understand what she was all about. "Never apologize, never explain." In a timid urban setting that sounded like a riotous motto, but down here it was meaningless. You might as well say "And never use a handkerchief." Audacity lost all its luster, became rude and finally pathetic in these surroundings.

Living freely, living beautifully—somebody had to know you were doing it, or you might as well give up. She tried to conjure up Pierce, but he had become twelve again and insisted on imitating the Lone Ranger. In Bloodbury, people took her seriously; at least they had the grace to be a little alarmed by her. But here . . .

Her mother brought dessert and fiddled with the bed covers: this is where girls like you belong, blanketed in wholesome stupefaction. Late nights are behind the whole thing—late nights and not enough green vegetables. When she had gone, the room seemed suddenly very bare and stupid. The bookcase was full of children's books. Alison got down her school atlas to trace once more the possible escape routes. Thinking she could master Stapleton, indeed. Her finger wandered vaguely over Viet Nam. Even old fraud Stebbing disapproved of her. That was pretty hard to take.

Women without husbands went to bland places along creamy highways and sat around in sunglasses. Their faces were brown and stiff, the temperature was perfect. They wore white trousers in stucco bungalows. The people down here thought that Alison was one of those. Well, was she?

Las Vegas, Miami, Acapulco—Alison could just see herself. Straw hat, striped shirt, face a little gaunt from chronic hysteria, morale beginning to give in places. Irritatingly casual, except when the waiter brings the wrong change, and then terrible chokes of rage. She put the atlas away. Pierce was trying to show her his bubble gum cards, what a little pest; she didn't want to go away, she couldn't bring herself to go away.

Her parents were perfectly right. A defeat was a defeat, however trivial. Life among the wet gums of Stapleton was better than no life at all. Next time she'd take the job, even if it meant embalming corpses.

She thought she would.

3

Stebbing had completed his autumn harvest in time for the early snow. He was doing silver branches now and snowmen made of warm white bleach, and antiseptic peace on earth. He wore a knitted blue cap and a canvas windbreaker; and he squinted into the raw grayness, scavenging for prettiness. Alison had her hands crossed into her sleeves and shook with cold.

"I don't think I made myself clear the other day," she said.

He didn't answer, being half buried in professional coyness, and he probably couldn't hear anyway through his knitted hat. But the illusion of communication was important. "I may have sounded a bit shrill and silly . . . I'm really not like . . ."

Good grief, he was actually changing the color of the sky. The thickening cumulus of grays was being rolled back into that frightful all-season blue. Was there any point in talking at all to this man?

Yes—because Stebbing had it in him to understand. He might have sold out, but that took brains didn't it? " 'What was that, dear?' " she said. "If you wanted one phrase to put on Fred's tombstone, it would be 'What was that, dear?' "

No, not on Fred's tombstone—on hers. It suddenly seemed to her that she had spent a lifetime talking to inattentive men. Stebbing was smiling slightly, as they all did . . . other American wives must get used to it: the glassy eyes, the regular breathing; the flaccid eagerness to please and, finally, the hopeful interjections. "Yes, well, that's Sam for you" or "You never know with Sam." Some instinct, acquired in some classroom, or while trying to please some girl, directed the American male to the main points, even made it possible for him to carry on authentic conversations at times: not bright, but authentic. Such as: "you know who Sam reminds me of? Joe Pfennig!"

She thought of all the other wives with their big vague husbands—Bloodbury and Stapleton seemed to be in the same zone for that—and thought, Perhaps if Fred weren't quite so *conspicuously* inattentive . . . She could take "What was that, dear" in the privacy of the home and pretend it was like other people—just as she could pretend that Stebbing was listening to her now. Hey, he was: he'd raised his ear flaps and was pouring out the coffee. A brown splash sizzled against the snow.

"It was when he did it in company—I admit this is very petty, but I couldn't help noticing it more when there was company. He would ask visitors about their plans when they'd already told him about their plans. I tell you, I writhed."

Stebbing must understand about that. He wasn't a real artist, but he must know the rules: awareness, consciousness. He must have heard of that somewhere. He scratched his chest through the canvas windbreaker and drank some more coffee.

"A lot of men are like that. It isn't so very terrible. It's life."

"Oh, don't be so Confucian about it. What could be worse? Than not hearing, not seeing? What's the phrase—fire in the belly? Fred had none of that—although, heaven knows, he had room for it. Just a tiny pilot light of attention going out every few seconds."

"You've had a hard life all right," said Stebbing with unusual sarcasm, as if he had had almost his share of Alison.

"I'm not saying anything like that, it has nothing to do with hard. It's a question of what terms"—but the fraud had already lowered his flaps and was ready to go back to work—"you're going to accept in life. I just happen to think . . ." She was shouting into a void; quite sure that she was right and he was wrong; and infuriated by the smug wool that he pulled over his ears to keep her words out. Quality was important in life; it was no virtue to endure the second best.

His scaly fist swarmed over the canvas, weaving fresh mediocrities—Stebbing was the enemy, if anybody was. She wanted to shout at him and claw at his painting. But she had lost the verve for that kind of gesture. The best she could do was walk away, and even that she did rather shakily. If she didn't find someone who agreed with her soon, she would lose every ounce of strength; she would just lie down in the snow and die.

. . . And being right didn't help. Reflected off a thousand blank Stapleton eyes, she was wrong. Tottering over the snow in high-heeled boots and a fur coat—that's what happens when they stop going to church you know. Because she had been raised here, she could see it just the way they saw it, as well as her own way. She might be occupying an extraordinary subtle and worthwhile position, but to them she was just another gaunt woman in sunglasses who had messed up yet another marriage.

She drove over to the post office, hoping to find some solution in the mailbox, hoping, let's face it, that someone had written a note telling her what to do next. But the box just yawned at her—couldn't be more bored. Not even an organization shrieking for help today.

Eleven-thirty . . . one more hour to a drab lunch. She drove over to Stapleton's only travel agency and looked through the frosty glass. A thin anxious face superimposed itself on a picture of Bermuda. A group of tanned, brainless people boarding a plane. An open model of some monster plane with thousands of tiny seats. Now. Come on. It's *worth* doing.

She walked in. The inside was quite dark and small. There was a rack on the right full of splashy folders, and a small desk in front. A fat woman was haggling about Europe, so Alison looked at the folders. They seemed to specialize in the Caribbean. Fabulous hotels, our own golf course, our own tennis courts; and pictures of people who had gone three thousand miles to play tennis. White sand and palm trees, people lying with their eyes shut in the midst of plenty. Were people really so dense and unfeeling? Of all the subhuman occupations, sun bathing—

"Can I help you, madam?"

"I'd like some information, I guess."

"Anything special?"

"Well—Europe."

"Yes, madam. Which part of Europe?"

"France . . . Italy"—then she thought of Mexico, too. "Not just Europe. Mexico would be interesting, wouldn't it?"

He was already pulling folders out from under the desk and handing them over automatically. Italy—more fabulous hotels, more people playing tennis; a disconsolate family visiting the ruins. (Couldn't find the tennis court, probably.)

"Where would *you* go?" she asked the man.

"It depends what you want."

"Yes, of course. I want . . . something the opposite of Stapleton."

She smiled slightly and waited. This was a Stapleton boy him-

self. It went without saying that her wish was completely meaningless to him.

"I'll take these folders home and see."

He nodded that that was all right.

"Italy might be an idea."

Just nodded.

"Spain, even."

Said nothing.

"Well, thanks very much."

"You're welcome, madam."

She had a feeling from the way he kept looking past her that
a lot of people were waiting for service. But there was no one
there. He was probably just waiting to pull out his sandwich and
his little container of milk.

Little things like this that she used to handle without thinking
were now a morning's work. She hated leaving this man without
demonstrating that she made some kind of sense. That (a) she
was joking, but (b) there was something to it, about getting
away from Stapleton. But she had an armful of pamphlets now,
and there seemed to be no excuse for staying.

"Good morning, then." To think she had actually tried, a few
months ago, to like this town.

"Not at all."

She was looking at her watch as she left the travel agency.
Pierce was waiting outside with a cap pistol. She jumped a foot
even before the gun went off. Not really Pierce, of course, just a
regular little Stapleton boy: but it could have been Pierce.
"That isn't funny," she said, "frightening people." But he
thought it was and ran off laughing, leaving her almost blind
with frustrated rage.

4

The Willoughbys' house was one of those buildings that managed to be old without being interesting. Quakers, as far as Alison could tell, had no history in the usual sense; it was against their principles for anything to happen. Two wars had passed fairly close, but the Willoughbys had paid them no mind; they kept no records except for births and deaths in the family Bible. Grandfather Seth did his damnedest to live the same life as great-grandfather Job, and to have the same face on the dining room wall to show for it. Alison had spent a while scratching this dry surface in township records and Mrs. Fisk's fifteen-volume memoirs. Nothing.

The whole house was bare of associations. The furniture was old, but that was all, just old. Her father never brought up his family, and when she asked him about them, he couldn't remember much. His father had been a doctor, with a beard; Mr. Willoughby's youth had been neither happy nor unhappy. Mrs. Stetson down the street remembered him as averagely playful. It didn't seem worth going on with these inquiries. They all turned up the same gray material.

The lively part of the house was upstairs where Pierce worked frantically at his hobbies and his love of life. But his ectoplasm wouldn't cooperate any more, he was always changing his face and doing imitations: she had lost her contact with him, and upstairs was beginning to seem as bad as downstairs. Her schoolbooks were still wrapped in brown paper, and they looked as flavorless as the other things that were just old. The white wickerwork table she used to work on was chipped and gray; she felt no affection for it, but didn't want to part with it either.

(That combination of feelings was right in the Willoughby tradition.)

She sat with the light off, and the grayness inside was reinforced with winter. One of her first memories was of her mother fidgeting at light switches—ostensibly to save Depression pennies but really because darkness seemed more proper. Light was too gaudy, it clashed with everything they owned. Alison was beginning to feel the same way.

She had rounded off the long afternoon by having a talk with Mrs. Stetson and felt enormously enervated. Mrs. Stetson was one of the few neighbors who was even slightly excited about the past, but she didn't really bring it to life; she just got excited about it. There was something sinister about her animation over listless events:

"And then the Ponsonbys moved out here, and oh, my!" She was going blind, so that her mind's eye was happy to be occupied with anything at all.

This afternoon, Alison had asked again after her father, and Mrs. Stetson had come up with a whole new trove—Mr. Willoughby's college period.

It turned out that this was Mr. Willoughby's golden age. He had a sort of brief flowering at Waterbury College.

"I have the yearbook. He didn't want it himself," said Mrs. Stetson and began groping along the shelf for it. Alison had never noticed the old Waterbury yearbooks before, four volumes of red leather and dust on Mrs. Stetson's bottom shelf.

The old lady told her which page to open and then, while Alison skimmed through the profile, chuckled in a detached way because she was using her eyes again on one of her brighter memories.

"Great practical joker," it said, and a list of his accomplishments in that line—"ready wit." Alison stared and stared. It was a joke, of course, putting down all the opposite things. She looked at the picture, and that was a joke too. It was a real smile.

"Oh, yes, he was funny all right. In a gentlemanly way, of course."

Alison felt slightly sick. "What happened to him?"

"Happened? What do you mean happened?"

"He isn't funny now."

"Well, a man gets more serious, I suppose, it's only natural. He had a very hard time, out of work, you know. And then losing his boy in the war."

Mrs. Stetson was right—theoretically, it was all quite natural.

"Anyway, it wouldn't do for a man his age to be larking about."

Talking about theoretically, it was possible theoretically even to feel sorry for him. Her father *had* had a hard life. But she just felt sick. If Mr. Willoughby had ever been cheerful and friendly —which she doubted—he ought to have kept it going somehow.

She left Mrs. Stetson, who was still in a high good humor over hitting on such a nice bit of past. When she got home, her father was back from work, tinkering with the big clock in the hall. She looked at him closely and he smiled pleasantly, distantly. He was always at the wrong end of the telescope.

"It's been gaining," he said. "The clock."

"Yes, as long as I can remember, it's gained."

He crouched over it in his pinstriped waistcoat and gave the pendulum a tweak.

"How long have we had it, anyway?" she asked him.

"I don't know. A long time."

"Thirty years, forty years, do you remember ever not having it?"

"I forget. It's pretty old."

She had nothing to complain about. He'd never said an angry word to her. He said many polite ones. She went straight to her room and had sat there frozen ever since.

It was quite dark, but her eyes made the necessary adjustments and by now she could see all she wanted. The blue-gray of the windows, the frame of the rocking chair against it. On the right, a tattered map of Pennsylvania hung like a shroud. Around Stapleton she had once drawn a desperate red circle; it was still there in shaggy crayon.

While she lived in Bloodbury, Stapleton was a dream; now that she was back in Stapleton, Bloodbury was a dream. It worked like a pendulum, or a rocking chair. She hadn't really been out of this room more than five minutes in her life. She was still sitting in the dark because her mother used to say, "If you're not reading, you don't need the light," said it, said it, said it until Alison didn't have to be told any more. She was sitting up here because downstairs was galoshes, daddy tinkering politely among the galoshes. . . .

Man shouldn't have to be polite with his own daughter. What a terrible, new vice. Right after Pierce's death he began it—a kind of relentless courtesy worse than a whipping. Villains in the movies were always polite, Pepe le Moko and all that; but none so polite as Mr. Willoughby, after Pierce's death.

Her mind jumped about wildly in the dark. A ring around Stapleton, a ring around Mr. Willoughby. Mr. Willoughby didn't drink or smoke. She had never seen him read a book. He had no friends. He was never bored. What a terrible man.

She suddenly remembered something about Pierce's death

that deepened and enriched the chill. She remembered her parents standing in the hall as relatives stumbled past, a reception without a coffin, she was a bit vague about the details. Her parents behaved just perfectly, and one of her old cousins whispered, "They're being very brave"; and Alison remembered saying out loud, "No, they're not." Because after her own mechanical paroxysms, she understood. Their coldness did have a kind of terrifying grandeur, but it had nothing to do with brave. Coldness was contagious. She could absolutely see the point of feeling nothing. It was a voluptuous, number-one temptation to a Willoughby, and had *nothing* to do with being brave. If she stayed in this house, in this town, she would certainly become cold too. Her father waiting in the hall everyday with a kiss of ice. Something in the walls, in the furniture, and the family pictures in black starch said "Cool it"; a house that gathered no associations, people that allowed themselves no past.

People said she was pretty and vivacious, but she suddenly knew that she wasn't really. It was a family trick. So she had taken her red crayon and dramatically slashed a circle around the word Stapleton. Condemned area, must get away. Seventeen, eighteen, nineteen. The shape of the weeks and months were such that there was no place where you could just slip out. Her father coming home at night, her mother's rhythmic constipation, somehow it all made a tight, strangling weave, and she found herself hanging about, month after pointless month.

Pierce's diary was a great pillar of fire, and all that—but in spite of it she had hung on for two more years, battling the shapeless weeks. Now she knew, because she was having the same dream; but in between, she had completely forgotten—that the reason she had stayed at home was this same lethargy and panic that passed for calmness in her house and that held her still. She couldn't get up her nerve to leave; to pass her polite father and her ever-congealing mother in the hall, and just leave.

Pierce's diary was buried in a dark drawer. To read it, she would have to get up and waste some electricity. But anyway, that was a funny thing about the diary, too. The vitality there was rather hysterical, wasn't it—a bit like her own. A bit like, come to think of it, her father's at Waterbury. It was a brief fling that Willoughbys had before surrendering to their own dead-ness of heart. It had to be hysterical, overdone, to last even as long as it did.

If Pierce had lived, he would still be in the room next door, pursuing ever-diminishing hobbies, going off to the bank every day . . . she knew, because she had come back herself. Made up some silly excuse to leave her husband and creep back to the old flavorless house; creep back, through her own red ring to the life she really wanted, of coldness, inertia and controlled panic.

And there was her father, vivacious if not pretty in the Water-bury yearbook, and now his polite despair as he worked on his stupid clock. She felt no sympathy for him because that wasn't part of the rules: Willoughbys owed their first coldness to each other. But she felt a chilly kind of understanding. No wonder Pierce had hated his parents so much: they had planted the same seed in him—his father planted it and his mother had absent-mindedly left it there. He would have come back, all right; lived here for sixty years; left no records; lived the same life and worn the same face as his father, George—with the extra, excruciating boredom of "interests."

Alison gave the rocking chair a trance-breaking heave; she

was wasting more and more time on these crazy constructions, as a substitute for action. On winter evenings, you could make anyone's life sound sinister by these methods. She was impatient with mystical melodrama as a form. In Bloodbury, she had always swept the tendency aside with vivacity, with interests. She could do so here. In the spring she'd get into politics or something; teach a course, write a book. Meanwhile, forty minutes to supper and then, just this once, television.

"The library here is terrible," she said at supper.
"Is it?" said her mother. "It's a brand-new building."
"It cost enough," said Mr. Willoughby.
"They forgot to put in the books."
"Oh."

Her mother seemed vaguely embarrassed. Heaven only knew why. Mr. Willoughby was at his most detached. Neither of them had ever responded to this kind of conversation, or ever would. At times she had thought that they didn't want her to be intelligent, that they thought it shaming—but it wasn't even as firm as that. She also had a notion that her mother was embarrassed for the sake of Mr. Willoughby ("Not while your father's eating"). And that Mr. Willoughby was detached out of some strange delicacy that he'd forgotten the reason for.

It had given Alison a certain blind aggressiveness in these matters, and she went on about the library for a few minutes, listing some of the shocking ommissions: but their total lack of interest, and her mother's "Is that so?" defeated her finally, and she felt herself flouncing, with ungovernable irritation, into the next room to watch television.

5

"Why do you live here, when you could be living anywhere you liked?" Fred had failed to answer her note and she had to take it out on someone. "And why do you paint like that, anyway?"

Stebbing was anticipating spring with a host of synthetic daffodils. His flaps were up, so he couldn't help hearing. But he ignored the interesting part of the question. Instead he said, "Why do *you* live here?" He held his thumb against the sky.

"Because it's lovely and unspoiled, I suppose. And because its part of us. Right?"

"Oh, right, I guess."

If she could ferret out what contentment this complicated old man found in Stapleton, she might know better what to do here herself. Of course she could never make such a perverse adjustment as his, but she felt that at some point his problem might have been not unlike hers. Something in the outside world had driven him back here; some joke he couldn't cope with, some situation Stapleton hadn't prepared him for. (Like having his French laughed at or being frightened by a trans-vestite—something that a non-Stapletonian wouldn't begin to understand.)

She felt for the moment a sort of bond with this vulnerable man. He understood about irony, you could tell from his face. (Pierce wouldn't have liked him so much if he hadn't.) Perhaps he had decided, since he couldn't live anywhere else, to embrace Stapleton with sardonic overemphasis—it wasn't quite her solution, but it wasn't a bad one either. She wished he would be friends and talk to her about it. "I didn't mean to say

I didn't *like* your painting; I meant, why that particular . . ." but there was simply no chance of his hearing a remark like that.

Stebbing's silence was not as irritating as usual, because it was such a nice day. Winter was shrinking on all sides. There were pockets of snow all the way up the hill (which the old rascal would turn into crocuses); the air was wonderfully clear and cold, knifing through the thick lethargy of winter. Alison's vitality peeped out cautiously, and said that it was safe. You stay indoors for weeks, massaging your paralyzed will (in fact, she had even begun to hit her mother's prune juice on the sly) and then spring comes and you see it was all a winter dream, you're free, you can do and say whatever you like. George Pyke stopped calling her up at last, and a new girl was observed in his front seat; a neurotic-looking blonde from Harrisburg.

"Have you ever been patted on the head, Mr. Stebbing?" she asked good-humoredly. (You could say almost anything you liked to Mr. Stebbing, because he only caught one sentence in three.)

"Eh?" It was like talking to someone who was knitting or cleaning a pipe. Stebbing dabbed at his canvas and was always a little bit slow and a little bit stupid: destroying the timing that was necessary to making a point.

"I hate to bring him up once more on such a lovely day," she said, "but my husband actually used to pat me on the head. After dinner, as if I was part of his stomach. I was terrified he was going to say 'There, there.' "

Stebbing's face thinned distastefully; she knew he didn't like her to sound clever-clever. His own wife was an elemental type girl: womanly, and all that. Trudging through fields of hay singing contralto folk songs.

"I know you think I'm being frivolous, but do try to understand, Mr. Stebbing; I didn't do this thing lightly. I had many good reasons. As I'm sure you have had for, for . . ."

Stebbing went on with his knitting. His painting gave him an excuse not to answer, so she couldn't tell whether his silence stood for anything special. She had seen very few people lately, and her poise was going rusty; she talked in a hopeful rush.

"If you could just see this one point . . . I'm not what you think at all. Fred wasn't stupid, I wouldn't have minded stupidity, it was much worse than that. It was, oh, I don't know. Well, I'll give you an example, if you like. Every Saturday we used to make love. Saturday, for heaven's sake, and he always—"

Stebbing stopped her just by looking at her. He had a tight grip on his brush as if he was about to lash her with it.

"That's quite enough," he said. "How dare you talk to me about things like that? Private things."

The Stapleton face. He looked suddenly like a whole committee of outraged mothers; the face that every Stapleton child fears instinctively from birth, and all through life, disapproval gone mad, in a dull setting.

Alison saluted it with terror. "I don't understand you, Mr. Stebbing. I thought you were—" What? The people down here had repealed every passion but one; but that one was a beauty. Disapproval. You didn't argue with it. Alison knew totally, as she knew few things totally, that she was in the wrong now. Later she could work out why.

"You thought what?" echoed Stebbing. "You thought because I was a painter, an artist—"

Alison nodded.

He shook his head. "People have funny ideas," he said.

That hurt, so she said, "And also with your young wife and everything—"

Oh dear, not again. The committee, the terrible Stapleton committee, kept assembling in his wide face. "I'm sorry, I mean—"

"I don't know what my wife has to do with it."

"Yes, of course—I mean, nothing."

"My first wife died, after thirty wonderful years. Perhaps you think I was wrong to marry again? Is that it?"

She sat there miserably watching him pack up his things again. His hands seemed to be trembling; oh, good God, she hadn't *hurt* him? How had she done that? Such a corrupt man shouldn't feel hurt. It couldn't possibly mean that he was sincere, after all. He was so *totally* artificial—sincerity could only be a terrible new perversion. His stinking, lying paintings—if she brought those up, she supposed he would say, "I do the best I can. Is there anything wrong with that?"

To think, she had felt a bond—he stuck the easel under his arm and said good morning, and that, she knew, was the end of Stebbing. He seemed to pull the hill up behind him and vanish with it into the house.

She tried some disapproval herself. Stebbing wasn't very hard to despise. If she was damned by his standards, he was triple damned by hers. Making a living by blaspheming nature, and then festooning the rubbish dump with lace valentine morals. Here was corruption of a delicacy and thoroughness . . . look at it this way: any amount of overstated gush was perfectly O.K. with Stebbing, but you couldn't admit that you made love to your husband, well it was laughable.

She was right, she was right, she was right. But still, a visit from the committee— She might be right, but she certainly didn't feel right. Stebbing's disapproval of her was so heartfelt and sure of itself; hers of him was sort of a fake. He was the Spirit of Stapleton, set to music. The committee somehow made you see things their way. Her words about lovemaking did sound brassy and vulgar as she heard them now; the allusion to Stebbing's young wife sounded unforgivable.

Words didn't die in this still air but hung there until you were sick to death of them. Thinner, shriller, "Saturday night, for heaven's sake, my *dear*, too, too awful, fancy making love on Saturday night—" What kind of terrible wax doll had she turned into saying things like that?

She couldn't tell *what* she was, one hardly even existed without someone to talk to. She hadn't the courage of her own attitudes, letting an old hypocrite like Stebbing put her in the wrong with his synthetic standards. She hadn't the guts to be what she wanted to be.

But the really horrifying thing was that Stebbing *was* sincere, he hadn't been joking for a minute: that was almost too grotesque to bear. . . . And he had been Pierce's friend, and probably still was Pierce's friend. She could just picture Pierce walking beside him up the hill, whispering, "She didn't get any of that stuff from me." ("*I* know that, Pierce.") And on top of that, it was only 10:25 in the morning, with another lank day ahead of her.

Since it was a Saturday, her father was home doing something in the garage. He was always doing something.

The garage was musty, smelling of old magazines and rubber-leather; she had learned to drive years ago by wriggling the car in and out of this garage, cannonading off the bushes and at least once splintering her headlights against the far wall. (She forgot to put the car in reverse and started her up and saw the wall rolling in, followed by a dismal clunk.) Except that the *Saturday Evening Posts* almost reached the ceiling now, nothing had changed.

"Hello, Father."

"Hello there."

"What are you doing?"

"Just fixing things up."

He was on his back in old clothes, but still the soul of courtesy.

"Do you want the car?" he asked.

"No, mine's been fixed." He never knew anything about her affairs, but he looked much younger down there and more accessible. His business clothes tended to make him seem so small and old and unattainable.

"Can I help you, Father?"

"Well, yes." He surprised her again. "You can hold this." He handed her something which she didn't notice, a wire of some kind. She held it like a silver cord between them and said again:

"Father?"

"Yes?"

She didn't know what to say, but hoped the cord would convey something. I've wanted to talk to you, but you understand I can't *say* that. Silent people should be extrasensitive, he should get that much at least from the cord.

She waited desperately, hopefully.

"Yes, Alison," he said after an empty while.

"I was wondering," she said slowly, "don't you people want to know why I left Fred?"

"Give me that," he said and took the wire. "Thanks, I think that'll do it."

Why the people she talked to were always plunging into something else, she would never know. *She* couldn't be a bore, could she? He puttered inscrutably for a few more minutes, while she waited, leaning against the car, and running her finger over a bump in the paint. The car had changed slightly; they used to have a black Plymouth.

"Father? I was saying—"

"Yes, I'm sorry." He wiped his hands on an oil rag. "Well, your mother and I figured that some things are best left unsaid—"

"Most things, don't you think?"

"And we figured you must have your reasons. Your husband must have done something pretty bad. Isn't that right?"

"Well," she flicked at the puffy paint with her long nail, "in a way."

"Some people are just no good. You can't tell until it's too late, of course. But when you do, there's nothing for it but to admit your mistake; make a clean break . . ."

Did he mean it? Did he talk this way in his heart of hearts, like the wise, pragmatic old ladies in the movies? Was there anyone left who *didn't* talk this way, then?

"Fred wasn't exactly rotten," she meant to say next. But the words stuck hopelessly. As long as he thought that Fred was rotten, Mr. Willoughby was on her side; he even seemed to hover on the edge of sympathy.

"Your mother and I appreciate the way you haven't complained; the way you've kept going," he said dryly.

For even this amount of understanding, Fred could be sacrificed.

"I'm glad you think that," she said. "I didn't know."

"Don't mention it," he said.

"I didn't know whether you and mother approved, or what."

"Naturally, we have to stand behind our only daughter."

It wasn't much, was it? To sacrifice Fred for. She looked into her father's mild, unaccented face and smiled at him—you see what I'm doing, Father, I'm simply asking you to make a small gesture, a little effort, and then you can have your rotten version of Fred and anything else you want. Mr. Willoughby smiled back, dammit, politely, and looked quickly away.

"I think that's everything. You can have the car now."

"I have my *own* car. Look—what about Pierce," she said suddenly. "What do you think of him?"

He looked surprised. "What do you mean, what do I think? He was a very brave boy. He died for his country. Naturally, we're very proud . . ."

There was a sly look in his eye, and she could tell he had read the diary and hadn't forgotten; there was infinitely modulated mockery in his voice. (She couldn't be mistaken on this point.)

No, it was worse than that—he *was* Pierce, laughing at himself in this clapboard necropolis. Laughing at *her*. He hadn't lost any of that old Waterbury humor. The pseudosmile was stiff with suppressed laughter.

She went around to the kitchen where her mother pottered away her days and said, "Mother, what do *you* think?"

"About what, dear?"

"About me and Fred."

"Well, nothing special, I guess. I mean, we're both sure that you're in the right . . ."

"Why? Why are you sure?"

Her mother looked vaguely alarmed. She backed against the

kitchen table and her fingers reached behind her for the Stapleton *Gazette*. She's going to find me a job, thought Alison wildly. But the fingers, having closed on the paper, dropped it again. "I told you we were having someone to tea on Thursday, didn't I, dear?" Mrs. Willoughby said irrelevantly.

"Yes, Dr. Somebody or other."

"Yes, well, that will be nice."

"Why do you bring him up now?"

"Well—he's a doctor, you know."

"Yes, that I understood."

"And, well, we thought you'd seemed a little rundown lately, not quite your old self."

Alison took a step forward and her mother actually flinched. "You did that? You asked him to tea to look at me?"

"It's not just that, it's really a social visit." Her mother ground herself nervously against the table. She was getting old, wasn't she?

"I suppose he's a psychiatrist, is he? an analyst of some kind?"

It didn't matter whether her mother's silence meant "yes" or "no" to this preposterous question. Things were quite incredible enough—sneaking a doctor into her presence without discussing it with her. What kind of person did they think she was? What kind of a nutty freak? All these months whispering, waiting, "Poor Alison"—they were sorry for her, but it was like laughing, too. Finally, as a last straw, bringing in strangers with modern ideas to consult; it was like bringing in George Pyke—a complete, cheerful betrayal of *themselves*.

She left the kitchen in rage and terror. Tempered with a kind of wild boredom at the way they'd done it. Pierce must have felt like this the night the Pomfret Inn was raided. Your own parents—Good (yawn) *God!*

She wrote a note, so that there would be no misunderstanding this time, and left it under the fancy telephone and walked to the service station where her car had been fixed, and five hours later she was outside the red ring and back in Bloodbury.

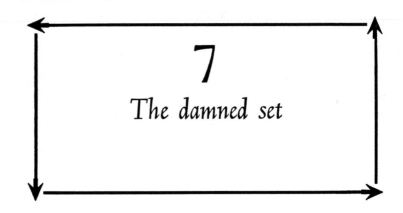

7

The damned set

1

The south of Spain was having its wettest winter in ninety years and Fred understood why Pete Glasser was having his house designed adulterously rather than by a Spanish contractor. The mountains behind Fred's new apartment bounced the same set of clouds back and forth, and every cloud was an upturned ocean. The rain wore a hole in Fred's roof, just over his bed, and the dampness worked its way along the walls making the paints run dismally; his abstract of Jonah in the whale was already a soggy shambles, and his "cross section of my mind" was just starting to gleam ominously. The wind kept ripping into the external wiring so that with the rain came darkness, and painting became practically impossible. Worst of all, on rainy afternoons Frieda was likely to call, and there was no escape from that.

No comfortable one, anyway. She cased all the cafés as a matter of course, so the obvious sanctuary was out. The church was always locked in the afternoons. He didn't like to visit the

Glassers. (He'd have felt silly going to church, too, just to get away from Frieda.) Some afternoons he walked along the beach in his raincoat and plastic hat, but the wind and water took turns on his face, and the beach was desolate, even the Swedes having given up, and after half an hour or so—his usual time thing—he was ready to throw in the sponge and face Frieda.

He wasn't exactly afraid of her. And you couldn't call it bored either. What would you call it then?

"Hello, Frieda."

One anonymous day in November, as far as he knew, a Tuesday, and there she was again, panting and wet at the top of his stairs. Now what did he feel exactly?

"Am I disturbing you? Were you working?"

He used to say, "Yes, I'm working," but it didn't make any difference, she always came back later.

"What a day," she said, "whew."

"Yes."

She took off her coat and there was the black shapeless sweater again. It hung in loose, coarse folds, vaguely puzzling, the different aspects of its shapelessness. Fred offered her a drink. The inevitable brandy, but she accepted it as if it was a wonderful new discovery. "Oh, yes, please."

She sat on the sofa and Fred gave her the drink and went and sat on the other side of the room. Between them was a defunct fireplace surrounded by clammy logs, olive wood that didn't burn even when it was dry.

"This damn coast," she began; and then, "I'm sorry, I always seem to be grumbling, don't I? But you're the only sympathetic —and I always seem to be saying that too."

"It's all right," Fred mumbled.

"Did you get anything done today, any painting or writing?"

"No, not really. No."

"I don't blame you, this damn weather."

She had made a lot of tiny adjustments for him. She never said anything worse than "damn" now (atlhough he'd never brought this up); she didn't flatter him quite so much; she apologized for things. In many ways, it was worse. She was always looking at him tensely to see how she was doing, and he could only smile, or look meaningful, and hope for the best.

"I really do think your 'cross section' is very fine, a marvelous concept, the more I think about it. Perhaps the 'Jonah' didn't come off quite so well"—question here, is that all right, you don't want a yes man, do you? You so strong, Mist' Cope—

"I like the 'Jonah,' " he said.

"Yes, well. There are many fine things in it, of course, the gunmetal gray suggesting the liver, and so on, we've talked about that. I was only speaking comparatively."

Something very puzzling about her appearance lately. But he was getting trapped in Frieda's special super-glue and couldn't stand back from the situation to observe.

He said, "It was all an accident, you know; I only called it 'Jonah' after I'd finished."

"I believe many great paintings are done that way."

"It seemed, as you say, liverish, and that reminded me of Jonah; but I wouldn't call it a great painting."

"No, of course not. But it's got something. I think you have a wonderful talent, Fred, really I do."

She leaned forward in all earnestness, and he felt the thing that frightened him most about Frieda: let's face it, an offbeat kind of lust, based entirely on pity and availability; or contempt and availability; or shapeless black sweaters and availability.

There *was* something strange about that sweater, a listlessness . . .

"Have you lost weight lately, Frieda?" he asked. "You look different."

"Yes," she said. "On my trip to Germany last month, I lost some weight."

"Really? Germany?" There had been a week back there when he hadn't seen Frieda, but she hadn't said anything about Germany.

"Yes, I told you about it."

His mind wandered, he just couldn't help it; monologues, even miniature ones, were just beyond him. He thought, here is this girl with enough enterprise to go to Germany, and I haven't even been to Seville.

He had been to Granada, tooling around the Alhambra with Pete Glasser; but after a moment's excitement over the Moorish fretwork, he had felt boredom like a roaring motor, the worst he had ever experienced. He wondered if he was going to have a stroke. There was this damn tracery everywhere, and you had to look at it, that's why you'd come; a real vertiginous feeling, a fear of falling into the ceilings . . .

It was worse than his usual blank reaction to beauty, his hopeless attempts to make something out of it; this was really quite painful. The old Moorish architects were laughing at him: boy, this stuff will drive Cope absolutely crazy when he sees it. He cut the visit short and ducked into a café; Pete seemed relieved to go with him.

Later on he figured it might have been the big lunch they had had at the Parador, four big courses, wine, etc., on a hot August day. In all the time he had been here he hadn't come across anything half as interesting as his own stomach. But he felt badly out of key with this Moorish stuff and tended to postpone seeing other specimens of it. Without a woman to *make* you go sightseeing . . . Apathy in Spain only needed a toehold, a little encouragement. There was always the problem of making plans, and leaving the flat empty, and I don't know, if he had a car it would be different he bet, but—and there was his painting to think about . . .

The painting was Frieda's doing. Every day she said, "How's the work?" And he said, "Oh, *you* know," and she said, "When can I see it?" and finally he did some, just to end the suspense.

He wasn't the kind of idiot who thinks that any six-year-old can do modern art; he was the kind of idiot who things that any six-year-old can't, etc. No, kidding aside, he was embarrassed even to try. He daubed in his bedroom where no one could see what he was up to, even though it was dark in there and he could hardly see himself. The paints ran wild in the dark, getting on his clothes and his blankets, but he got his two pictures done somehow and out into the living room. Frieda came around the day after and looked stunned; stood there with her fingers to her mouth and then really sickened him by saying, "They're, I don't know, kind of, I don't know," and glowing at him.

The terrible thing about Frieda, her source of strength, was that some specially retarded part of his brain was always half inclined to believe her compliments. That gray mass surrounding Jonah, for instance, was arresting enough in its bleak way. He had chosen gray because it was unpretentious, so it was just a fluke; but the retarded lobe said, don't sell yourself short, boy, that choice was no accident. And Frieda said:

"Don't sell yourself short, Fred, you're worth all these damn phonies put together"; and he was idiotically annoyed and grateful.

She brought him some more canvas, saying that her husband would never even miss it, and he set to work on another painting. But now that he thought he might actually be good, he became totally paralyzed; he stalled and puttered. Mixing the paints every day became a terrible drag. Cleaning up the mess afterwards was another. But the part in between, waiting for his greatness to assert itself, was the worst of all; and pretty soon he knew, even the backward lobe knew, that he'd been had once again.

He kept at it stubbornly for a few weeks. But he found he had no aesthetic ideas at all, beyond simply repeating himself, couldn't do real shapes and couldn't think of abstract ones, wasn't really interested in shapes anyway, but only in renewing Frieda's synthetic praise.

"What the hell is this?" said Pete Glasser when he saw the two paintings. "Cross section of your mind, you say? Christ, Fred, things can't be that bad in there."

"It's an abstraction."

"Yeah, you better stick to writing, Fred."

"So anyway," said Frieda, "Mort kept insisting, and you know how it is, you get so tired. You understand that, don't you?"

Fred scrambled back, "Mmmm, yes."

"You don't sound very convinced. Do you think I should have gone on refusing?"

"No—I guess not. I mean, you know best."

For a moment she had that Alison look, a thunderous suspicion that he wasn't listening, a rumble of disgust and a flash of rage, three seconds apart. But she decided not to call him.

She said, "It's very difficult. If I'd had someone to turn to— but it's dog eat dog around here, honestly it is. If I'd told one of the girls, it would have been all over town in five minutes."

The retarded lobe said, there's always me. And Frieda, who had a special closed circuit to this lobe, said out loud, "I didn't know you so well then, or I would have gone to you."

"Yes—well. That might have helped."

The most uncomfortable part came now—treading water, hoping to get the drift of what she'd said. Maybe she would come right out with it; otherwise he would have to keep foraging for clues. What did people go to Germany for? Animal vegetable or mineral? Goods or services? Meanwhile there was a real danger he would miss it again, on the second go-round. For all his feverish concentration.

"It isn't the first time, you know. Mort is quite pathological about this thing. He just won't hear of it," she said.

Fred shook his head. She waited. "That's awful," he said.

"I knew you'd think that," said Frieda. "You'd make a wonderful father."

Which is how good old Fred got the message at last. The slack sweater had been trying to tell him something.

He'd heard so many stories like this down here, he should have taken it in his stride. But other people were so remote; this girl with her drab insistence, her fanatic face and clothing, had forced her way much closer. He felt the quick, cheap emotion, instant music, Fred Cope faces life, that he had felt for the girl in New York. He found himself pitying the black sweater, wanting to put his arm out and comfort that. It was all and more than he could do to stay in his chair.

He made it to the fireplace and braced himself like Ulysses against that. Remember, you don't like her, Fred. She was watching him like a cat, breathless, cruel with passion. Just too much; too crazy.

"I see what you mean about cesspool, though," he said, and went back to his chair.

2

She didn't just disappear, like the girl in New York; and Fred couldn't very well stumble off down his own stairs. If only she was just a *little* crazy, it might be a different story, he thought— but that was one message she couldn't seem to decipher. She left, but that was just one afternoon, and there would be plenty more like it. More thrilling episodes, while Fred waited, either for her to sane up or for himself not to notice or care any longer.

His only other friend was Pete Glasser, who sometimes came round after supper—although he didn't invite Fred to parties any more; Fred didn't get to the parties at all any more—and sat brooding at Fred's spines (ten penguins and the fifth volume of Proust's thing.) After seeing him cry in the café, Fred thought he should do something about Pete—keep an eye on him anyway.

"Christ, why don't you get some new books? I've been staring at that Camus all winter." Pete was a hard man to help.

"I'm sorry. Why don't you move your chair?"

"You want to borrow my *Justine?*"

"O.K."

"You still got my *Ginger Man*, I see. Didn't you finish it yet? Didn't you like it?"

"I found it somewhat opaque."

Pete grunted. Fred had hit on this trick more or less by accident. He happened to say one day that Glasser's copy of *To the Lighthouse* had density—and, boy, did it ever—and Glasser snickered and said:

"Shit, Cope, you're a sarcastic bastard," and Fred had never looked back.

"How's Marilyn?" he asked, not wanting to push his luck with "opaque." (One of these days Pete would say, "But seriously, Fred—")

"I don't know how's Marilyn."

"What do you mean, you don't know?"

"She went away."

"What do you mean, 'went away'?"

"Went *away*, for God's sake. What does went away usually mean?"

"I mean, where? Did she take the kids, or what?"

"No, she left the kids with Janet. I don't know where she went to."

"When do you expect her back then?"

"I don't know. She went with Frihoff."

Glasser looked at the floor. Fred Cope Faced Life again, briefly. But this wasn't life; this was charades. Frihoff was the first syllable of *Gone with the Wind*. Pete was a gnome who narrated the various tableaux.

"She'll be back," he said.

"Yeah, with my lousy luck, she prolly will." Glasser's whiskers trembled. "It's mainly Mort I feel sorry for."

Fred went over and started trying to build a fire. He had never felt so cold, clammy-cold through the two sweaters and his shrinking lumber shirt; but the olive wood mocked him. He doused it with kerosene and it flared for a moment, and subsided again into wet apathy.

"Shit, don't you know how to build a fire?" asked Pete.

"It's this crappy wood Frank Waters sold me. You try lighting it."

Glasser came over and started reconstructing the fire carefully. "Hey, this stuff is wet. Where you been keeping it?"

"Up on the roof. I don't have any other place else big enough." Glasser shook his head. "I've got some canvas over it, Pete. Waters sold me the canvas too."

"Yeah. I bet it leaks."

"So. I hear that Frieda Frihoff lost her baby," said Fred over Pete's shoulder.

"Yeah, that's right. A month ago. Where you been hiding?"

"She said that Mort made her do it."

"Frieda said that? You don't want to listen to that crazy bitch. Mort wouldn't do a thing like that. Give me that petroleo a minute."

Fire shot along the wood, zipping along the surface like mercury. Glasser began redeploying, although he must have seen it was hopeless.

"If Mort had a kid," he said, "he might stop hellcatting around. And we'd *all* get some peace."

"You seem very sympathetic with Mort."

"Well, how would you like to be married to that neurotic bitch?" Pete said angrily. "All that bloody whining and posing, *you* know . . ."

Except that Pete Glasser was standing proxy for one of the parties, it was just like those divorce counseling things on television where the husband and wife wind up shrieking: *you're* a maniac; *you're* a monster. Fred always turned off the set at that point, embarrassed that anyone should see such things.

"I suppose there's always two sides," he said.

"The hell there are. The kid's a whazit, hysteriac. Ten to one she just miscarried . . ."

The thing about those television shows was that you always started out curious; two nice-looking people, sitting calmly across from a kind old bless-my-soul doctor—what little thing has gone wrong here? And then slowly they would warm up and strip off the blandness and begin to swing: "Don't you listen to him, Doctor, he's a liar, he's a liar," acting out the whole marriage in a few frantic minutes; and Fred, sick from sated curiosity, would wonder why they allowed such programs.

"So what else is new?" he asked.

"Nothin', I guess," said Pete, startled.

"You might as well give up on that fire."

"I guess."

Pete sat back on the sofa, anger slipping away from his face, confusion moving in. The Frihoff thing was really too much for him, though he wouldn't admit it. Toss and turn between rage and casualness, but his natural mood now was this becalmed anxiety. He wasn't ready for such a density of mess, give him another year or two down here.

"Pete."

"Yes?"

"What do you say we blow this town for a while? Go someplace where we don't know anybody."

"I was thinking of that very thing myself," said Pete, brightening. "It sounds good, doesn't it?"

"I've about had this place, too, if you want to know it. Frieda—"

"Shit, yes. I know what you mean."

"You know?"

"Hell, yes. The guys at José's are taking bets. You're three to one against."

This place was really ridiculous. You couldn't get mad at it, in a way. Three to one against what, though?

"Where do you think, then?"

Glasser shrugged. "Morocco?"

"O.K. with me."

"Get some of that good grass?"

And what was grass again? Oh, yes, that stuff. Marijuana.

"I never did fix that up for you, did I, man? Here's your chance. The shit grows in the streets down there, man."

Third question: What was all this "man, man" about? Pete squinted at his cigarette: it's like a role, man, a persona. Come on. Pete was himself again, and they spent the next couple of hours making plans for a quick getaway the next day.

Taking bets, pretty funny.

He put some of Frank Waters' canvas over the leak in the roof and moved the bed over to the far wall and climbed in. They were going to start hitching early in the morning—Pete had wanted to take bicycles, but Fred was in no shape for bicycles —so he wanted a good night's sleep.

Funny, people taking bets. Tickled the vanity. Hard to say why.

He could already hear the water gurgling through Waters' lousy canvas. Sharp splashes on the tile floor a few feet away. What a character, that Waters. Every autumn it seemed he dumped all his junk, olive wood and porous canvas and weak plaster, on the new people in town, and nobody saw him again till spring. They said he lived with the gypsies back in the hills. He probably taught them plenty.

Funny, about the bets . . .

There was a new sound, somewhere between a squelch and a tap down by his shins. He bent forward to investigate. The blanket was beginning slowly to soak: another vein had just opened in the roof. Damn it to hell, Fred swung his feet onto the wet floor and began groping for his flashlight. The water looked ominous under the narrow beam. There was no room for his bed between the two lines of drip: the head was already rammed up against the wall so he couldn't push any further in that direction, and the other way led right into the drip. The only alternative was the window side, where the spray was constant but light.

He sat there with his feet on the cold, wet tiles trying to decide what to do. He fingered his amputated beard (loss of nerve there). Well, do something. It was awfully draughty outside the covers. He began to move the bed, which grunted and scraped, over to the window.

He could see now that it was no joke about Frieda. Poor kid. He wished he could help. Losing a baby seemed terrible at this time of night. And Pete talking glibly about miscarrying, as if a miscarriage was nothing; as if it was just another gossip item for the gang at José's.

When you were cold and tired, you saw things as they really were. Everything became suddenly very sad and serious. Even sex became serious. Send Alison some more money, better not think about Alison. That poor kid, though. No really, I mean it. Terrible thing a miscarriage. Terrible, terrible thing, having to go to Germany. Trying to hitchhike in weather like this, what are we, crazy? No and then Mort and the girl, it was just terrible.

He was trying too hard and he knew it. The compassion was

real enough, but fatally thin and unimaginative, and soon he could sense it beginning to run down. He found himself repeating the words, Mort, Marilyn, miscarriage until they didn't seem serious at all. It was like standing in front of a painting and saying "It's beautiful, it's beautiful" until it was nothing at all. He had no real moral ideas any more than real aesthetic ones.

What was actually wrong with these people? Their lives were sloppy, but was that a moral offense? You couldn't prove it by him. Lives in Bloodbury were tidy, was that good? Something a little frightening about a *completely* pointless life. Bloodbury knew that instinctively and pretended there was a point to their lives, but there was no virtue in it. He felt dimly that the people here might be excused if their paintings were just a little bit better. Good painting would justify the human mess; but you couldn't really blame people for painting badly, could you? Still, it was a sort of formula, bad painting or sloppiness but not both, that was *real* morality, boy. He wanted to disapprove of these people without lapsing into intolerance—and this might be the way. He was getting used to the wet and seemed to be dozing off in the ooze, pretty sure he was onto something important, which he could work out later when he felt less sleepy.

3

They started off in gray drizzle, watching for headlights. No regular Spaniard would be up for hours yet, but they might catch a stray truck, or a foreigner. Pete was bunched up in a windbreaker. Fred had on his raincoat and waterproof hat. The conditions were ripe for misery, but they both felt good to be moving, at least trying to move. The early rain was like a blessing. They trudged to the outskirts, past silent white row houses,

then past the chintzy villas with their pale, artificial lawns, out
to the stump of an old alcazar, where they stopped and waited;
watched, to the left, a sluggish lump of light trying to rise behind the sea; listened to the right, for the ghostly rattle of
trucks in the dark.

Very good not to have to think anyway; must be very good for
Pete; just a little action, boy, and your brains got beautifully
scrambled, your nerves were unplugged one by one. Pete was
frowning but serene. Switching off slowly.

A dull gleam edging around the ruined alcazar. Fred stepped
onto the tarmac to make sure he was visible. It looked, from the
way the lights jiggled, like some kind of jeep.

"Hi, Fred, hi, Pete."

The Land Rover stopped and, oh hell, they knew every damn
person in it. Three in the front seat, four on the ledge in back.
Jeff whatzit driving with Linda's knee tangled in the gearshift,
and Heiny thingamy crouching, in his duffle coat, by the window. Couldn't make out the faces in back yet, but you knew
somehow that you were going to recognize them all.

"You haven't got room for us, have you?"

"Sure, we can squeeze in a little fellow like you."

Fred climbed over the tail gate and floundered upon darkness
and legs.

"Fred, you can sit here"—oh no, not her too! He felt the
breathing presence, a hand on his coat; she wanted him to
crunch down next to her and feel the pulse in her hip for a
while. Pete shuffled around behind him, forcing him down.

"All aboard?" shouted Jeff, and started the motor. Fred grazed
off Frieda's lap and landed next to her.

"Hello, Fred," she said, her voice already full of hot treacle.
"How are you, Fred?"

It was dark a while longer and the car bounced and made barking noises; Frieda kept lurching against him and, unwillingly, he lurched back. Smell and touch were sharp as razors in the dark, and he was grotesquely aware of her body. She had for now neither face nor voice, but a fantastic amount of body. Why oh why did she have to be a nut?

"Where are you going?" he shouted, to bring words into it and to spotlight her crazy mind.

"What was that?"

"Where are you going?"

"Gib."

"Oh." He nodded. It got brighter even in the back of the Land Rover, and soon he could see her a little and her presence subsided. She wasn't just Woman but Frieda, the all-American Nut. What was this fascination he had for neurotic women, anyway?

"We're going to Morocco," he yelled.

"Oh. That's very sudden, isn't it?"

"Yes, just last night."

"It sounds great."

Pete's slowly emerging features had lost their early morning sparkle; he looked haunted, nonchalant, anxious, changing with every bounce. Fred made a face at him—we had to run into this gang, huh—but Pete didn't catch it. Better keep talking so as not to feel the hip.

"You just going to Gib for the day?" She didn't answer right off, but looked at her nails: it sounds great about Morocco. I've never been there, you know. I don't suppose you could . . . no, of course not. She was sort of a whiz at extrasensory communication.

"Yes, just for the morning," she said, "just for some shopping."

Fred was relieved to get out at La Linea. Hobbling out of another trap.

"Christ, that dame," said Pete. Which was surprising because he hadn't seemed to notice her.

They hitched another ride with a chatty Englishman to Algeciras and got there in time for the Tangier ferry.

"Christ," said Pete, when they got on deck, "we made it."

"I wish you wouldn't keep saying that," said Fred on impulse.

"Why not?"

"I don't know."

"You religious or something?"

"No."

"Well, what the hell."

"I can't explain it."

Pete seemed embarrassed at having attention called to it. It wasn't decent to bring up things like that. He stared down over the rail at the wedge of froth the ship was making.

"It's just a reflex from my puritan upbringing, I guess. It doesn't mean anything."

Pete said, "O.K., let it go."

"I guess I have this conventional streak.

"Let it go, for Christ's sake."

They didn't talk again for half an hour but watched Spain shrink, and then up to the other end to watch Africa expand. Fred expected to see a lot of mosques and things, but there wasn't much. Tangier was a modern type port, like, oh, Liverpool or somewhere. He felt stupid about bringing up the swearing; if he could have said: "Yes, I'm religious," it would have been something. Pete would have honored that; it wasn't hip to sneer at religion, just punk.

These empty, conventional reflexes—Alison's very own phrase

about it. She had some friends who used to say "Jesus" and "Christ" all the time; and one evening he had brought it up afterwards, and she said, "What's Christ to you?" and of course he couldn't say. The funny thing was that she seemed as uncomfortable as Pete; as if it was *Fred* that had done the indecent thing in bringing it up . . .

"I am sort of religious," he said to Pete as the ship started to sidle in.

"Is that so?"

"Yes, I am."

Fred felt like the comedian who is still trying to explain himself after his wife has slammed the door and left the house. Pete wasn't interested, and Fred could think of nothing to add to his embryo statement of faith.

"Well, this is it, man," said Pete suddenly. "The home of fine grass." He patted Fred on the shoulder. "Let's go, man."

He took the gangplank at a fast slouch. Fred half expected to find Frieda waiting on the quay—nothing like that, of course, just the usual Hitchcock crowd: swarthy men in robes, or sharp suits, looking sinister as hell. They bore in with their shoe-shining equipment and outrageous suggestions, but Pete proved quite sharp at brushing them off, and once you got a few yards inland, they thinned out.

"I got a contact," Pete said, "guy knows where to get the good grass. None of this cheap shit, if you'll pardon the expression."

"I don't mind," Fred said quickly. "I'm no prude."

"I thought it might be against your religion."

They started looking for the Arab quarter. It was still spitting rain, out of an unbroken gray cloud, and the Moslems had their hoods up. Fred was bored to discover that he felt good again. There were postcard smells and sights even in the square outside the Arab quarter; one specially persistent smell that seemed to sum up the whole place, a *totally* foreign smell. He felt someone nuzzling his sleeve—gad these people were persistent—but it was only a donkey wanting to get by.

"Hey, Pete, that was a donkey"; he was happy, excited. It waddled past them, under wide saddle bags, and they followed it through the gates into the Medina.

The smells thickened and crowded into your nose. Every stall had its own special flavor—a riot of herbs and mustardy powders, plus the owner, plus the donkey droppings in front. Fred and Pete were hustled over the cobblestones by implacable Arabs; in no time Fred was dislocated, from being plunged down one alley too many. The tide of life spumed and beat on their backsides; and if you stepped out of it for a minute, the merchants were on you in a flash. Still, jolly exciting, as the Anglo-Spaniards would say.

"I think it's around here someplace," said Pete.

Surprisingly, pleasantly, they came into a more open place. It was studded with cafés, and in each, people with beards and slacks, and American Negroes—they were back in the Village, safe and sound.

Pete picked a café and Fred ordered a beer. The waiter shook his head and Pete said, "No alcohol, what do you think?" So they had some mint tea, really the only choice, and started looking around for Pete's contact.

"He's a little guy with a name like Paracelsus. Jeff stayed with him."

"Where's he from?"

"I don't know. He's just a little guy."

It became clear, as they ordered the second glass of tea, that Pete would have to make inquiries. He began fiddling with the beard, which was his way of saying, you do it. But Fred didn't feel much like it either. The smells and the taste of tea were beginning to get on his nerves. Usual thing: at first he had thought, hot dog, I'm responding spontaneously; and the moment after he thought it, the glass broke and he turned to salt.

"I'll ask those people in a minute," Pete said, "those people over there." Three lounging Americans with friendly, decomposing faces. "They'd know him, I bet."

They drank their mint tea, and Pete asked if Fred wanted a third round. Fred said no. Pete pulled his beard down to a point, then scattered it again, then to a fierce point—

"O.K., I'll go ask," said Fred.

Pete dropped the beard and said carelessly, "You want to ask? Or you want me to?"

You could only stand so much, watching someone else playing with his beard. Fred went over and tried to get the Americans' attention. "Excuse me, fellows." They heard him, you could tell that, but the response took thousands of years. Dinosaurs came and went, and man began fashioning crude implements. They looked at him first—let's get that settled: there's somebody there. Now, then. What was the next bit? Man out there wants to make contact. You wanna try, Harry? Don't look at me, you guys, I talked to somebody last week.

"Excuse me, fellows."

One of them sort of blinked, so Fred seized his attention, trapped it in his handkerchief.

"You know a guy with a name like Paracelsus? . . . I know it sounds crazy . . . but that's the name we were given . . . so, anyway."

The dots were because they looked so vacant. It certainly was a goofy name, and Fred felt he ought to apologize for wasting their time with it.

"That's him over there," one of them said at last, not pointing but inclining his head slightly.

"The little guy sitting by himself?"

Very slight incline of the head.

"Thanks."

"O.K., man." The fellow made a limp gesture, as if replacing the "Please don't disturb" sign, and Fred went back to Pete with the hard-won information.

4

Paracelsus was an anthology of a man. His skin was slightly yellow but he didn't seem to be Oriental. His accent was hard to decipher; it could have been central European with a Brooklyn overlay—but then, where did he get the English *a*'s? Or the Swedish *j*'s? Fred had heard some crazy speech in the south of Spain, but never such a breathtaking amalgam as this baby's.

"I'm Pete Glasser. A cat named Jeff Flood told me to look you up. This is my friend."

Paracelsus was slow-speaking too, but alert and quick in the face, so that you didn't feel it was quite so hopeless.

"Friend got a name?" he said.

"I'm sorry, Fred Cope," Pete said nervously.

Paracelsus nodded. "Don't be sorry, man. Don't ever be sorry."

"You remember the cat I'm referring to? Jeff? He shared your pad for a while, he said."

"Yeah, I remember the cat."

"And another cat . . ." Fred had never heard Pete talk about cats before; he did it awkwardly, but maybe Fred was just receiv-

ing it awkwardly. Fred was afraid his buddy might be making
a fool of himself; but Paracelsus seemed to find him authentic
enough and answered in kind:

"Yeah, and a chick called Linda."

"That's right, that was the chick."

They had some more of that dreadful tea. Fred began to
wonder if Glasser was ever going to get round to the marijuana.
It was beginning to get dark, and still Pete was circling, digging up mutual cats and chicks.

"You know Gregory Corso?" asked Paracelsus.

"Not really," said Pete.

"He was here," said Paracelsus. "You know Ginsberg? You
know Bowles?"

"I got a friend knows Ginsberg."

Poor old Pete, he's really at sea, thought Fred. He doesn't
know Ginsberg, for God's sake. Then he realized that Paracelsus
was looking suspiciously at *him*.

"Your friend don't talk much."

Pete looked over, hopefully: say something, man. The cat
named Cope yawned and said,

"It's been a goddamn long day."

"You want some more tea, man? Wake you up?"

"Nah. I already had four glasses and it didn't help worth a
goddamn." He couldn't drum up any other slang; and he certainly couldn't say anything like "pad" with a straight face.
(He could think it, but he couldn't say it.)

Then he got an idea, "Hey, Pete, ask about the, you know,
grass."

Pete looked embarrassed and Paracelsus uncomprehending.

"Yeah, well, we were wondering—Jeff said, you could fix us up
with, you know . . ."

Paracelsus looked around and then squinted at Fred.

"Jeff said, *you* know, the real good stuff, the best. What do you say?"

Still squinting at Fred, "Is this guy O.K.?"

"Yeah, sure, he's my friend."

"He likes the stuff?"

"Sure he does."

Fred looked depraved, examined his cigarette, did a little squinting himself. Felt like an Intellectual For Eisenhower.

"O.K.," said Paracelsus. And then they sat there for another twenty minutes or so, not referring to it again.

"You know a cat named Mailer?"

"I saw him once at a patry. He's quite a cat."

"So I hear."

At last, casually, Paracelsus stood up and began to move away.

"Are we going to get the stuff now?" whispered Fred.

Pete looked at him in wondering dismay and then scooted off to catch up with his contact. Fred followed along, feeling huge again: the spirit of Wall Street, in his raincoat and hat, and with his small suitcase. (Pete had the appropriate rucksack.)

The alleys were dark now, and the tempi were different. People scurried like rats in and out of the smells or drifted along the walls, staring with glistening eyes. They weren't so picturesque now, but alien, sneering at the big man in his all-American raincoat; Fred began nervously to hate them; then saw that this was unfair, and lapsed into nonthink and vague discomfort.

Their guide didn't say "This is it," but just glided in, past a row of sleepy Arabs. It was a minute café with two thin tables inside, both smothered in customers. Two, three long-stemmed pipes were going in slow circulation, and in a minute Fred was sucking on one, tasting the thing he had smelled everywhere, the definitive Tangier smell. That was it, of course.

Paracelsus talked to the proprietor in Arab, which meant more mint tea. (The café didn't sell marijauna, only tea.) Pete was watching greedily while Fred smoked, and licking the top of his beard.

"You pull it in real deep, man, right down to the bottom of your lungs."

Fred was afraid he wasn't doing it right. Paracelsus was watching him again. Which way was out, which way was in? He handed the pipe quickly to Pete who grabbed it and took a deep grinding puff, and looked well and truly sandbagged a moment later.

"Good stuff," he said, "good Kif."

"Yeah," said Fred, who hadn't felt a thing yet. "Very good stuff."

Paracelsus took his turn, and seemed a bit more genial after it.

"Where you cats going from here? Any place good?"

"We didn't decide yet," said Pete. "Last time I was over, I never got out of Tangier. I went into, you know, orbit for three, four days."

"Where's it good?" asked Fred.

"What do you want, man? The grass grows good in like Marakesh."

"Yeah?" said Pete. "What about like Fez? I hear that's O.K."

"Yeah, well you get good grass there too, but not the same kind of grass you get in Marakesh, you know what I mean."

"Rabat? Casablanca?"

"Yeah, well if you know where to go. But I really recommend Marakesh. The stuff grows in the goddamn streets."

Fred had the pipe again, and again had the feeling he wasn't doing it right. It was supposed to go just like regular smoking, but nothing was happening yet. He puffed and passed. What else besides grass, he wanted to ask. Is Fez like a pretty town? But he didn't want to act suspicious, so he let it go.

Pete emptied the pipe with a couple of gasps and Paracelsus refilled it for him.

"Can we pay you for this?" asked Fred.

"Please, man." Paracelsus shook his head.

"Are you sure?"

"*Please*, man."

The Arabs on the other side of the table were glassy-eyed and shrunken, folding gently inwards. Peter was looking glassy-eyed too, but a little wild; he had managed somehow to get his hair mussed, a zany tussock stood up in the back.

"Take it easy, man," said Paracelsus, "you'll be here a few days. Don't have to smoke it all this evening."

Pete stared as if he hadn't understood.

There was no point talking to him after that, so Paracelsus went around him to Fred.

"I'll give you some addresses in Kesh where you can get the stuff."

"Thanks."

"You feeling it yet?"

"Yeah," said Fred, "just beginning to." Hoping to anyway.

"Your friend isn't used to it, huh? That's no way to smoke shit, you know."

"He's got things on his mind."

"Yeah, well that's no way to smoke, man. Ever drink three martinis on the trot? Yeah, well, that's it. Booze? Not me, not this cat. I like to sit here with my pipe and watch the people go by. You dig that? Right out there in the street. That's how I like to do it."

Fred was afraid he was losing Paracelsus too. Everyone was sinking into the group coma, leaving Fred by himself on the bank. Why wasn't the stuff getting to him?

"Man, like the lights go on, and the cars come and go. I *like* that, yeah, sure. But I'll tell you this. If I could take a bagful of real good shit to Paris and find me a chick, *phhht* boy, Paris, that's the town. You like this stuff? You feeling it yet?"

"Yeah," said Fred, trying half consciously to sound as goofy as his friends, "yeah, I dig it."

"Sit here with my pipe, and watch 'em come and go. You digging me at all? What more you need? But I'll tell you this— you know I tried injecting the stuff in oranges, take a bag of oranges to Paris, but it didn't work out, tell you about it sometime. If I could just get some up to Paris, oh man, you know what I could get for it?"

"What you get, man?" asked Fred.

"And another thing I forgot to mention. Got this chick in Copenhagen, man, she's really stacked. I mean, you know, money as well. And she writes me every day begging me to come on up. One time she even sent me the fare."

"Why didn't you go?"

Paracelsus shrugged and looked uncertain.

"Did I tell you about this other chick in Berlin? She writes me all the time 'dear George,' that's my name, she writes me—listen, living off some rich chick, that's what we're here for. That's what we're here below for. You digging this stuff the least little bit?"

His accent was hard to follow, and Fred missed a good deal

of what he said after that. Pete had gone to sleep with his head on the table, and the pipe kept going round over his head. Fred was hungry and tired, but he couldn't very well leave without Pete.

George Paracelsus leaned over Glasser and poked Fred with the pipe stem.

"You know my philosophy jumble jumble? I don't ask nothing of no cat. Just leave me alone with my pipe and I'll do O.K. You dig me? I mean in general? I don't own *nothing*. That's one thing. Look at those crazy cars, will you," he chuckled, "coming and going, coming and going."

"Hey, man," said Fred, "they got food in this pad?" Was that right?

"Whawhazat? You know they cut this stuff with tobacco. The Arabs actually prefer it that way . . ."

Fred sank back among the hairy robes of the Arabs. He was missing all the fun. Just his luck to be immune to grass. At the same time the taste was making him a little bit nauseous. It was so damn foreign—not European foreign, but foreign foreign. He couldn't help it, he wished he was to hell back in Spain. Marijuana was a disgusting habit, not convivial like booze, but keep-off-the-grass private: it locked you up in your own head and threw away the key. Besides which, it tasted awful.

"You better take it easy, you don't look too good," said George.

"Feel O.K., feel like roses. Let me out of here please. Excuse me, sir. Will you for God's sake excuse me?"

The Arab next to him didn't understand. He looked so tired and fuzzy. But Fred got over his woolly knees somehow and out in the street, where the crazy lights were on and the cars came and went and it was like flying under water and lo, Vesuvius, the great excuse me, earth-mother, don't like this place one bit, it isn't *Christian.* Whoops.

5

They went to a café which had no stock in hand but two old bottles of orange squash stranded behind a wooden counter. The owner sent out for coffee and food, and Paracelsus explained how the place had been virtually wiped out by post-independence prohibition and was getting by now on one lung. Boy came back with three cups of muddy coffee and a big gray chunk of pastry. Pete, very white and frail, managed to say:

"I really dig Morocco, you know? After Spain, especially. The people here are awfully friendly."

Fred wondered where he had seen all this. Must have dreamed it.

Paracelsus said, "Yeah, well, Spain's no good for me. The chicks are like ice up there."

"How are the Moroccan chicks, then?"

"You want to see a belly dance tonight? It'll cost you, man, but it'll give you the picture."

"Maybe tomorrow night, huh? We're a little tired right now." Only post-Hemingway pride kept Pete from sliding into unconsciousness then and there.

The pastry had no taste at all, which was a switch. Fred had already eaten a square meter of it, and he still thought Morocco was just lousy. Everything tasted except the food.

Paracelsus said, "You name it and I'll take you to it. You dig?"

"Thanks," said Pete.

Fred nodded.

"So what do you want?" he asked Fred.

"I don't know, what is there?"

"Oh, look now, come *on*. What do you want to see?"

"Come on, man," echoed Pete, "say what you want."

"I don't *know* what I want." Fred gestured helplessly. How in hell had this suddenly happened? What looking glass had he stepped through this time?

"I'm getting out of here," said George angrily, "if that's the way it is."

"Where you going?" asked Pete.

"Don't fuss me. Just going to *go*." George sat for a moment chewing his lip and staring at the orange squash. Then he changed his mind.

"It's a good life I got down here. I got it licked, you know that? Get up late, grab a quick pipe to settle my mind, get the rhythm going, cruise around, see my friends—I got a pad for three francs a week, you know that?"

"Geez," said Pete.

"How much is that?" asked Fred.

"About sixty cents."

"Geez."

"So you don't want to do anything, huh?" George Paracelsus wheeled on Fred again.

"What *kind* of thing?"

"*Anything*, for God's sake."

Fred just gave up. Why didn't he ask Pete? "Why—"

"Nothing can bug you when you got your pipe. Right?"

"Right," said Pete.

"I had a good job back home, wife, children, you know the bit. Or at least, I think I had. You know how that is, a man gets confused." He smiled; was he joking or what? "Anyway, I said one day 'The hell with this, jazzbo, I'm getting out.' Right?"

"Right!"

"And you know, with a pipe, you've got it all. You've got the kind of past you want, chicks everywhere, adventure—I'll tell you about it sometime—and the kind of future you desire. And the overhead is really laughable."

"Great," murmured Pete.

"And I'm at peace with every man. I don't want to start no war. You give all those politicians pipes and there wouldn't be no wars."

"It sounds like a great idea. Doesn't it, Fred?" Pete glowed.

"Yeah. Look, I'm getting sleepy. Let's go find that hotel."

Paracelsus knew of two hotels near at hand, a cheap one for twenty cents a night and an expensive one at sixty. Fred insisted on the sixty-cent one. He waited to do the colorful thing, but he was tired and wanted a good bed too; do the colorful thing tomorrow, maybe.

"See you cats around midday, then," said Paracelsus after steering them to their hotel in the middle of the Arab city. He dwindled off down the alley.

It was still raining and Fred's feet were wet. The hotel looked pretty crumby; the twenty-cent one must be a pip, boy. Their room was up four flights and was brutally cold. There was one thin blanket to each bed and they couldn't find anyone to give them another. The people in the next apartment were chanting and playing the flute. Fred hated that chant already; it was stupid, insolent, whining, like someone trying to sell you something: a rug with a filthy design. He was sick of being tolerant, too tired and edgy to take the mature view.

"What a wonderful character," said Glasser, while Fred was trying to shut the window. "I'm really glad we came, you know?"

"Who? Who's a character?"

"Paracelsus. And a nice guy too, I thought."

"Window's stuck. It's set all crooked."

"Two complete strangers, and he offers to do anything we like. I'm afraid you hurt his feelings about that, you should have said *something*."

What am I a nice guy for, thought Fred, what's in it for me? He bet there was steam coming out of his head, that was what was clouding up the window.

"I thought he was just an average kind of bum," he said. "That kind of thing can be done much better. Look at this jerky window, will you?"

"Cope, what are you saying? This guy's completely natural— how often do you see that?"

"Too damn often."

"He's a philosopher, with a wonderful way of life. God, Fred, I thought you'd be the first to see that. The guy is truly simple, like a saint or something."

"Yeah, well, I guess I missed the point there. He seemed just plain retarded to me. That stuff about giving the politicians pot, and there wouldn't be any wars—"

"Well, it's true."

"That was just the kind of thing my grandmother used to say. 'If that Hitler just had a nice hobby or something—' " He shut the window with a tremulous bang.

"It isn't the same thing at all. It isn't the words a man uses, it's his feeling for life. Paracelsus has a wonderful feeling for life." Pete stood by his bed, shivering defiantly in his undershirt. "If you're not onto his wave length, I'm sorry for you."

Pete went to bed in grumpy silence, still looking sick from the pot. Fred was pretty sure Pete was wrong; but if words didn't matter, it was going to be hard to prove it.

"Look, I've got nothing against the guy, but stupidity is stupidity. He's smoked his brains out, that's what it adds up to."

"I hate to say this, Fred, but Americans have forgotten how to live, and you seem to be an American in that respect."

A hell of a thing to say. Fred almost snapped out "You're an American too," but checked himself; the insult would hurt Pete more than it had hurt him. And Pete looked sad enough without that.

"And another thing," Fred remarked instead, "I'm not all that crazy about marijuana."

"It's a great experience. Didn't you get high, man?"

"What do you say we forget Tangier and hit out for Fez in the morning?"

"What do you mean, and hurt George's feelings?"

"George won't remember a thing. George is too goddamn stupid . . ."

Pete got up on his elbow. "Christ, Cope, don't you know a real human being when you see one? Of course he'll remember. And of course he'll be hurt."

Fred turned out the light and got into bed in his pajamas, undershirt, sweater and raincoat. That dreadful chant was still coming through the window along with the endless rain. The room was still cold and beginning to get stuffy as well.

"I don't want to see the little bastard again. I'm sorry, Pete, I don't like him, I don't like what he stands for. Just because he's incoherent, you think he's smart. Just because . . ."

Pete was nothing but a wretched snort in the dark, "Christ, Fred."

"Tell me again why he's so good, then."

"You must be hopeless, Cope. What are you, insensitive, or what?"

"Just tell me, that's all. We meet a guy has all the earmarks of being an idiot, a bore, and a fake—just tell me where I made my mistake."

"Let it go, for Christ's sake." Pete's voice was thin, angry, tired. "I can't put it in words and you don't seem to know any other language. Let's just forget it."

The neighbors chanted and blew their flutes until morning.

The next day there was nothing much they could do about the strain. They breakfasted on monosyllables.

"Shit that rain."

"Shit that rain is right."

They sat under an awning watching the stuff pizzle down interminably. Glasser looked as if he'd lost his friend. Didn't he know I was like that, thought Fred. Alison said it stuck out a mile. No use saying, sorry about last night; one would have to say, sorry about my whole life.

Pete was embarrassed to bring it up, but after breakfast they had to decide what to do next. So he said, "Christ, Fred, did you mean that stuff last night, or was it the pot talking?"

"Look, Pete—just take this one point. You say he's so generous, showing us around. I question that right there—it seems to me that anyone would do as much."

Pete writhed. "O.K., forget it," he said.

"Well, that's just one point."

"So what do you want to do? Go on to Fez or what?"

"No, we'll see your friend—I don't mind."

"Christ, Cope, you're just incredible."

What have I done this time—Fred just didn't see it. It wasn't as if Paracelsus was an artist or something. Glasser, slumped way down in his wickerwork chair, looked like the only man left after a terrible accident.

"It's not that important," said Fred, "is it?"

Pete grunted and moved down in the chair. The waiter took the cups away.

"What do we do then?" asked Fred.

Pete shrugged.

They sat there for an hour and a bit more watching the Moslems cruise by in their soggy robes. Fred's behind took up too much of the chair: which annoyed him. What was Glasser being so petulant about? What was this guy, a woman or something? To have moods like that.

Pete's face was all screwed up. He probably wanted Fred's friendship more than anything in the world. But a man had to live by his code.

Fred was willing to admit he might have made a mistake and was more than willing to talk about it. But this damn coy business—"If you don't know, I can't tell you, you, you thing"— well, he took that from his wife, but not from this little punk. O.K. to try to make yourself sensitive for a woman, but not—

A great weltering grossness that both pleased and appalled him: up off your knees, Cope. Be yourself, at least.

He squeezed out of the chair and said, "O.K., see you," and went back to the hotel to collect his things.

6

Fred didn't go on to Fez, there didn't seem much point. Morocco tasted of mint tea and marijuana; it would never smell right if he lived there a hundred years. He could sense the chil-

dren giggling inaudibly just behind him as he made his way out
of the Arab quarter.

He was a Westerner, no a European, no a Christian—some-
thing different anyway. Civilization stood for something, by
George. Hadn't we fought these people for hundreds of years?
Damn right we had. The Crusades and stuff were fought mainly
because these people didn't drink, because they were *different*.
Something in that.

Unfortunately phrased, though. He didn't want to sound
prejudiced.

"I've been living with the damn wogs for a year now," said
the Englishman a few minutes later, standing next to him
against the ferry rail; Fred didn't want to sound like that, for instance.

Kidding aside, what Fred meant was, it was all right to be
different, diversity was grand, but when a man like Glasser actually prefers a Moslem society to a Christian one, it could only
be affectation, couldn't it?

"It's good to breathe clean air and talk to a fellow human
again," said the Englishman, unconsciously satirizing and dis-
torting Fred's thoughts.

Cope moved off along the deck, and the man followed him
with worried eyes.

"I was in Kenya before that," he said, "and the damn niggers
booted me out of there without much ceremony. I can't afford
to live in England, and I can't take the wogs." You *do* understand, he said mutely, a small withered man with only an echo
of dead hatred in his voice.

"I guess so," said Fred, losing his own train of thought again.

"The British Government let us down utterly, you know. In

the end, my wife had to go to bed with a gun under her pillow. Women shouldn't be asked to do that, should they?"

"I don't know what the issues were," said Fred, "But I agree with you, about, er, women."

"The *issues?* Oh, the *issues* were always clear enough. It's a question of whether we were going to allow a lot of damn niggers . . ." but it still wasn't real hatred. Those were just the words one used.

"Adored our houseboy, of course . . . just not ready for it, of course . . . Bible quite unequivocal on the point."

On the windy deck, the man's voice didn't carry very far and Fred had to stoop to catch it, although he didn't really want it. Man was saying something about an iniquitous act passed and carried out to sea which gave the niggers carte blanche with the ship's motors led by a few demagogues very hard to follow.

All Fred had ever meant was, he really liked Spain, that was his home now. No need to knock Morocco, but civilizations *did* stand for something, not just loving the houseboy of course.

"And finally," said the man, "They *did* burn the house down after all, and my wife was very nearly scorched alive. She was ill at the time, and tried to ring for the houseboy, but for some reason Bwando couldn't come. I think the bell had been disconnected."

Shouldn't make any difference, of course: but God, how a thing like that blurred your judgment.

"How is she now?"

"She died shortly after we got to Morocco. The general effects, you know. And lordy, what a time I had trying to get her a decent Christian burial. We were in a small village with nothing but wogs, who didn't speak a word of English—really a comedy of errors."

It must have been horribly painful for him, but he managed to talk about it in the same detached, slightly unreal way that he talked about the niggers; in a life that had gone so bewilderingly wrong, it was obviously best to keep *every*thing unreal.

"I find it hard to grasp general principles when there's something personal involved," said Fred.

"Oh, there's no difficulty about the principles. It was the signing of that iniquitous Act . . ."

Man plunged back into his shrubbery of argument, documenting it so exhaustively that he had barely got to 1949 by the time the ferry landed. Fred tried to think what it would be like to find yourself, say, sixty-five, with no bottom to your life, no meaning; he couldn't help comparing it with Paracelsus, who had carefully divested his life of meaning while he was still young, to avoid unpleasantness later. (And then there was Fred Cope, who didn't know *what* the hell he was doing.)

"What are your plans now, Mr.—?" he asked the Englishman.

"Mr. Paterson. Bob Paterson. I thought I'd look for something in the south of Spain. I gather I can still afford the south of Spain. And at least it's run by white men, eh?"

"Yes."

"Dagoes, anyway. I don't care if I never see another nigger."

Wonder why he assumes I won't object? Wonder why I *don't* object? Well, the wife lying in bed, tugging on the bell, waiting for the beloved houseboy downstairs; houseboy probably fiddling with his matchbox.

They got off the ferry together and Mr. Paterson asked Fred if he had any ideas about lodgings. In spite of all he'd been through, or maybe because of it, he looked quite frightened to be in a new place, and dependent. Pretty pathetic for a racist, Fred thought sternly, and resisted a temptation to take the old fellow home with him. He did, however, find him a fifty cent pension with a potted palm in the lobby.

Kill the old fascist with kindness. Perhaps he should have helped the man even more and shouldn't have been put off by his childish opinions. Anyway, you meet so many people as you travel, and they impinge slightly and are gone again, that Mr. Paterson soon became diaphanous and then mythical, and finally just something to bring up when people talked about Kenya: something to show that things weren't as simple down there as they, the people in question, thought.

He got a lift this time with an American couple that lived only two streets away from his own apartment; not really a wild coincidence in that part of the world. He had never met them before, although he had heard of them all right: Baines, they were called, and they said they didn't have much in common with the people he knew because they didn't write or paint, or even pretend to write or paint.

Harry Baines was a businessman, representing an ever-ramifying soft drink company; Marion was a glossy credit to him. They drove a plush Buick and Fred felt a certain guilty pleasure in being in a car that fitted him properly; guiltier pleasure in finding ease with the kind of people he was used to.

"You an artist?" asked Harry. "Did you say you were called Fred?"

"Well, sort of. Yes, Fred, that's right."

"Another one," said Marion.

"So where's your beard? Where's your uniform, son?"

"He looks awfully clean. Are you *sure* you're an artist?"

No mistaking Baines, anyway. He was pale and chubby from

desk work and from thinking pale and chubby. He had those thin strands of anonymous hair—who the hell was he to make fun of artists? His wife was bright and standard as a carnival doll. You could see them in their paper hats at any captain's party. Fine pair to talk about beards and uniforms. Still.

"It's nice to be in a big car again," he said.

"Yeah, well, we don't go for these orange crates."

Fred already had a funny feeling about the Baineses. He liked them, rather in the way he liked Ernie Peabody, and yet he felt a marginal scorn much nastier than anything he'd felt for Ernie. The scorn came from Glasser, and the pseudo Alison in his head. Right now he was imagining Baines with a big button called "Ed" and a squirting posie. "Cope, you old son of a bitch." Squish, ha ha. And yet he liked them.

"Were you always an artist, Fred?"

"No, I was in insurance."

"See, I knew he was one of us."

"Who were you with? . . . I had a friend with that outfit . . . well for petesake . . ." He despised them and yet felt comfortable with them. He seemed to be getting slowly stranded between the two cultures. For now, he sank back in plastic surrender.

Another light impingement, quickly forgotten. They said, you must come and see us, and left him at his door. The sun came out, making it a bright, glossy evening. The clean white houses looked fine and well, clean. This was his civilization, good to know that anyway.

You think a thousand things in a day, all of them contradictory and you're lucky to have one thing left at the end; but he had that. His mind fell solemn as a *Life* editorial. This was his culture, boy: the Christian, all right, Judeo-Christian, West.

He strolled along to the grocer's to get some food for supper, and of course he had to order the whole thing in English and he thought, You're a jackass, Cope: let that be your thought for the day and let's get the hell home and to bed before you have another one.

("Your culture"—shit, Cope, you're really rich. Glasser's melancholy voice had the last word after all.)

7

The rest of the winter came in two-week blocks of bright-and-windy, and wet-and-windy. (It was a weathery kind of place.) On bright days the central café was filled with winter faces: people down from Berlin for Christmas; gaunt English girls in slack leotards; investors who talked about opening bowling alleys ("We could convert it to a supermarket during the day"). With Fitzwilliam down for Eton, the way was clear for the divorce—that mob was on hand too; start a little business, buy up all the houses, yakety, yak. Fred could hear them now on every side, crass and earnest, with big, red mouths and sunglasses motionless on chalky cheeks. Then the rain would come for two weeks and with the next sun you would get a whole crop of fresh stale faces and plans.

With Glasser still in Morocco, Fred had no wedge into the permanent arts group. There was nothing to prevent him sitting at their table, but no encouragement either. They greeted him with nods as though they had forgotten his name, and never asked him what he'd been doing. He bet *real* artists weren't as rude as that.

On the other hand, if he sat by himself, he got Frieda or the newly discovered Baineses. Frieda didn't lean on him so hard out of doors. Her musk was diffused in the open air and she didn't put her chest on his elbow so much. All the same, her presence fretted him and he had to be thankful whenever the Baineses got to him first.

Marion Baines played a lot of bridge and tennis, and as a way of getting clear of Frieda and the café, Fred began to accept invitations to play with her. It meant visiting a whole new lot of houses up the hill, with picture windows and three-level living rooms, a class he had hardly been aware of; playing bridge all morning and tennis all afternoon, or vice versa, and then scooting along the coast to Torremolinos to dance the twist all night.

His old passion for big spiffy hotels came bursting back and he underwent a mild surge of vitality, and a tendency to shout in the lobbies. The sporting set also went to bars where you paid American prices; and this fellow called Jack Stagmeyer did feats of strength, and one Perry Mulloy tried to lift people over his head, and Marion said, "It's all relative, the whole thing is relative." The expensive barmen simpered warily and said their tame English phrases: "Cheers," "Tank you very moch," "Bloddy good show, yes?"

The tennis kept them fit, cleaning out the hangovers and raising a fresh thirst. It made them consistently tanned and bouncy. It made Tony Wilkins want to wrestle everyone in the bar and Robert Frith to do handstands, and everyone to shout.

Fred knew who they were—they were the lost and damned. At last he had found them. They ran with the bulls at Pamplona and jumped into the Ritz fountain. Inside, they were bitter and empty. The pain of the old wounds was pretty constant. They gave themselves ten good years, and then poof! Have another drink, old man.

(God, how Alison hated that kind of patter. Wit-substitute,

she called it.) Anyway, they remembered his name and seemed to like him. He wrestled with Tony Wilkins and frolicked with Perry Mulloy. He sang "Ol' Man River." He got rid of a lot of pent-up energy talking into the general roar.

There was a vacuum in the group into which he was halfway sucked. Ed Baines worked all day and didn't go out at night. He was as hearty as anybody, but it seemed to be based on something different. On Sundays he played ruthless bridge, and made endless gags to cover the ruthlessness. Everyone else felt like death on Sundays, so it was no joke tangling with Baines at bridge.

Otherwise, Ed wasn't very visible. He took a lot of trips to Seville and Madrid—"firming up deals" as his wife satirically put it. He was sort of a local phenomenon, the only man in town who actually worked, and people made a lot of jokes about it, which seemed to please him rather frantically.

It left Marion without a natural partner, so Fred inevitably hung on to the part. There was no sexual possibility here: she was noisy and flirtatious and talked conventional dirty after midnight, but there was no possibliity. Hard to explain why if you didn't know her.

His orbit swung out wider. He spent less time between his moldy apartment and the beach. During the wet cycles, one of the gang always came and picked him up in a Volkswagen and whisked him on up the hill. On sunny days, he found them at the café, planning the day's sport from there. He sometimes waved to Frieda at the artists' table, and received slight waves back of unease. She seemed to have taken up with a young colored boy, which should have let Fred neatly off the hook; but she looked so wistful and the colored boy jarred him too; she shouldn't be with a colored boy. No, why not? The jet-set girls were a lot better-looking than Frieda, but he supposed he had certain proprietarial feelings about her still.

Christmas he spent with the Baineses, and Washington's birthday he spent with the Baineses. The time in between had been killed by a thousand shuffles and feats of strength. After the initial burst of friendliness, you didn't get an inch closer to the Baineses, or a foot further from them either. Fred was inclined to be an affectionate drunk who said be my brother: but not to the Baineses, you just couldn't to the Baineses. Marion flirted incessantly, but like a robot; real intimacy bounced off her harder than it landed. And Ed was the equivalent in male buddies. Always happy to see you, but let's not push it.

At Christmas lunch, Fred did try to push it a little. He talked about his wife and his muddled life. He wanted her that day, for a change, and thought the Baineses would understand, at least enough to be tactful.

Marion was shining with curiosity. "You mean you don't even know where she is?"

"That's right. I know it sounds crazy."

"Have you tried the police?"

"No."

"Have you written to her parents?"

"No."

Ed Baines said, "I don't understand." He looked grumpy about it, and Fred thought, I'd better drop it, in a moment, after I've explained myself.

"It's hard to explain, I know. But the thing is this: Alison left me because I bored her. That's what she said, 'You bore me.' So, if she felt that way, what good would it do if I found her again? I'd only start boring her all over, wouldn't I?"

It hurt to admit those things. It was the kind of confession

that pleads for a gentle response. But Baines looked just furious:
"What do you mean, bore her? I don't get it."

"*You* know, *bore* her. I'm very dull, basically dull. I know just what she means."

"I'm glad somebody does. It's beyond me."

Marion had gone quite blank too. It wasn't sensational or sexy after all. So there was nothing in it for her.

"Carmelita—*terminado con los platos,*" she called to the kitchen. "Shall we have coffee here or on the terrace?"

"It's cold on the terrace," said Baines.

"I'm sorry I brought it up," said Fred. "It's no business of yours."

"That's all right." Marion was bored numb. "It's good to talk things over with a friend. You don't want to bottle it up. Carmelita, *tenemos el, la, café en el* whatstheword, *fuera?*"

"*Sí,* señora."

They went out through the plateglass door. Fred felt his confidence had been abused. It did hurt to admit that you bored your wife. More than he had expected. Couldn't they at least have kept silent?

They looked peeved too, as if Fred had ruined the meal.

"I said I didn't want coffee on the terrace," said Baines. "I said it was cold."

"Oh, did you?"

"Never mind." He had a natural pout, so you couldn't go by that. "It's colder than hell out here, but never mind," he said.

They sat in frosty sunlight. Baines looked puffier than ever, slumped in his canvas chair.

"I expect your wife would find *us* very boring," he said at last.

That brought the festering thing out on the table. Fred was nonplussed for a moment. The words "I expect she would" held pride of place in his mouth, and wouldn't allow any others to pass. But under Baines's baleful eye he did manage. "No, no, it was just a personal thing."

Baines relaxed a little. Fred felt as if he'd just removed a tiny growth from his host's brain. The subject was changed to something grossly trivial, the relationship was restabilized and Fred took Alison back to the privacy of his head. Which really suited her better.

The wrestling and handstands continued right over Christmas. There was no beginning or end to the lost and damned year. Now and then, people took trips, that was all. By the end of January, Tony Wilkins had wrestled with everyone in the troupe and was talking about re-enlisting in the Royal Marines. Jack Stagmeyer was moving into the bowling alley phase. Robert Frith cut his hand doing a trick with beer bottles—that was something to talk about. They came clunking, splintering gorgeously down and Robert shouted "Bugger!" Well, that was really all that winter. Fred made a medium-heavy pass at a girl called Rhoda and was turned down, which was much more like normal.

There weren't too many suitable bars along the coast, although new ones were being planned all the time. So the setting contracted: the same pet barmen with the same quaint phrases, the same swordfish for Perry Mulloy to take down from the wall and challenge people with. But it wasn't altogether monotonous. Every now and then there was a shriek of pain. Somebody would yell something wild; a woman would cry.

On January twelfth, Perry Mulloy pulled a real gun and shot two bullets into the bar ceiling. On February eighteenth, a woman was found in the ladies' room of another bar with her head cut open. And on March first, Ed Baines tried to commit suicide.

8

There were lots of interpretations of that. Jack Stagmeyer, who had known the Baineses in Milwaukee, said it was a chronic thing, that he tried it every year around the same time. "Spring fever," Jack called it. Perry Mulloy heard that he had been fired by his soft drink company—Coca-Cola was getting too far ahad. Sue Mulloy said that he was jealous of his wife and thought she was being unfaithful. ("Grand weather for suicide we've been having," said Jack Stagmeyer.)

"This is no place for a guy like that to live," Sue said.

"What kind of guy is that?" asked Fred.

"You know, hard-working, serious. Business vamerica z'business. Pillar in search of a community. All that."

"And who was Marion supposed to be being unfaithful with?"

"Well, you, I guess."

Fred sat at the café, bewildered even by his standards. Me —oh, look fellows; I'm not that good. He had always been the original Blob with women. What was getting into everyone these days? A more desperate bunch of broads he never hoped . . .

"He told me," said Sue, "I mean he told Marion, that he didn't see why you didn't go back to your wife. It seemed to worry him a lot. You didn't make any sense at all."

Fair enough. Still—

"He said he could understand the other people down here, but not you; you just didn't seem to fit in."

Fred put his sunglasses on, mainly to hide. It had never occurred to him that Baines had given him two thoughts. It was
always embarrassing to know that people were thinking about
you. He shut his eyes behind the sunglasses.

Honestly, Baines must be nuts. Marion's metallic flirtation
couldn't have fooled anybody; once you were satisfied the flirt-
ing didn't mean actual hatred, there was nothing more to be
thought about it.

Sue apparently thought the sunglasses meant, go ahead, you
can talk freely. She was a gossip with a kind heart, so people
went on telling her things. And it seemed that Marion Baines
had told her plenty.

"Just between ourselves, Fred, Ed asked Marion to stop
seeing you. She just laughed, of course. And he said, well look,
is there anything between you, and she said, that isn't worthy of
an answer. . . . He was terrified of this place, you know. He
saw people going off with other people's wives, and each time he
thought, there goes Marion."

"I wish somebody had told me."

"Marion thought it was just too silly. Anyway, it amused her
too, in a nice sort of way. Marion is really a very fine person."

Sue had to say that if she was going to go on getting people's
confidences. Even the cruddiest confidantes received a pat on
the head. Fred was surprised when Perry chimed in with:

"It's going to be hell for her. Seeing her old friends every day.
What can she say? that her husband's a poor slob who just can't
take it—"

"Perry!" said Sue.

"Well, it's true. Ed's O.K., but he hasn't two guts to rub
together."

"Perryyou'reawful."

"I think trying to kill himself was the smartest thing he ever did. What do you say, Jack?"

"It doesn't mean a damn thing. He does it every year. Just to show that he's around."

Fred had never heard the group discussing a moral problem before and he was fascinated. They seemed to have criteria out of the *Arabian Nights.*

"He should have been more considerate," said Robert Frith. "People don't think of the trouble they cause."

"I don't think *that's* fair. He left Marion well provided for. And I know it sounds awful, but he was quite tidy about it. Sleeping pills may be dull, but they're tidy."

"I hear they were drifting apart anyway. This may have been his way of releasing her."

And the best one of all: "I believe divorce is against their religion."

Fred rocked in his wickerwork chair, listening to the unreal crash of voices, an unconvincing radio sound effect meant to be human voices. They were already on their third round of drinks, stoking up for an evening's horseplay, as if nothing had happened; but talking earnestly, because this thing had its serious side too.

"What'll you have, Fred? Same again?"

"Nothing for me, thanks." Fred got up and left them. He went for a very slow walk in the back streets of town; where it was shady and quiet, and you could feel the firmness of cobblestones under your stupid sandals.

He wandered down a white glade of houses that came out on the beach where the fishermen were fixing their nets in icy sunshine. They had to get in a lot of fishing before the bad weather began again. Those that weren't hovering over the nets had sprawled under and around the fishing boats, resting and talking quietly. Their houses were small and crammed with children and grandparents; so that even on cold days they rested on the beach.

There was a great stillness except for the shrugging of waves. Fred noticed a familiar face: the father of the girl who came to clean for him.

"*Mucho sol*, eh?" said Fred. The man smiled and said something quickly that Fred couldn't follow. One "*Qué?*" would be enough. The man repeated it, at the same pace. Fred smiled too and said, "*Sí, sí.*"

He stood on the beach until dark. Two teams of four men were pulling endless ropes out of the sea. They had started before he came and didn't finish until sundown: hauling the wet, heavy rasp of rope onto the sand and coiling it there. Every hundred yards or so a cork buoy was attached to each rope, which Fred expected each time to be the fish they were pulling in. But the buoys only announced a new installment of rope.

Towards sundown they began to work faster. The front man coiled the rope and ran back to become the rear man, faster and faster, pattering through the sand, until with the dipping of the sun, they had what they wanted: a tiny netful of fish which they flipped into a small drawer.

For a minute they stood, looking solemn and dark-faced at the fish wiggling in the drawer. There was one squid which had to be segregated, a poem in slime. An old man picked it up and tossed it into a bag. The beach was suddenly dark and the fish were wiggling slivers of dull silver. The rope pullers, a mixture of two old men, two boys and four in-betweens, seemed satisfied with what they'd got; although it looked like a bad joke after all that work.

They started back over the sand, carrying their drawer of jumping fish and talking softly. They seemed very sweet-tempered, although Fred had been told by one of the gang that it was all a string of obscenities. You never knew who to believe around here. Fred followed them over the sand and back into town.

He went to see Frieda, for the first time in three months, and found the colored boy there, drinking Nescafé and fiddling with a guitar. He was very polite, and so was Frieda. Polite and sober. Not desperate, not available.

Fred said, "Ed Baines tried to kill himself."

Frieda said, "Yes, I heard that."

"Did you hear why?"

"Somebody was saying that he got the maid into trouble. But somebody always says that, don't they?"

Fred expected her to launch an attack on the lost and damned set and say perhaps that they weren't really lost at all, everything on this coast was bogus and second rate; the *real* lost set were probably in Greece by now.

But something about the colored boy thrumming the guitar seemed to compel in her a grotesque, for her, moderation. He had succeeded, where Fred had failed, in de-hipping her, in giving her a style.

Frieda said, "It's a pity." Not even a damn pity, he noticed idly. The colored boy smiled and hit a chord. Right across Fred's face.

There was nothing here for Fred. Certainly not what he had, he now realized, come for. He could have made Frieda what he liked too, it would have been a good winter's work; but he was so indeterminate himself, she never did find out what kind of women he wanted. And now it was all over, absolutely.

"How's the painting, Fred?" she asked.

"Slow."

"Fred is quite a talented painter," she said carelessly.

"I'd like to see your work, Fred."

He got up to go. Couldn't take much of this. The colored boy got up and showed him to the door.

And said, "I'd really like to see your work." Smiled.

"Come and see us again, Fred."

The lemons were bitter this year, baby. The vines had tender grapes for the young foxes. Cope went quickly over the stones. He couldn't believe it. Ask the fairies for a genuine emotion, and this is what they gave you. Jealousy, unmistakable and amazingly painful. Jealous of a colored boy. Over a woman one didn't want.

The hell one didn't. He wanted wanted wanted, better think about something else, for instance think of a puffy soft-drink salesman sitting on a bed in no doubt gorgeous pajamas, holding his little bottle of pills, weighing them, thinking God knows what—get even with Marion, or Coca-Cola or whoever the villain was; "How could we have been so heartless, Baines was *worth more than any of you.*" Thinks Baines. O.K. we'll do it. Shaking the pills onto his hand, sweeping them triumphantly over the pouting lip.

Marion probably had been out merrymaking while Baines was working it out. Fred could just hear her braying good night to the gang; coming in, fuzzy, with metallic echoes of funfunfun jangling in the dim brain. Whispering into the bedroom, some thing on pillow, part of the design, no, piece of paper. Note for milkman perhaps, funny place to leave it, in a way—

It was hell for Marion, the gang was right about that, anyway.

That was the kind of pain they might even feel themselves someday.

Instead of picking at his own dreary little emotion, Fred decided to do the serious thing and go and comfort Marion. . . .

His shadow swooped along under the street lights, now long, now short, out of the side streets, onto the main drag, where the crowds congealed at the corners or stared into the windows of the chintzy new shops. Fred wondered what he was swooping into. Would Marion laugh like ice in a glass or cry wildly? And what would Cope the Clumsy do for her tears? Pat her head like a great whale or stand by the window mumbling reassurances over his shoulder? The Spaniards must think he looked very funny bustling along with his big determined all-American do-gooder face; he saw himself like a man in the movies, montaging the hell along.

It wasn't for Marion, it was for Cope: therapy for Cope. Well, so what? You just do it, that's all. Don't worry, you'll still hate yourself afterwards. The colored boy with the courteous handshake, "Come and see *us.*"

Cope had dithered Frieda away, hadn't helped her, hadn't helped himself. He had somehow refused even to hear the colored boy's name. It was all fantastically painful.

"*Esta señora aqui?*" he said to the Baines's maid, Carmelita.

Behind Carmelita stood her big fisherman fiancé. Which meant that the señora was out. (It wasn't proper for courting couples to be left alone, but Marion Baines said, "They've been engaged at least five years, what the hell?")

Carmelita said, "No, señor."

"*Dónde esta la señora, por favor?*"

He tensed himself desperately to get some of the answer. It sounded as though the señora had gone out with Señor Mulloy.

To Torremolinos. To go bowling perhaps. (*Bolera* meant bowling? Funny.) Carmelita couldn't say when she'd be back. Her fiancé was breathing heavily through his nose: some sort of bull-like obstruction, but it made him sound impatient.

"Well—*muchas gracias.*"

"*De nada*, señor."

The maid watched him go, and as he turned the corner he heard the warped door crash shut. There was nothing to do but go home.

9

Ed Baines recovered and went back to work. The rest of the gang continued to pullulate—Fred saw them at their table in the café every day, brassy and amiable as ever: the Baines episode was as trivial as anything else that happened down here. Fred had been suckered into taking it to heart. All the same, he couldn't sit with them any more. Nothing personal, just couldn't stand them.

One or two of the girls were still theoretically desirable, but after you'd talked to them awhile, you lost the taste for it. Now Frieda— (And quite apart from sex, why didn't they love their country, godammit? Fred began to sublimate with patriotic thoughts.)

He noticed a funny thing at the café, which made nonsense out of his recent researches. The athletes seemed to be on much better terms with the artists than he had ever managed to be. They stopped at each other's tables and there was a kind of hearty, neutral raillery that came over in gusts. They should have been enemies, but they weren't. Only Fred, in the full flower of his ambiguity, was anybody's enemy.

Creeping paranoia at the lonely table. No one to talk to, the old difficulty of looking occupied, the coffee and brandy sliding down swift and tasteless; he wasn't really anyone's enemy, everyone in town said "Hello, Fred"; just get your role straight and we'll come play with you.

Frieda did come over one day with her friend (whose name was Wally) and said, "You look so disapproving, everyone's afraid to sit with you."

Back to that too. He hadn't moved a damn inch.

"You must be working on something very important," she said. "Artists are so manic depressive, aren't they?"

("I'd really love to see your work," said Wally.)

In the zany permutations of the place, Frieda and Wally, patrons of the arts, seemed to be becoming friends of Perry Mulloy and Marion Baines, well-known socialities; the four of them were breaking in a new table and threatening to become a bowling team. Mort Frihoff came back without Marilyn Glasser and took up right away with Jennifer Frith. That was just plain silly—Fred was beginning to recognize definite grades of foolishness in this place, from his lonely corner seat.

Frieda's character had simply changed completely. Wally had rendered her altogether fit for Fred: but of course she didn't want Fred any more. She also ignored Mort and Mort ignored her, without rancor or embarrassment. Did nobody have any feelings at all? Or were these a whole new kind of feelings?

He wished Glasser would come back. In a fumbling, incoherent way, you could communicate with Glasser. Fred wanted to ask him if these people were really the only alternative to square. Or if he ought to start looking somewhere else. Meanwhile, he went back to reading newspapers.

Slowly at first, and simply to look occupied; but then, overwhelmed with existential despair, he began hitting the stand early, and even jostling the other tourists to get at his rock. Pushalong with Sisyphus. On a cold March day he threw his Penguin Camus into the fire and watched it fail to burn because the fire wouldn't burn, but the gesture was existentially valid; and with bitter exhilaration, he went back to clockwatching and taking things out of his pocket and hoping for mail.

This was the kind of liberation Camus had promised—living without hope, baby. He watched the mailboy cycling his rounds sometimes early morning, sometimes late evening, with a wallowing curiosity. It was getting hot again, and the spring flies were returning, another dusty summer was on its way; a break might come in the mail.

He had just about decided to go all the way in degradation and write Ernie Peabody, when he did get some mail after all— not very exciting, just a card from Pete Glasser. Saying that he was going back to the States, with Marilyn, to try to get a job in the Peace Corps. (Hoping to see you again sometime, no mention of the Morocco caper.)

The card made him feel pretty damn good for a moment. Glasser was out of the plague area. Leaving his still unbuilt house down here. He would have to shave now and wash and wear a suit, which was pretty funny right there. (You think people should shave, Cope? You think people should wash? He didn't quite, but all the same, he found himself rooting sadly for the proprieties and liking the idea of Glasser combed and braided.)

He stuffed the card into the big, empty pocket of his seersucker jacket and ambled away from the post office. From a block away he could see them, the whole gang, grouping, regrouping in their slow afternoon dance. A shimmering haze seemed to rise from them, of sheer boringness; each contributing his bit to the great international dullness. They were, he was just the right distance to see it, terribly uninteresting people. The tolerance he had brought down here had been totally eroded; he hated these damn people and everything they stood for.

And again, if a man was going to read the papers among boring people, he might as well be in New Jersey. Crisp bacon, milk and a sense of purpose. Shit, Cope you slay me, but there's something to it. He was suddenly awash with homesickness. New Jersey—you baby.

Two days later he got the piece of mail that did the trick. Three months old, a letter from Alison, smothered in wrong addresses, no only two, thanking him for the money: forwarded in Ernie Peabody's handwriting. It had been sitting at his old pension, probably for months (the Andalusians didn't take mail too seriously.) Her voice had lost its coolness and become as shrill as the voice in his dreams. But the pawky sarcasm, the righteousness, seemed pathetic now because they were dated "November" and this was March.

The address was Stapleton, which was even sadder. A big, free spirit shouldn't go home to mother. It didn't make his memory of her any pleasanter, but it made it a bit smaller and more manageable. Call his year a shambles if you like, but hers— Of course he should have written to Stapleton, for a routine check. The truth was, he supposed, that deep down he hadn't believed anybody could be lucky enough to lose a wife.

Now every last excuse was gone, and he supposed he ought to do something about her. He hardly remembered what she looked like—beyond a vague sense of doom. But it still went without saying that he ought to do something. Not looking for her was one thing, hiding from her was another. You couldn't just let a marriage vaporize away, not if you had Fred Cope's household gods. You did, well, something.

8

In which Square hands in his sword

1

Bloodbury shrugged off the snow, changed its act.

Bob Wilkins said, "One more party, I go out of my mind." Half laughingly he said it, because you couldn't be too careful.

Fran flinch-winced. "I thought you liked parties, I thought *you* were the one . . . "

"Well, maybe I was." The slightest hint of confusion in Fran's eyes was enough. Bob believed that everyone, especially Fran, was closer to crazy than they knew. That look of blind confusion, you saw it more and more.

"We can't let Alison come back without a get-together. Alison of all people," said Fran.

Especially on the bus you saw it. The low threshold of craziness, the frightened eyes peering down from the dark area near the luggage rack. "I guess you're right. Sure, Alison," he said, "get-together." Boy.

Everywhere you walked in the Wilkinses' house was fawn

carpet. It ran along the passage and lapped the walls and streamed into the closets.

Ernie Peabody went squishing over it, tugging at his gabardine spring coat. "Hi, everybody, hi, Fran," "Daffodils, Ernie, you're sweet." Daffodils for Christsake, thought Bob, but didn't say it, because Ernie had the confusion worse than anybody.

"Where's the guest of honor?" asked Ernie.

"She's inside."

"Isn't it great," Ernie said confidentially, "having her back?"

Alison was back. Standing by the false fireplace, pale and drawn: kid had suffered, damn shame about that. Talking to Betty Flax, wonderful human being too, but not about to cheer anyone up. Ernie sensed a role.

"Al, how *are* you?" He went with open arms, and then held them there. Some people weren't designed for bear hugs, especially Alison. But Ernie had committed himself, and touched her shoulders.

"Hello, Ernie. How are the birds?"

"Birds?"

"Or was it music?"

"It's fine. I guess." Birds, music.

She laughed, but kindly. She looked more humble, or something. "Listen, Alison, it's great to see you."

They were standing in their natural clusters, the MacIntyres, the Spodes. They kept a little away from Alison, as they always had: something cold and frightening there. It didn't bother Ernie too much though, he meant it was kind of stimulating.

"Did you bring Bert?" he asked Betty Flax.

She shook her head.

"Too bad. I guess he's baby sitting, huh?"

"He doesn't really care for parties."

"Well, he's certainly got a point there," said Ernie vaguely. Bert with his breakdown and all, better not go on with that. "So. Alison."

"Yes?"

Where you living, what you doing, how you keeping—his wife had massaged it into him not to press the questions tonight. He saw her point too, in a way. Tact was obviously important, although he frankly thought people overdid it sometimes. If you were sincere and showed the other person you were on their side —Ann Peabody had been upstairs powdering her coat or what-thehell; she came down and was on her way over to supervise.

"Isn't Alison looking great?" Ernie said to his wife.

"Nice to see you, Alison," said Mrs. Peabody. "Ernie, get Alison a drink, why don't you?"

The living room shuffle. Ernie swinging out along the wall by the canapé table, Alison edging the other way towards the window. He had started out to get her a drink but ran into Duckworth Miller, who wanted to dissect the recent upturn.

Two, three drinks later Ernie noticed Alison again looking out the window. Poor kid, not kid either, *woman*. The thing about tactfulness had never really been proved to his satisfaction. When he had that bit of trouble back in 1957, he could have used someone like Ernie Peabody, a friend to, well, help him back into his trousers at least. (God that was a terrible summer.) Anyway, Alison looked just as sad with everyone being tactful. They didn't even say "Glad to have you back" for pete-sake; they wouldn't even admit she'd been away. Now wasn't that worse?

He went over. Man had to use his own judgment sometimes.

"Alison?"

She looked up with a pleased smile.

"I—tell me if I'm speaking out of line. But what about Fred?"

"What about him?"

"Well, I just thought, it seems such a damn shame"—play it by ear now—"two wonderful people. Fred has so many good qualities, and you have so much to offer, too." Both looking at the dark window: Alison had pulled the curtain back and they could see themselves on the glass. "I don't want to pry, but if ever two people had something to give each other."

Sledding down the wrong path, Peabody, try to get back. "I know it sounds awfully corny."

"No, that's all right."

"But Fred is . . . "

"A fine man."

"Yes, I guess that's it."

She looked at him, not at the him in the glass, but the real Peabody, and said, "It's very nice of you, Ernie, I appreciate it."

For a moment he thought, You do? and then sagged. What a dumb idiot. His wife was behind him, too far away to hear, but quite able to see; and she smiled at him kindly too, rubbing the embarrassment in like liniment. *Ernie you're not like other people, just take my word for it. They don't think like you. Don't try helping them, please.* Ann had had the whole family psychoanalyzed after his "trouble" (like a great dose of castor oil) and he was always slightly afraid she was going to do it again. He shambled across the room for another drink.

Fran had her doubts about tact, too. She meant, what are friends for? She made it a point to smile at Alison whenever she could: tenderly, you-don't-have-to-explain-to-me-honey. (Unless you want to, of course.) Alison smiled back politely, little darting smiles that didn't fool Fran for a moment: the poor thing was going through hell, trying to be gay, spontaneous, a good sport. Still very much in love. If only she could confide in someone about it. But Alison was a loner—another smile, oblique through the Spodes and MacIntyres, a smile of hopeless invitation. Well, what do you know—Alison was cleaving through for a chat.

"Is everything all right, dear?"

"Yes, fine. It's a splendid party."

Fran patted her hand. "There's nothing like old friends."

A few years ago, in Akron, Fran would have taken the opportunity to come right out with it—have you heard from Fred? can we be of any help?—but here—just in Bloodbury, you wouldn't feel it in, say, Nutley—there was a paralyzing something in the air that said you better be careful, you might set her off. Or if not her, that quiet little man in the corner. Bob Wilkins was very much alive to the problem. He sometimes said after parties, "Did you see the look in Duckworth's eyes when Ernie said that about whatwasit? I thought he was going to clobber him." Life was full of narrow escapes.

So Fran just smiled.

Duckworth Miller wanted to show that he understood more than anybody. Lucy Spode acted natural, that was the best thing in these cases. Harry MacIntyre winked at one point, but Alison probably didn't see it. Everybody underplayed their therapy to the point where Alison didn't know it was there at all. She thought, to be frank, how inhuman they all were, except for Ernie and Fran; and she thought how even Ernie and Fran were only a little bit human.

Maurice Stebbing had been right about one thing. Deep down, lots of people were dull. It was a relaxing thought. She could be kind to these people because she no longer expected anything from them; her disgust was no longer shored up by Pierce's pieties, but ran, swarmed, over everybody.

She took her wrap and kissed Fran like an adder, shook hands, kissed, around the room, gently, sibilantly; went out into the harsh spring night by herself. Betty came out behind and offered to drive her home. She was sorry to have to accept. The dampish night, with the faint violet glow coming from Bloodbury through the wet spindly branches, was just made for disgust.

They drove in silence. She had a feeling that Betty was empty too, dried out—but that might have been a superficial reading of Betty's thin face.

Later she walked around the house without turning on any lights. She knew enough magazine psychiatry to know that the disgust was mostly with herself. It had never occurred to her that she might be a coward; being a coward made everything else impossible. All roles became equally ridiculous. Without courage, you were nothing but attitudes. No more attitudes from now on, nothing but kindness.

They were all cowards, that little weakness stank up the Wilkinses' living room, stank up the whole world. And Alison was the woman's open champion. She used to think, Come on everybody, just try, you can do it. Girl scout leader Alison Cope: tons of effort, everybody. Not understanding that deep down *she* was the one who was bored. And frightened.

She turned the bedside lamp on reluctantly. As the light came on, she could see the stupid traces of Fred, a Matisse reproduction he had given her hopefully, a chest of drawers full of fat complacent underwear: if she was going to be kind to people, she ought to be kind to Fred. But she fairly shrank from it. If she couldn't disapprove of Fred, what was the point of anything?

Undressed quickly, and turned out the light: Fred was impossible—you had to draw the line somewhere. Marrying Fred was part of the Willoughby death wish—just as Pierce's interest in dull people was part of the Willoughby death wish.

Almost the only encouraging thing about her situation was that she still couldn't take Fred.

2

Everyone wondered why Alison had come home at all; and being puzzled, they began to feel again that there was something queer about her. Was she going to turn into a gaunt widow in a boarded-up house? They said: *She's been through a lot, I know, but still, and maybe Fred had something at that. I never could see what was supposed to be so bad about Fred: I knew how Betty explained it, but then again, look at Betty—*

In ever smaller circles, the most far out speculations being privately distributed to one person at a time; there were no group orgies of gossip in Bloodbury. The MacIntyres wouldn't even say nasty things about her in front of each other (Harry used to say "meow"); Duckworth Miller went as far as anybody ("I think she's frigid, that's her trouble." "Duckworth, you're always thinking people are frigid." "Well, they are.") A nice, polite town, up to a point.

Alison had come back because she felt safe here. If she was going to be a coward, she might as well go all the way. That she could ever come to depend on Bloodbury was the kind of bitter medicine that was almost exhilarating to take. Bloodbury the bogus, the home of the pseudoevent, was chock-full of people of her own level of courage and wisdom. For several days after the party she phoned them up, just to chat. Gradually she became aware of a sort of metallic withdrawal: sounds of phased-out politeness that she knew so well.

But before that had time to get on her nerves, the flat surface tilted and Fred came home. She heard from the incredible Peabody (was he really an investigator of some kind, a plain-clothes, second-story man? he seemed to know everything) that Fred was back in New York.

Her first response was humble panic. Fred might be second-rate, but she didn't want to face him right now. She packed up her things and fled to the Flaxes, wondering, as she scrambled into their car, whether life-as-a-work-of-art included the possi-bility of farce. Cowardice was certainly a galloping complaint; one surrender took you halfway to the next. (Only this wasn't a real surrender, just a tactical withdrawal.)

She had been finding out, since the party, that Betty Flax was a more serious kind of person in a serious kind of world. The silence that she had taken to be understanding was simply because Betty and she had less to talk about these days. They belonged to different plays with different sets and different orchestras. All the same, Betty was the only person who could give her halfway intelligent sanctuary. So to Betty's she went.

The community, in the form of Duckworth Miller, who ran into her next day at the supermarket, seemed guardedly amused and promised, smiling, not to tell Fred. She turned away regally and heard laughter down the aisles, laughter from the canned vegetables. It brought back old nightmares. Being laughed at was something that happened from time to time to serious little girls; but she hadn't expected it to erupt in this situation. She had braced herself for the idea of humility, but on the understanding that it meant cruel self-knowledge, not silly giggles.

That was certainly the worst week of all, the dithering week at the Flaxes. Betty didn't laugh and Bert seemed uninterested, but outside, all Bloodbury must be whooping it up over her crazy retreat. She tried to take an interest in Betty's children, but felt that they carried the community amusement around like radioactive dust.

She wasn't even absolutely sure that the situation *was* funny. Humor (as opposed to wit) was rather a silly accomplishment that she had never much bothered with. It meant systematically emptying everything of importance, it meant mechanically twisting events and people to see a "funny side." Fred, for instance, had a sense of humor.

And speaking of Fred, there he was in Bloodbury now and she had to do *something* about him. Betty said he had moved back into their old house and was once again carrying his briefcase to and from the bus station. Bert said, with chilling innocence, that he would like to talk to Fred about a job someday. (Bert used to be some kind of writer, but had given it up since his breakdown. Alison had always been rather vague about Bert.)

Nobody seemed to know what to do with Fred—Alison got the backwash of the gang's conferences—and for a full week he walked in an invisible hoop, watched but not touched. Then Fran said, "Well this is silly, nobody in Bloodbury seems to know how to respond to anything, but *I'm* going to give a party this evening *and* I'm going to ask Fred." ("Nobody talk about Alison, though," she said, in concession to the local diplomacy.)

The gang really had no idea whether the party was a good idea or not. Fran was quite right: outside of the vague feeling that one ought to be tactful, nobody in Bloodbury had the faintest notion how to respond to the unusual. They knew that Fran was usually wrong, but they had no suggestions of their own.

Alison said she would baby sit for the Flaxes that evening and she talked a little, though not about Fred, to Betty as she dressed. Betty would have been sympathetic perhaps: but there was a somberness about her this spring that made one's problems seem sillier than one cared to have them seem. Stebbing had made her strictures on Fred sound flashy and movie magazinish; they weren't really, but they might sound like that with Betty, too.

"You know," said Betty, as she was leaving, "I don't think Fred is so dull. I think he's rather interesting."

"You never had to—"

"I know, live with him."

The heavy click of a car door, the sober voices of the Flax children, who went to bed quietly these evenings, and then silence. A sad house. What was she going to do about Fred? Was there anything sadder than a cheap clock ticking in a dark kitchen? do about Fred?

She would have to face him sometime. Big pink face, quasi-interesting eyebrows—the eyebrows her only possible excuse for marrying him (and they weren't *that* interesting); the face that responded with agonizing inappropriateness to whatever line she took with him. "Look here, Fred"—the first words would be simply impossible. "I think I should explain myself, dear. (Don't look like that, dear, stop trying to look so concerned, just listen quietly.)" If she could just get past this interview, a new life would be possible.

A year ago it was no trick at all to dress down Fred; it was sinfully easy and pleasant. But now he was a rather formidable stranger again. Perhaps he had not spent the last year so unprofitably as she had. He had, everyone said, been abroad. Perhaps he had learned something over there—she felt a childish awe of sheer experience, although of course no amount of experience would help Fred much.

Because of her own childish year, she had no platform to address him from any more. Maybe the best thing would be to start straight in about divorce terms. Practical, no sermon, no platform.

Yes, that was something she felt up to. Maybe if she did it quickly, before it froze into a set piece in her mind, and before the complications had time to cluster—she went quickly to the Flax's phone and began dialing for Mrs. Pelotti, their number one baby sitter, whose number was printed large on the blotting paper.

Mrs. Pelotti took forever to come quavering along the street (she lived three houses away, but her arthritis made it into an odyssey). Alison tapped her foot and kept her mind fretfully blank of larger issues. She had ordered a taxi, which would get her home a good deal before Fred—that would give her an advantage: catch him panting and confused in the doorway; catch him in full flounder.

"Look here, Fred—"

Mrs. Pelotti slowly mounted the porch and cautiously invested the house. She was one of those old ladies in whom dimness and shrewdness are so tightly intertwined that you never can tell how much to explain. "I have to see my husband," Alison said. "He's been away. I'm sorry . . ."

Mrs. Pelotti's mouth gaped, but her eyes were sharp as needles. Alison knew that a year ago one would have sailed out without another word: one didn't have to explain oneself to people like Mrs. Pelotti.

But there was nowhere to sail to because the taxi hadn't come yet and she had forgotten the fundamentals of regal composure and she found herself, incredibly, saying, "I haven't seen him for a year. We agreed to, you know—" *Now* the taxi came, locating itself with a derisive blip of the horn.

Mrs. Pelotti, gaping and needling, took the five-dollar bill without looking: what kind of a nut does Mrs. Pelotti think she's dealing with? "Good luck, Mrs. Cope," the old woman said, surprisingly.

Alison leapt, unstrung, at the taxi. She was so certain she didn't belong in a farce—perhaps that made her just perfect for it. Tangling with Mrs. Pelotti, plunging distraitly into taxis, this wasn't her role at all. She pushed back a strand of yellow hair and sat up straighter. Farce was a quality of soul—now that was a pompous way to put it, the clown in the baggy suit would probably paddle her for that, oh dear. But seriously, if you could just laugh at yourself, people said—very healthy thing to do.

She tried to smile, felt her face crack like plaster from inside, oh dear. Trying to laugh at herself in a dark taxicab and failing.

The clown would kick her across the footlights for that and into the bass drum.

The house was already full of Fred again, cigarette butts on top of the television, a newspaper crammed viciously into the armchair. Can of your favorite beer. Light up a cool mild refreshing white owl teabag tastycake, yum: the set had been erupting again, you could just tell. It looked guilty and pleased with itself at the same time. She took the ashtray into the kitchen. The sheer size of Fred, the massiveness of his imprint on an armchair seat— The number of butts a big man could smoke.

She was home first, her advantage; catch him off guard, her advantage.

She moved nervously about the living room, reminding herself of her advantages. Waiting for the clown to strike again.

For reasons which were strong but not clear, she turned out the living room light after a bit and went and sat in the kitchen. Waiting, the simple act of waiting for anything, was unpleasant; but the kitchen was the best place for it.

From there she could scarcely hear the sigh of tires, the car door's own special complex of sounds, the stuttering of feet on the porch, a pause of several seconds as of keys being searched for—and the final melancholy incision of Fred into the house.

3

Rumbling around the door, snapping on the hall light, "What the hell?", the heaviest footsteps she had ever heard; now quieter across the living room carpet; another light going on fiercely, heavy breathing, around the corner—

"Hello, Fred."

"Alison. What the hell?"

His eyebrows were still interesting, but that was beside the point.

"I just came back to say . . ." she said.

"What are you doing in the dark?"

"I don't know. It seemed . . ."

He pulled the chain on the kitchen light. She had only seen

him dimly, by the light in the next room. Now she saw him clearly. He hadn't lost any weight. His hair was longer than she remembered it. "You didn't get a tan in Spain."

"No, it rained."

"Well, I just came to say. Divorce . . ."

Movies like this. They used to make them in the thirties. She almost smiled nervously. Light comedies in dinner jackets and tweed skirts. Ocean liners, horse shows. An arch reconciliation in about twenty minutes, Cary Grant winking at the chambermaid, throwing the key out the window: she handled her throat painfully. She had wound up watching a lot of television in Stapleton in spite of her principles.

"Yes, fine," said Fred. "Divorce it is."

"Yes, well I thought"—what was he saying? that was a typical Cary Grant tactic, wasn't it, agreeing to the divorce; enlisting her vanity against it. "What do you think would be fair for a settlement?" she asked quickly.

He shrugged. "I don't know. You name it."

She looked beyond him to the sofa, to the television, to the sliver of Matisse. I want this, don't want that: it *wasn't* her kind of story. "I don't care, you can stay here, I'll get a job." She gestured generously.

"All right. Whatever you say."

"I'll spend the night in the guest room and be gone in the morning." Guest room. Clark Gable bumping into Irene Dunne outside the bathroom door. Her backing off awkwardly in a pair of his pajamas. Alison felt the nervous smile again.

"Is there anything you want to say?" she said.

"No."

He just stood there. Raised on the same movies as she, taking the same artificial view of things. She could see him creeping downstairs to the guest room, oozing his own version of glamor. Was there a key to that room?

Oh, stop it. She was a serious person, not a foil for Cary Grant; she would change the kind of scene they were having, call in a new director. "Do you think I owe you an explanation?"

"No."

"You don't?"

"No."

"Well." She began to move restlessly. Kitchen movements. "You must think *some*thing."

"You want to know what I think, is that it?"

She moved right past him, shrugging, to put a glass in the sink. She turned on the water, which came with a grinding rush and rinsed the glass carefully. (Couldn't care less what you think.) Fred usually stumbled over his words, trying to please, while she did the laconic bit. Try it once more. "All right, what do you think?" she said five minutes later.

He waited a bit longer, rubbing his chin.

"Well?"

"Well, I'll tell you, Alison. I don't think it makes much difference what I say. It would just come out in clichés, and I know how you hate clichés."

"I'm used to them."

"All right, here's a couple of quick ones. About the divorce— I'm for it. I don't want to try living with you again. I don't want to talk to you again. You give me a pain."

"I'm sorry. If only you'd made a little effort—"

"Yeah, a little effort. So that's the main thing. Make any damn settlement you like, only leave me alone."

This wasn't Cary Grant. More like Edward G. Robinson. Get out of my life, sweetheart.

"I didn't mean to bother you," she said stiffly.

"Yeah, well you bothered me all right. Now let's forget it."

She hated being compulsive, but she *had* to talk more than that. "I only wanted you to be at your best, to be all you could be."

He, on the other hand, didn't seem to care if he never talked again. He took an apple from on top of the icebox and began chewing it slowly. Was he *kidding?* His face looked heavy and depressed. "I don't want any more of your crazy games," he said at last. "Let's go to bed."

"What do you mean, my games?"

"You know."

"Anyway I thought you were conventional about marriage."

"I am."

"So, how can you talk about divorce?" It was such a degradingly silly conversation. But she couldn't seem to improve it. Fred passed up the obvious answer, that he *hadn't* talked about divorce, or anything else.

"Look, Alison, I'm tired. I've just been to one of Fran's parties and I want to go to bed. Once upon a time, I didn't mind sitting up all night trying to make conversation with you, but I'm not up to it any more."

"I didn't know it was such a trial for you."

"As a matter of fact, it was one sweet hell of a trial. And I don't want to reopen it. Good night."

He tossed the core into the garbage can and started for the kitchen door. "Do you want a pair of my pajamas?" he asked her on the way out. The movie became an old-fashioned two reeler, and Cary Grant waddled off down the Ritz corridor in a series of frantic spasms.

She still half expected him to tiptoe down to the guest room, and she spent a bad night thinking up rebuffs.

She got up early, to tackle him once more over breakfast. He came into the kitchen quietly, and there was a speechless embarrassment between them over who should cook the eggs.

"I'll be out of your way in a minute," she said.

He nodded.

"Do you want them scrambled?"

"That'd be O.K."

He went out for a moment, checked dressing gown, same old flapping slippers, and came back with a newspaper. He sat by the window and read it in sunlight, without apology. He chewed his toast loudly.

"Here are your eggs."

"Thanks."

"Look, Fred,"—she creaked up a chair. "Would you mind putting down the paper a minute?"

"Hold on, I want to finish this."

Very clumsy defiance. Very childish. Not such a very good act after all.

"When you're quite ready—" she said tartly.

"Listen, Alison, to hell with *that*. I don't have to take any 'when you're quite ready' falsetto crap."

He went on with the paper, and she tried freezing him out until that silly feeling began coming back. Oh, this was absurd.

"Don't you think we should talk this over like adults?"

"No."

"No?"

"No."

"What do you mean?"

He looked at his watch. "I've got to go." He brushed the toast crumbs off his dressing gown.

"Fred—what sort of an act is this?"

"Act?"

"Yes. You usen't to be like this."

"No?"

"Look, I'm asking you to talk, will you please talk?"

"An act, that's pretty good."

"Will you just tell me what you think? Do you hate me, or what?"

He stood up and started shuffling to the door. Too terribly theatrical. He must have spent the year at the Actor's Studio, doing exits. But instead of wheeling at the door and saying, "Yes, you bitch, and I've always hated you," he kept going right through the living room and up the stairs.

It was really undignified to follow him. But if she didn't he would be out the front door and off to work with nothing settled. So she trailed dismally up the stairs and said, "Fred, you haven't answered my question."

Fred was knotting his hand-painted tie. If he didn't speak now, she was going to scratch his eyes. Even if he said "what question?" she'd scratch.

But he said, "Let it go, Alison, for Godsake. I'm not acting. I just don't want to start the crap in motion again."

Could she scratch him for that? "Look, it isn't just you," he said. "It's people like you. I've spent a whole year surrounded by hundreds of them, and I've had them up to here."

"What kind of people are like me?"

"Well, if you must know, cruel, second-rate people are like you, among other people. Beautiful people are like you."

He still didn't express himself very well, poor dear. Good to have him talking again though.

"You prefer kindly first-rate business people, do you? Four-square Americans, good eggs." This was what she had been last year, someone with a definite set of values. She would drive Fred back into *his* old position, too.

"No, you've fixed that," he said. "I don't like good eggs either. You've fixed this whole town, and everyone in it."

"Well, what do you like this year?"

"Not much. One man I met in Spain. Being back at work. I may add to the list in time."

"It sounds thin."

"It is thin."

"Thin, I mean, even by your standards. And God, what standards." She felt her face contract sharply—"Tenth-rate, empty, borrowed, fat-faced standards. Thin by those standards."

The screen was small and old-fashioned. A bedroom mirror in real life. What she had said was very bitchy. But that was right, she had been given a bitchy part. If you left your husband for some silly reason, it soon showed in your behavior. Her face in the mirror was thin and sharp and superficial—that was just right for the part. She wasn't like that really, but divorcees had to look and act like that for the camera. It was demanded by the Legion of Decency.

And Fred was acting just right too. Muffled and bearish. How banal can you get? His hand came up and washed against her cheek, rattling her teeth.

"You useless, selfish bitch"—a hopelessly stilted line in real life, but fine for this kind of movie. He moved off screen, massive and righteous, and out of the room. She lay down on the bed, still sort of watching herself, and wept just beautifully.

4

There was no avoiding Ernie Peabody on the bus. He or his
equivalent bounded beside you like a retriever: the real Ernie
today, and he had been thinking about starting his own company again, two or three fellows, keep it small and manageable,
what do you say, Fred?

"Keep it small, is a good idea . . . these things tend to get
topheavy."

Fred was deep in thought (his newspaper lay becalmed in his
lap) and Peabody couldn't really penetrate. Fred would have
sworn he hadn't changed substantially in the past year, and
now he had socked his wife the way they did it in Spain—
well, no, a real expatriate would have put a bullet through her
foot; but still, it was a big step forward for Fred.

He brooded about the de facto nature of conduct, how you
didn't know what kind of person you were until you did something characteristic. Deep waters. All those nights trying to read
Camus made a man profounder than he knew. Look at it this
way. Even if what you did was something of an act, your choice
of act says something about you. What do you say to *that*, Ernie
baby?

Peabody's round face worked obliviously on his project. Did
he really have one in the works, or was it a device for extending
the possible limits of conversation? I mean, you couldn't ven-
ture outside of business, but within those limits you could at
least, well, discuss projects . . .

Stalking angrily out of the room, now that was the most interesting part of all. He had made up his mind to stalk out, so

in that sense it was an act; but he had feared the inward deprecating smile, the joke about the Moose, the cut it out Fred, that would have made it an out and out fake; and instead he had simply stalked out; he had observed it, a genuine action based on an artificial pattern. Wonder if big Ernie would follow that one?

Not only that, he didn't rush lumbering back and take Alison in his arms, didn't throw the situation away. The rage was real enough to get him safely onto the bus; and even here he felt a certain genial anger. Ambiguous but honest-to-John anger. Teach her to tangle with the Moose boy.

He examined his own behavior with extraordinary Camus-type interest. He had been flustered to find Alison crouching in the kitchen last night, but had taken sanctuary in the first and most obvious lesson of the past year. If he just kept quiet, people misread him completely. They thought he was judging and condemning them—perfect for this situation, if he could simply stifle the nervous desire to explain and to conciliate.

And this was where de facto came in. For he found that his mind had matched his behavior perfectly. No nervous smile, no apologetic gestures, even in embryo. By George, he was actually judging and condemning: possibly had been for years. That's why he always looked as if he was.

Can you believe it, Ernie? Chief Justice Cope; but he was losing the desire to put himself down, to have a wonderful sense of humor about himself. What he had said and done was serious in its way. He didn't really think it was funny. Not really.

He meant what he had said to Alison a few minutes ago. She was a destroyer—for the best possible reasons, no doubt. That horse's ass brother of hers had given her a splendid point of view, but no right to it: she wasn't a saint, she wasn't an artist, she had never made anybody happy; she had made a few people nervous, maybe.

You could make a brutal case against Alison. It was part of her point of view to talk about compassion, but just take the things she used to say about her parents, for a start. They had always struck Fred as decent, kindly enough people when he met them; the kind of people you see at Howard Johnson's restaurants. But to Alison, they were card-carrying ghouls. (She said her father didn't smile properly, although the smile looked quite kosher to Fred.) Her own coldness railed at all this coldness going around. She talked about maturity and relatedness (before it became hackneyed to do so, that is), but her father was quite charming and invariably kind and she didn't relate maturely with him at all. Why had he noticed none of this before?

"So what do you say, Fred?"

"I'd have to think about it, Ernie."

"You could come in as a full partner. Put your name right on the letterhead. Cope-Peabody, consultants." Cope, Peabody— blood brothers. Quintessential squares. Consultants in squareness.

"I don't think so, Ernie. But I appreciate your thinking of me."

"You don't have to decide right away—" Ernie was shot through with moonbeams. Tomorrow he would pull another fantasy out of his briefcase—festoon it with business jargon, of course, but the heart of it would be wild; or he would take this one to one of the other regulars. But nobody would want to be seen dead on a letterhead with Ernie Peabody. It was like admitting you liked the suburbs or that what the country needed was more conformity.

On the subway, Fred had a small shock: he thought he saw Austin Gold. Everyone looked so wretched in the subway, especially this girl at the next strap. She had the same reflective pallor as Austin and the surprising, lustrous hair (as if she had nothing to do every evening but wash it over and over); he felt first pity, then "in that case, it must be Austin," and then of course not, why this one in particular, there were two or three other girls that could just as well have been Austin. Austin Gold day today, everyone down into the subway.

The New York compression took some getting used to. He wanted to touch the girl and say, "It's all right, Cope is here." But the girl was probably as tough as she needed to be. City-rat toughness; Austin's blank hard face when he stopped making love to her; the face under the driers as he passed the beauty shop in the arcade a few minutes later. A strange beauty shop where everyone was ugly. He always looked in there on the way to work, and he had never seen a good-looking person yet. Not once. What are you staring at? . . . the hideous cashier in the doorway filed her nails ominously. The customers glared at him through plastered slits. Good to have you back, Fred.

Disturbing to remember about Austin though. Talk about cruel and second-rate, boy. That was just the way they treated them in the south of Spain.

He decided to give Austin a call when he got to the office. By now he could talk to her like an old friend, ask about her brother Otto, was it? with the three fingers, was it? better not bring up her brother. He found the number in his shabby black book; but when he dialed it, the girl, the angry New York girl, said, "That number has been disconnected."

So—Austin had broken out. Great. Teaching piano in the country: to orphans with artificial fingers (Herman—*that* was her brother's name?) Or perhaps she had found a kinder man than Fred—well, it was possible, there must be a few hundred million of them knocking about.

If one just took one's conduct at its face value, not realizing what a warm human being one was underneath, one might conclude that Fred Cope was pretty much of a rat with women: first Austin, then Frieda and then, to crown the year, belting his wife. Quite the killer, quite a year. If his dossier arrived in a manila folder on his desk right now . . .

He bent to his work, which certainly hadn't become any more interesting in his absence. Mr. Thurman had taken him back with gleeful indulgence at $25 less a week and was probably giving him tiresome cases as a punishment. He found that he could concentrate longer on a single case than he used to: but apathetically, resignedly, with a bleak but steady half interest. Coming to work every day was no longer a fun reflex, but a somber, pointless effort.

He wondered if Alison would be there when he got back or whether she would have disappeared again. She never had said where she'd been all these past months—he opened another folder really expecting to find his own case. F. Cope, good risk, very cautious fellow. Strange taste in women, though. (Women have strange taste in him, if it comes to that.) Twenty-eight, very young to have given up like this. But consider the choices: he isn't hip and he's no longer perfectly square, and he sure as hell isn't an individualist—tell you what he can do, though. Maybe he can live with the squares, has got the coloration for that, and cultivate irony on the side. Surprising lot of people do that. Open the next folder and you'll find a prime case, Ernie Peabody . . . yes, Ernie.

Fred could rattle on like this without missing a beat in his work. He thought about Alison again. If she had left once more, his life would be formidably pointless. Waiting for the next neurotic woman to claim him: lusting meanwhile in a vacuum (good for the irony no doubt). Although you never knew for sure. Mr. Thurman had put him fifteen desks behind the equivalent of his old one, next to a great-looking secretary. Very sane-looking kid. And not conspicuously hostile either.

This morning he had felt almost mature. But this place made you regress fast. Could maturity come and go like that? By three in the afternoon he was looking at the girls around the water cooler and thinking the old thoughts. He went back to his folders with asperity: Alison Cope, thirty-year-old prig. Nice-looking, when her character isn't showing— Very nice-looking, in fact.

He was soon thinking about her the same way he was thinking about the girls at the cooler. In that sense, anyway, she was a stranger again: his feelings were boyish, sly. If she spent another night in the house with him, never mind about maturity, boy. It was tough enough last night, secretary, girls at the cooler, his eyes swiveled around the folder—this kind of sex was just emptiness, afternoon emptiness. The blank, bland work got to you, the empty green walls and the men in the white shirts. You could either be a boy in a place like this, kept alive by bursts of concupiscence, or you could be old, and feel nothing. There was nothing in between. The girls were the only living thing: regress or perish.

He had had a certain grumpy stature when he left home this morning—but how long would that last if he stayed here? Cultivate irony. O.K. if you say so, but irony implies some control over the contents of your skull: and that is the first thing you lose in this wasteland. Remember how it was last year, when your mind was a half-assed catalyst, an agent for pointless impressions, and when it never occurred to you to have stature? That's what the old building did to you. This new one was much worse. One thing had changed anyway: he saw this stinking mausoleum for what it was.

Last year he *liked* the office, the daily surrender of coherence: wonder if they hired these girls for just that reason—like the Ministry of Pornography in 1984. . . . Well, this was stale stuff, of course, everyone had known these things for years; he had known them himself, he had clucked and clucked over the impersonality of modern life, cluck cluck like a machine, but now, as he looked around, the whole place seemed to be saying, never mind about Modern Life: we've emasculated *you personally* before and we'll do it again; we'll fill your fat head with gossip and modulated, continuous sex and old newspapers, and cut down the attention span so that you're at everybody's mercy, wondering what they just said—oh, you know the things we do, just look around in any direction; just look at yourself in a few more days.

The sallow beach and the crumby foreigners (were they really so crumby?), the corruption and hysteria, was that life worse or better than this? Was there any other life? (Had Alison discovered another life maybe?) With a little imagination, one might work out something. But who had a little imagination these days?

Four o'clock—O.K., admit it, five minutes to four. Supposing he walked into Thurman's office and said "I'm quitting" again: boy, Thurman would have a heart attack, wouldn't he? Don't give any reason or anything, just act as if it was the most natural thing in the world. "I'm quitting, Mr. Thurman. Mr. Thurman?" Thurman swooning away.

If Alison was home—stop thinking of her in terms of secretaries and shoulder straps, Alison is a different thing altogether. What should the policy be then? This morning it was so beautifully clear. But by now, in nightmarish revival of last year, his brains had undergone the afternoon scramble and could only churn up half sentences and scraps of thought to work with. Suppose Alison and he tried going somewhere together in shoulder straps and thirty-five-year-old history of heart trouble what's this? The folders twitched at his attention, the glaze of afternoon, once you got to four-fifteen you were over the hump; he looked down the long tunnel to the green glass door that said Paul Thurman. It would be pretty damn de facto if he went roaring down the tunnel into Thurman's office. It would prove something about himself.

He gripped another folder with tight fingers and ripped it open so violently that several pieces of rice paper went fluttering smugly to the linoleum floor.

5

Just lying absolutely still seemed the best idea: listening to the cars and the very mild street noises. The spring breeze dried her face quickly, parched it and starched it: her cheeks felt like huge rock faces, packed with gorges and furrows; her eyes were choked with dust. She felt like the far side of the moon at the planetarium.

That kind of thinking got you so far. To eleven-twenty, to be exact. Alison sat up on the bed and looked at the mirror. Her face really was a little pale and stiff, so she went to the bathroom door and washed it back to life and combed her hair slowly. A Camille-like trance would be nice for the rest of the day: but worries kept crowding in—like what on earth was the *next* thing to say to Fred? Having played such a masterful game so far . . .

The other thing was simply to leave again—but that now seemed so profoundly farcical, like a child who keeps running away from home. She could do it with an acid note, but that seemed funny too.

Like stamping one's foot.

She thought of phoning Betty Flax about it. But even there she would catch faint traces of amusement. She suddenly remembered a scene that had been vaguely haunting her all that year. When she was nine, she had gone one afternoon to something called a Fun House. You walked down a dark passage, and as you walked you heard terrible shrieks of laughter. Yes, she could hear them now, cruel, meaningless shrieks. It was the first time she had ever been laughed at by machines.

The present situation was serious all right, serious enough to bring on a hot clammy dismay, as if she were a child (child again) lost in a big railway station. Thirtieth Street Station in Philadelphia, for instance. She honestly didn't know what to do next, and, you had to admit, that was serious.

Yet at the same time, she could see that it was tremendously funny. She had never seen a joke so clearly before. Alison Cope was a great comic creation, like Falstaff: floundering priggishly along, incorruptibly solemn; while the laughter clattered on all sides, like one of those garbage trucks that chew tin cans.

Why was cowardice funny anyway? She had no idea—but funny it obviously was. You couldn't be a tragic figure if you were cowardly. Tragedy and comedy were questions of character. Anything that happened to some people was funny. "Stop it, stop," she remembered shouting in the Fun House, but they went on cackling mechanically. They were probably laughing still at the memory of Alison, the perfect joke.

This hysteria had better be curbed, anyway. She piled her hair up in a businesslike sort of way. She could certainly handle Fred, whatever else she couldn't handle: memories of past handlings came back to reassure her. If you were going to be a bully, you might as well take every advantage. "Now look, Fred —after that childish exhibition . . . Let's try to act like grown-ups just once, shall we?"

Shrieks of mechanical laughter at that. Alison was a governess in a long black dress. Fred was a burlesque clown dressed as a schoolboy, smirking at the crowd behind her. She hit him with her ruler and it bent like a piece of hose. It was enough to make a machine laugh. She went out to the kitchen and looked in the icebox. Nothing there but bacon and eggs and six cans of peaches. What on earth did the man live on? There were some pickled herrings in the glove compartment or whatever they called it, but that was hardly an answer.

She settled for a can of peaches and a piece of toast. The new machines have a very good sense of fun, yes. Built into the new models. (Alison a very old model of course.) . . . One hundred eighty million senses of humor in the United States alone, and now the machines. Alison, you're unique.

"Look, Fred, I don't mean to be pompous about this—" Oh, to heck with it. Just be natural. Can handle Fred.

She went to the bookcase and tugged at a book with her finger. The book was stuck, as if the row had begun to grow together, the books had been sitting there for so long. She let it go and went and turned the television on. She was really too nervous to concentrate on a book at the moment.

At some point during the commercials, it came back to her —the woman was holding up a box of detergent, tapping it and smiling hypnotically—that Fred had called her a bitch this morning. The woman poured some soap in her washing machine and the next thing you knew, her husband and son were simpering over a pile of clean shirts, for Godsakes. Bitch, dirty bitch.

Ordinarily, she didn't much care what Fred thought. But when you were on a self-abasement kick—I mean, Stebbing and Fred, you could stuff them and put an apple in their mouths and nobody would know the difference. But they both thought she was a bitch, and that somehow counted. And George Pyke, what did he think? There was George now, on the screen. Yummier instant coffee, said George, it keeps you from thinking. Cretins swear by it. The millionth model of George Pyke sold that year smacked his lips and dissolved.

It was only these very slow unresponsive men who found her bitchy, she bet. It was her impatience with them that produced the effect, that and her desire to wake them up and bring out the best in (cackle, cackle)—the governess swung her hose and caught herself in the eye with it.

The funny thing was, she hadn't been half so difficult a year ago. (Except with Fred, of course.) She used to be patient with people like Ernie Peabody, patient to bursting point. And now she had watched herself change to something constantly itchy and querulous, transferring her bile from Fred to the human race: all in all, going back to Stapleton had been rather a mistake, hadn't it?

She wasn't really like that though, she only acted like that. If she was just around some nice, intelligent people for a while . . .

Go on out and meet some nice intelligent people, then. Nobody's stopping you.

I have no luck, I can't find any, I find people like Fred. No luck, that's all it is.

Find them and sneer at them. Isn't that the formula?

I didn't sneer at them a year ago. Who are you anyway?

Why, this is your friendly host at the Inner Sanctum, yock, yock, yock (Pierce again, doing his imitations)—you're going *out of your mind.* No one can hear you scream, I gave the servants the night off.

Alison thought, oh dear, not again, and tried to concentrate on the TV set. They were giving an electric wheelchair to an old lady with arthritis. The old lady was sniveling hopelessly.

Interestingly enough, said the pseudo-Pierce—that is, if you interest easily—I had the same weakness as you for people less gifted and fascinating than myself. Well, just look at Stebbing, for instance. But at least I never sneered at them, never once did this boy sneer . . .

—It wasn't Pierce of course, only her own head. She plucked off the set violently. She was too nervous to lie down again. In fact, the only thing that seemed worth doing was to go out and buy an enormous ice cream sundae; two enormous ice cream sundaes; and wallow in them.

She went out quickly and walked to the drugstore. The counter was lined with teenagers who watched her with what seemed like tremendous amusement. "A chocolate ice cream sundae," she said to the fellow. "Let me see your draft card," he said. He was a great joker, he might have said it to anybody —humor being the national disease—but she chose to take it personally.

"I asked for a chocolate sundae," she said sharply.

Review the bidding. Run away, that's funny; stamp your foot, that's funny. She was trapped by the comic possibilities.

"One chocolate sundae, coming up," said the fellow. "The first one of the day, I bet. It's tough waiting for it . . ."

It was three-fifteen. She didn't dare ask for a second one. A boy stood up, surprisingly, and opened the door for her. Another damned humorist, by the look of him. She walked home by way of Wensley Park where a real governess was steering a sailboat on the artificial lake, with a long stick.

Twenty to four. Fred would be home soon. The big breathy presence in the doorway; the indomitable strength of an insensitive man. How was it she used to handle him? Icy disdain? Katharine Hepburn sort of thing?

After a day spent like this, you couldn't look the milkman in the eye, let alone your husband. She had only bullied him in the past because he'd allowed her to; his flabbiness had created a power vacuum. By four o'clock she felt that her nerve had gone completely, she couldn't say "boo" to him. Icy disdain would just make him laugh. Was that what she was really afraid of? Fred's all-American sense of humor?

Or was it the laughter in her head? Pierce conducting the manchines at the Fun House: was she afraid of being left alone with that for another year?

6

She heard the muffle of slippers and the fumble at the door handle: Cary Grant was making his move at last. She held her breath and waited: Fred's shadow was slow and heavy; he must be squinting, trying to focus. He nicked a chair with his foot and caught the clothes as they slid off.

She felt quite luminous in the dark room. "I'm over here," she said, but held back the accustomed sarcasm: Fred was clumsy, that was simply part of his character. There was no point bringing it up indefinitely.

They made love more violently than they used to, not daring to speak. There was complete, exhausted assent in both of them. "It could be a lot worse," she thought. The pleasures of familiarity; the pleasures of inevitability.

Afterwards they both expected depletion and the quick return of sarcasm. She would say, "You realize this doesn't change anything," and turn her back to him, denying what had happened.

They still didn't dare to speak: so many mistakes could be made that way. They embraced again, more peacefully, trying not to think any more, not to analyze any more.

Let's go to Greece, you should have seen Thurman's face, I didn't really miss you, neither did I, it's just that I can't face going back to Stapleton, ceramics, neurotic women, freedom, I understand what you mean; I haven't changed, take me as I am, still boring, still bitchy, newspapers, art, why didn't you write then? I told you where I was staying, what was that dear what was that dear?—it was certainly better not to talk. Their ideas still lagged well behind the de facto situation.

He squeezed her hand and she squeezed back—a gesture somewhere between resignation and friendship. They must have had *some* reason for marrying. He remembered her gray rage across the pillow from him the last time they met; she thought, if he goes to sleep now, it's all over—there's no hope for anybody.

Possibly to avert that, he turned on the light and looked around for a cigarette. With his eyes blinking, he looked very young: twenty-eight was all he was in fact, really rather soon to give up on somebody. Maybe they could stagger on a bit longer, he might still learn some new tricks. God knows, there were duller people in the world than Fred.

She was beautiful and relaxed now against the pillow. Not ruining her face with talk. Nothing like as bad as he remembered. You could see that the bitchiness was a mannerism. She wasn't the real thing at all; he'd seen the real thing lately, and he knew. Laughing at Baines's suicide was sort of bitchy, for instance.

The worst thing you could say about Alison was that she was sometimes heartbreakingly silly: and that was hardly incurable: she already looked a little less silly than last year. Only thirty, after all.

Then again—maybe with Fred, if you didn't talk for too long, and too abstractly, he might be able to follow some of it. In a crisis, you could always remember George Pyke.

And I—what have I learned?

He lit two cigarettes, like a man in the movies—unreality enshrouded them still—and handed her one. They looked at each other and smiled simultaneously. Pretty funny.

They smoked silently: talking would still raise a whole new set of problems. But they relaxed in the sight of each other. All evening, ever since he had come in from work, they had moved about the house in petulant mime. Now at least they were at ease.

Before turning out the light again, a thought occurred to him. He was sure he'd read somewhere that marriages were often better for a year or so's separation. Where was it he'd heard that?

—He bit back the thought viciously. That he could even think such a thing. Peabodyisms at a time like this. Things were certainly looking up; but no marriage should be asked to take the strain of that.

Constant vigilance would be needed to keep this show on the road and get this marriage moving again.

He turned off the light with a slightly uneasy smile . . . feeling in some obscure way that couldn't be literal truth, that the past year had made them not the least, but the most, typical couple in Bloodbury. . . . And she thought that not being the stuff of tragedy perhaps had its advantages, and if you were going to marry a square you might as well marry a good one; and for once, she fell asleep before he did.